"SEE YOU IN HELL!"

With her smart-gun, Chapel sprayed a clear gelatin over Simmons's face and down his body. Wynn flicked his cigarette and it twisted through the air. Simmons strained to knock it away with his good arm. He managed to hit the cigarette and smother it in the gel. It smoldered and went out, but a thin stream of smoke curled up from his arm where part of the burning ash had landed. Then the gelatin ignited, sending flames racing up his arm and over his neck and face.

He frantically batted at the flames, but they quickly rushed over his chest and abdomen. Within seconds, he was entirely engulfed. His arms flailed as his skin bubbled and popped. He tried to stand and fell over. He rolled and rolled, but the flames burned hotter and brighter. Then he could feel nothing, his nerve endings gone, and Simmons knew he was doomed.

Amid the horrific smell of his own burning flesh, he saw Wanda standing before him. She was smiling, waiting at home for him to return.

Then an enormous explosion rocked the building.

Avon Books are available at special quantity discounts for bulk purchases for sales promotions, premiums, fund raising or educational use. Special books, or book excerpts, can also be created to fit specific needs.

For details write or telephone the office of the Director of Special Markets, Avon Books, Dept. FP, 1350 Avenue of the Americas, New York, New York 10019, 1-800-238-0658.

S P A W N

Novel by **ROB MacGREGOR**
Based on the comic book by **TODD McFARLANE**
Screenplay by **ALAN McELROY**

AVON BOOKS ◆ NEW YORK

This is a work of fiction. Names, characters, places, and incidents either are the product of the author's imagination or are used fictitiously. Any resemblance to actual events, locales, organizations, or persons, living or dead, is entirely coincidental and beyond the intent of either the author or the publisher. This work is a novel by Rob MacGregor based on a screenplay by Alan McElroy, based on the character created by Todd McFarlane.

AVON BOOKS
A division of
The Hearst Corporation
1350 Avenue of the Americas
New York, New York 10019

Copyright © 1997 New Line Productions, Inc. All Rights Reserved.
SPAWN AND ALL RELATED INDICIA IS TM and © 1997, TODD MCFARLANE PRODUCTIONS, INC. ALL RIGHTS RESERVED.
Artwork © 1997 New Line Productions, Inc. All Rights Reserved.
Visit our website at **http://AvonBooks.com**
Library of Congress Catalog Card Number: 97-93052
ISBN: 0-380-79441-1

All rights reserved, which includes the right to reproduce this book or portions thereof in any form whatsoever except as provided by the U.S. Copyright Law. For information address Avon Books.

First Avon Books Printing: September 1997

AVON TRADEMARK REG. U.S. PAT. OFF. AND IN OTHER COUNTRIES, MARCA REGISTRADA, HECHO EN U.S.A.

Printed in the U.S.A.

WCD   10 9 8 7 6 5 4 3 2 1

If you purchased this book without a cover, you should be aware that this book is stolen property. It was reported as "unsold and destroyed" to the publisher, and neither the author nor the publisher has received any payment for this "stripped book."

SPAWN

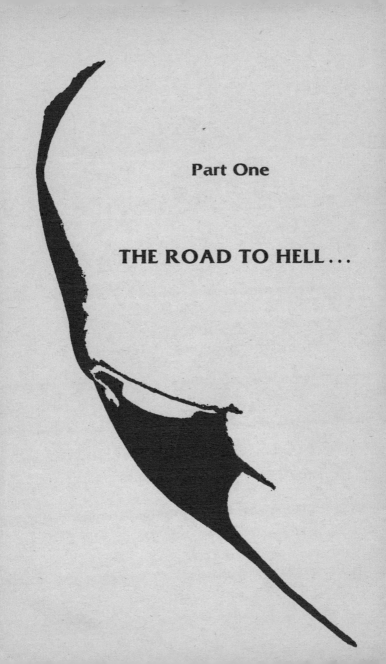

Part One

THE ROAD TO HELL...

A NOTE TO READERS

THE GREAT Battle has waged eternal. The Army of Light and the Army of Night, as always, are fueled by souls harvested on Earth. It has been eons since the dark forces last assaulted the heavens, but the steady decay and violence of earthly civilization has provided a constant flow of new recruits, as well as those willing to sell their souls in exchange for wealth and power. All the Dark Lord needs now is one great soldier, someone who can conquer Earth and lead his hordes to the gates of the heavens . . . then rip them down and surge through to victory.

I may sound like just another hell 'n' brimstone preacher when I tell you that one day there will come a great battle, when the heavens will touch down on Earth and Hell will rise up to meet it, but allow me to offer my credentials.

I've gone by many names over the millennia. More names than I can recall. Most recently in history, at least recent in my terms, I have been known as Count Alessandro di Cogliostro.

I was in Babylon plotting with kings, and more than once as the Pharaoh's righthand in Egypt's distant past. Much later, I was the Roman soldier who speared the side of a man named Joshua, later called Jesus of Nazareth, a legacy that has followed me for two thousand years in the form of the spearhead—the Spear of Destiny. It has sur-

3

vived to this day and is a weapon of tremendous magical powers. As you read on, that story will unfold within this tale of the man who was finally chosen to lead the vile Army of Night into the great battle.

I've also been known as an alchemist, a magician, and I've even been mistaken for the Dark Lord himself. The truth is, I am a Hellspawn, an immortal re-born from the depths of darkness, sent here by Malebolgia, the blackest of evil lords who rules the eighth sphere of Hell.

Like many others of my ilk, I have been a curse to humanity for untold centuries. The death and misery that I have caused, by comparison, would make your worst criminals appear as innocent children. But one day several hundred years ago, I decided I no longer relished evil and carnage. The Dark Ages were over and I no longer craved the taste the blood or the sight of pain and horror.

I knew there was another way, one I'd always considered far weaker. The way of light, of justice, of hope. The way of Providence. I had come to realize that ultimately, like everything else, I was a part of the light, and that it was useless to fight and disavow it and its heavenly source. Sure, I heard voices from the dark side talking to me, first in my sleep, then even in my waking life, conniving, trying to draw me back. But I ignored them—I ignore them still—and I, Cogliostro, became Hell's first turncoat, a Lucifer to the Dark Lord himself.

I traveled the world seeking out other Hellspawn, hoping to find allies among them, to free them from their roles as puppets of Malebolgia. But for centuries, none joined me—and for that reason the Dark Lord tolerated me. He enjoyed torturing me by allowing me to pursue my fruitless ambitions. It was his way of demonstrating his power to me and to other Hellspawn.

Then one day I encountered a boy who was unlike any I'd seen for centuries. Even as an eight-year-old, he was bold and courageous. I knew he would grow up to be a fierce and fearless warrior, and I held great hope for him. I followed him over the years, but slowly my expectations faded. He had been blinded by a devious leader, a secretive general who today still roams free spreading darkness. The warrior was superior to the general in his power and prowess, and that was why Malebolgia chose him over the general to lead his armies in the conquest of humanity.

At the same time, I sensed he was inherently capable of defeating Malebolgia, but he had to overcome the hate and the overwhelming desire for blood revenge that took him from Hell's fire back to Earth. But I'm getting ahead of my story. Let's go back a few years and begin there.

Count Alessandro di Cogliostro
Rome

ONE

AL SIMMONS stepped through the door of the Hong Kong Hilton and casually surveyed the night—the passing traffic, the bustle of pedestrians, the shouts and the honking. The familiar odor of spices mixed with the acrid smells of exhaust fumes and fuel oil. But there was another smell that reached his nostrils tonight, the faint odor of smoke from a major fire. In the distance, sirens wailed.

He thought he detected a heightened awareness amid the usual clamor of the crowded city. The uniformed doorman seemed to twitch as he looked around. A frown creased his uneasy features when his gaze settled on Simmons. But maybe it was just his imagination. After what he'd just experienced, there was plenty of reason for Simmons to be edgy.

He wore a gray tailored Ruffini suit purchased a couple of months earlier in Rome. A garment bag hung from his right shoulder, and he carried a black leather briefcase in his right hand. The suit helped to disguise the muscular physique. To anyone who noticed him, he appeared to be merely a successful African-American businessman. That was exactly the way Simmons wanted it.

The doorman nodded, then signaled for a taxi. Simmons handed him a couple of Hong Kong dollars, then

7

slid into the backseat. He glanced at his watch. "The airport, please. Chek Lap Kok."

"Oh, it's good you want to go to the new airport, not Kai Tak," the driver said with a Malaysian accent. "Bad things happened there tonight. Very bad."

The driver stuck his head out the window, yelled something in Chinese at another taxi, then merged into the heavy traffic. With a population of more than five million, the streets of Hong Kong were congested at virtually all hours. Simmons had visited the island several times in the past decade, but it only took a couple of days before the pressure of Hong Kong's masses started to make him feel edgy. But tonight it wasn't just the congestion that unsettled him.

"So what happened?" he asked, trying to sound vaguely curious, but not overanxious.

"An army of terrorists attacked." He glanced up into the rearview mirror, then back to the road, and back and forth as he spoke. "They blew up half the airport, killed lots of people. They say it might be the rebels, but I thought they all left the country or were put in jail."

The taxi passed I. M. Pei's Bank of China, one of the island's bastions of capitalism. Since July, the land of silk and money was now under the control of the Chinese. In spite of promises that little would change, there had been a few rallies and several skirmishes between protesters and the police. But nothing as dramatic as the driver described had occurred. For his part, Simmons hoped the rebels didn't get blamed for the massacre. He knew, as no one else knew, that they didn't deserve it.

His thoughts rolled back three hours.

An incoming jet roared overhead as the assassin, clad in black overalls, slipped through the darkness toward the communications tower of Kai Tak Airport. He paused at the base of the stairs, then moved swiftly up the steps, taking them two at a time. He knew from the security report that there would be four men inside, including a single guard on duty.

When he reached the top, he double-checked his weapons, then shaped a small plastic charge on the lock. He backed down several stairs, dropped low, ready to rush forward through the doorway. He counted to three, then pressed a remote detonator on his belt. With the report of a muffled pop, he charge forward and slammed his heel against the door near the destroyed lock. Then he tumbled into the communications tower.

He leaped to his feet and whirled around. Three men were working at consoles. One had just taken a sip of coffee as he was watching a display with the flight number of the incoming jet. The guard, who had been standing near the door, was stunned by the explosion and had fallen to the floor. He was just turning over and raising his machine gun when the intruder—Simmons—slammed his foot into the man's groin, then his head. The guard groaned, rolled over, and flopped onto his back, unconscious.

Simmons kicked the machine gun to the center of the room as he menaced his weapon, a state-of-the-art, lightweight automatic pistol that looked like a ray-gun of the future. The smart-gun, as it was called, was made of plastic and easily disassembled and reassembled as a harmless green toy robot for the sake of custom officers. The weapon was quickly becoming the standard for him and others involved in the agency's fieldwork.

He ordered the men to get down on the floor. But one of them reached for an alarm and Simmons reflexively sprayed the room with bullets. The men collapsed to the floor, monitors exploded. The coffee cup was still hooked to the index finger of one of the men, but the coffee had spilled over the front of his shirt mixing with a spreading crimson stain of blood.

"Bad move," Simmons muttered toward the dead man who had reached for the alarm.

He saw movement on the edge his vision, spun to his left just as the security guard drew a gun from the holster at his waist. Simmons reacted instinctively, firing several times. The guard squeezed off one wild shot and collapsed.

Simmons moved to the center of the room and dropped a large backpack that had been slung over his shoulder. He unzipped it and removed an unassembled AK-830, a portable missile launcher. He spread out the glistening blue and black steel parts on the floor and went to work building his instrument of death.

He lifted the body of the AK-830 as legs snapped out to support it. A piston raised the missile mount into place and an electronic panel lit up. Tiny lights and figures indicated weapon system readouts.

Simmons picked up two cylindrical tubes and married them end to end, forming the missile he would fire at his target. He snapped out support rails and placed the missile carefully on them. A bracket closed over the mount, holding the missile in place and making electronic contact.

The intruder ripped open a shoulder bag and connected a cable from the missile casing to the chest computer he was wearing. Another cable linked the chest computer to a night-vision VR helmet. Simmons's black gloved finger pressed a VR interlock switch on the right side of the missile. The display indicated that the missile had been activated. Fins sprang out of the lower section of the cylindrical missile and the protective cover popped off, revealing the entire projectile.

Finally, he lowered the VR helmet onto his head. He touched an activation switch on the helmet's smooth exterior and a murky infrared night-vision image appeared. An indicator read **Aligning**, and slowly a three-dimensional VR representation of an airport and surrounding landscape came sharply into view. It locked in place over the actual image. The distant control tower, hangars, runways, and other buildings were identified with hovering icons. Targeting and weapon status were visible in small floating boxes.

Simmons's focus settled on a jet as it taxied toward an isolated gate. The flight was instantly identified and the aircraft was labeled **Primary Target**. Simmons pushed buttons on his chest and the image zoomed in as the jet reached its gate.

A small group of men awaited the plane's arrival. All were identified by their VR avatars on the screen while floating symbols enunciated them for targeting. Multiple-target acquisition indicators blinked **Ready**. Simmons remained calm, waiting patiently for the right moment.

Two men in suits and two men in military uniforms waited outside the gate for the plane's arrival. A limousine and a second vehicle with two bodyguards were parked nearby. A woman and a young girl stepped out of the limousine and joined the waiting men. He tensed at the sight of the child. No one had said anything about a kid. Portable stairs were rolled to the plane and the door opened.

Two bodyguards emerged from the plane and carefully surveyed the area. A man in a suit stepped through the doorway, smiled and waved. Several others followed him down the steps.

From Simmons's perspective, a VR avatar was superimposed over the man's image as he descended down the stairs. A sub-window appeared in which the man was magnified and identified as Josef As-Amifar. Like the plane itself, he was set off as a primary target. The sub-window dissolved and VR targeting crosshairs rotated into position, affirming target lock.

The image zoomed out. A sweep of the entire area was

made. An indicator specified Kill Zone Clear, and a signal beeped, indicating the missile was now armed.

Simmons felt neither tensed nor relaxed. He harbored neither hatred nor compassion for the targets. He was well aware of what was about to happen—he'd run through the scenario many times back home to work out the bugs—but through the same horrific wave of death he was about to unleash, hundreds, maybe thousands of other lives, innocent lives, would be saved. That was the justification that came with this assignment, as with most of his assignments.

In spite of the praise he received for his work, he hated the killing, and more and more he wondered why other solutions couldn't be reached to avoid unnecessary deaths.

He cursed under his breath when he saw the child still present. Who was the fool endangering the kid's life? She must have been a last minute addition, because his report had stipulated that no innocent bystanders would be in range. This was it, he vowed. His last mission. No more killing.

Simmons pushed a blinking button on his chest computer and a red light began to blink synchronically on the launcher. Three blinks later, the missile ignited and blasted through the communication tower's glass window. The projectile separated into four individual smart-missiles, all locked on their targets. Simmons knew there was no time for the victims to react. They might look up, they might have time for shock and confusion to register on their faces, they might choke on one or two words of prayer, but then they would be blown to pieces and incinerated into a thousand flaming bits of charred flesh and bone.

Simmons glimpsed several flashes as the strike virtually obliterated all of the targets. A perfect hit, devastatingly precise. In one sense, it was like playing a game, a game that was part of a larger ongoing game with many players in different parts of the world. A game that was fun. Except in games, real people didn't die. And the roar and the heat that rushed back at him made the mission very real.

The screen went black. The mission was over.

Simmons pulled the helmet off his head and stared impassively through the shattered glass at the destruction. Flames shot fifty feet into the air and secondary explosions from the plane's gas tanks hurled debris into the night. Confusion would reign for hours and he would easily slip away.

He turned away from the scene and placed an explosive charge on the body of the launcher in the center of the communications tower. He touched a switch and a countdown began ticking. He quickly removed his black operations coveralls, revealing a business suit. He reached into the backpack, took out an ordinary briefcase, dissembled the smart-gun, and placed it into the briefcase.

He hesitated another moment, made a final scan of the conflagration. A feeling of intense disgust gripped his gut. It was worse this time. Worse than he had ever experienced. He thought about the little girl and what was left of her and repeated his vow. It was over for him.

Finally, he turned and moved past the four men sprawled across the floor. He hurried down the steps and exited the communications tower. Fifty yards. That was all the distance he needed to cover. He glanced across the tarmac toward the employee door to the terminal. As soon as he was inside, he would appear to be just another confused, terrified traveler.

That was when he noticed a man standing just ten yards away from him, staring in his direction. He was garbed in a long black coat and a matching wide-brimmed hat that looked like the type Spanish monks had worn for centuries. With his silver beard flowing over his chest, he looked like a character from another time.

Simmons started to bend for the miniature .45 strapped to his ankle, but then he stopped. He wasn't going to kill anyone else, not unless he was being threatened. The man didn't appear intent on stopping him. The expression on the man's face was sad. It was almost as if he knew Simmons, knew all about him.

Simmons shook off the odd feeling as he remembered the explosive that was about to go off in the tower. He dashed for the terminal just as the tower exploded behind him, spewing a gusher of flames and debris. A wave of heat rippled across the tarmac, but Simmons was already safe inside the terminal, amid the chaos of scrambling passengers and employees.

Simmons glanced at his watch again as the taxi neared the airport, then nervously tapped his fingers on the brief-case, which lay across his lap. He'd recently turned thirty-three and it was time for a career change. His old life was ending. He sensed it as he often did probable future events. It was one of the reasons he was still alive. He wanted nothing more than to depart safely from this island and leave behind his career, his memories, his past. All of it.

"Uh-oh," the taxi driver murmured as he slowed to a stop.

"What is it?" Simmons asked.

"Roadblock. Soldiers. They must be looking for the terrorists."

Several armed, uniformed men from the Chinese militia, rushed up to the taxi. Simmons tightened his grip on the briefcase. Considering the circumstances, the smart-gun might attract attention, even though it was reassembled as a toy robot. He would be held and questioned. The longer he was held, the greater the chances he would be caught.

The soldiers peered into the taxi and ordered the driver

to open the trunk. One of the soldiers pulled open the back door and told him to step out. Simmons followed the order and stepped into the road.

"Open the briefcase," the Chinese soldier demanded in a firm voice.

Simmons held his position, showing no interest in giving up the briefcase.

"Now! Open it!"

"Aren't you going to ask for my passport?"

The soldier hesitated and as he did Simmons slipped a hand into his suit coat and pulled out his passport. He held it in front of the man's face. Across the front of the document were the words: United States of American—DIPLOMAT.

The soldier took the passport, stepped back, and called to one of the other men. Another soldier appeared, an older man with a captain ranking. He took the passport, glanced at it, then at Simmons.

"Open the briefcase," the captain demanded.

"I invoke diplomatic immunity."

Simmons studied the man to see if he was buying the tactic. He knew he could be taken into custody, interrogated, and searched. But he also knew that relations between the Chinese and Americans were tense and that the arrest of a diplomat could blow up into a major fiasco. A mistake by the captain could cost the man his career. He sensed similar thoughts going through the mind of the officer.

Then the captain straightened his back as he came to a decision. "You are a diplomat, but this is a state of emergency. Please, open the briefcase or you are under arrest."

He realized he shouldn't have tried to escape with the smart-gun. He should have left it in the communications tower with the missile launcher. The weapon had served him well on numerous assignments, but right now it was an impediment. He considered running, but he had no way of getting off the island. He'd be hunted down and caught before sunrise.

Just then he noticed someone watching from a few yards away. He couldn't believe it. It was the same strange character he'd seen earlier at Kai Tak—the guy with the long beard and wide-brimmed hat that reminded him of a Spanish monk.

The captain, following his gaze, turned and looked over at the man. He started to raise a hand as if to call one of his men, when he stopped. The two men locked gazes for several seconds. Then the officer abruptly turned back to Simmons and handed him the passport. With the flick of his hand, he waved the taxi on. Simmons slid into the backseat and stared at the stranger. The driver slammed the trunk, leaped behind the wheel, and drove off.

"Never knew I had a guardian angel," Simmons remarked.

"What was that?" the driver asked.

"Forget it."

Simmons puzzled over the peculiar encounter. He had no idea who the man was or why the captain had suddenly changed his mind. He glanced at his watch again. Right on time. In half an hour, he would be airborne, headed home and into a new future.

TWO

EVERETT ELEMENTARY in LeDroit Park on the outskirts of Washington, D.C., didn't look much different than it had in the days when Al Simmons had attended the school, except that it seemed a lot smaller. The "big school," as he'd called it when he was five, had shrunk as he'd grown up. Even though his perspective was different now, he knew that the school remained a sanctuary from the mean streets of the inner city, a place where a kid could still learn the three R's without any sense of fear.

Even though it was nearly four-thirty and the school had been out for more than two hours, there were still several kids in the playground. It took a moment before he remembered that Wanda had told him about an after school program the school had started for kids with working parents. She'd taken a position as supervisor of the program, supposedly to earn extra money. But Simmons knew that she had also accepted the post because he was gone so much, and if she were busy, she wouldn't sit around and worry about him.

He spotted Wanda's white Mercedes convertible in the parking lot. He smiled and decided to surprise her. He crossed the schoolyard and was heading toward her class-

17

room when he heard a young boy call out. "Hey, mister, can you help me with this thing?"

A five-year-old boy garbed in camouflage pants and a T-shirt held up a G.I. Joe in one hand. In the other, he clutched two small arms, one gripping a machine gun. He pushed one of the arms against the torso, but it wouldn't fit into the socket.

In frustration, he raised his eyes toward the big man hovering over him. "Please, mister, can you fix my toy soldier?"

Simmons knelt down next to him and the boy's pleading look turned hopeful. He took the disassembled toy and turned it over in his large hands. "Well, uh, I'll see what I can do."

He struggled to fix the doll as the kid stared intently at him. He felt incompetent and more than a little uncomfortable. This was not a situation he had been trained for. "Hm, harder than it looks."

The boy looked worried. "You can do it, Mister. I know you can."

"This . . . isn't . . . exactly . . . my specialty," he said as he pushed and twisted the arm against the body.

A pair of shapely legs appeared in front of him. "I'll say."

Simmons raised his eyes and took in the image of a lithe, statuesque figure. Both limbs popped into place at once. He handed the tiny soldier to the boy, who beamed and ran off.

"And what, pray tell, is my specialty?"

The young woman gave him an amused look. "Driving your girlfriend crazy."

"I'll tell her you said that."

Wanda Blake, his soulful, brown-skinned lover, met his gaze. She was thirty, intelligent, and strikingly attractive—the best thing that had ever come into his life.

They embraced and kissed as a couple of little girls

giggled. Wanda pulled back and studied Simmons, her arms draped loosely over his shoulders. "Maybe you should've been the kindergarten teacher. I know they'd pay attention to you."

"All I want to do is pay attention to you." He started to kiss her again, but Wanda placed a finger on his lips. "Let's wait."

"Yeah. How about going home and getting down to a little homework. What do you say?"

Wanda smiled mischievously and they headed toward the parking lot arm in arm. "Now where were you this time? What were you doing?"

"Never mind. It's far away and over. All over," he repeated.

The last thing he wanted to do was talk about Hong Kong. He didn't even care to think about it. If she knew what he had done in the last twenty-four hours, he doubted that she would be congratulating him. She'd probably think she was living with a monster. Only his training and his discipline had kept him acting month after month, year after year, as if his government job were nothing out of the ordinary.

A momentary frown crossed her features. "Until the next time," she pouted.

"Don't count on it," Simmons responded. "Don't count on it."

Across the playground, the little boy stood near the swings scrutinizing his G.I. Joe. He touched the arms, moved them forward and back. He shook his head, then glanced toward the parking lot just as Simmons was climbing into his car.

"Hey, you put the arms on backwards!"

Loud, cackling laughter was the only response. The boy whirled around, a frightened look on his face. He spotted a short, fat man seated atop a slowly rotating runaround near an oak tree in a corner of the playground. Without knowing why, the boy knew he better not go any closer to him. He was the stranger who would offer little kids candy and then grab them and take them away. You were supposed to stay away from him.

"Backwards . . . yeah, that's good . . . that's very good, Simmons," the man muttered. "I like that. You can take 'em apart, but you can't put 'em back together."

He laughed again and the runaround seemed to pick up speed on its own.

He went by the name Clown, partly because he looked like one—the scary kind of clown from nightmares, a dwarf. He was no more an ordinary man than he was an ordinary clown. He even scared himself sometimes.

He was concerned about Simmons right now. Simmons was a good soldier, but Clown and the boss had other plans for him. He laughed as he sensed that Simmons was disenchanted with his work. "You ain't seen nothing yet, Big Guy," he muttered. "Just you wait, Al."

But Clown hated waiting. He might just have to move up time itself and get to the fun stuff even sooner than he'd expected.

He grinned and his white teeth seemed to lengthen and turn blood red in the late afternoon sun.

The LeDroit Park neighborhood had retained much of its character from the turn of the century, when it had become a prominently black community. Located between Howard University and Howard Theater and Cultural Center, the neighborhood had been the home of many well known African-Americans. The houses, built in the 1870s, were detached and semi-detached and were originally advertised as offering the advantages of city living with the open space of the country. In the 1880s and 1890s, row houses were added to the neighborhood.

Al Simmons and Wanda Blake resided in one of the row houses on Third Street. The house featured many of the original decorative ironwork fences and balustrades. Its roofline was accented with turrets, towers, pediment gables, and iron crestings, and it featured unusual twisted porch columns.

Simmons and Wanda didn't waste any time when the front door closed behind them. Their clothing quickly fell away in a trail across the living room, down the hall, and into the master bedroom. They tumbled into the king-sized bed, devouring each other with passionate kisses, exploring and rediscovering familiar territory.

Each touch released a river of memories and a flood of ecstatic moments, both present and past. He recalled the day he'd met her in the parking lot of a grocery store after he'd backed into her car. She'd been upset because the car was only a week old. He'd invited her over to a nearby coffee shop to calm her down, and his life had never been the same.

Simmons felt as if he were drowning in Wanda's warm embrace, and willingly so. He ran his a hand over her cheek and jaw, along the silky soft skin of her long neck, and down her soft brown body. She trailed her fingers over his powerful shoulders and biceps, his muscular chest and thick, strong thighs. She murmured that he was bigger than she remembered him.

"Bigger all over," she whispered after running her hands over and down beyond his flat belly.

Then he filled her desires with his own as they eagerly entwined. She primed his passions and he answered with great ecstatic thrusts, until finally they could wait no longer and threw themselves into wave after wave of gushing rapture.

"Did I tell you how much I missed you?" he asked, gasping for air as he collapsed on top of her soft, warm body.

"Once or twice."

"Well, Wanda Blake, I'm telling you again."

She pushed him onto his back and then propped up her head with a hand as she lay on her side. She ran a finger over Simmons's moist, flushed chest. "Talk is cheap, Al Simmons."

He growled and Wanda laughed. He pulled her down on top of him and their lips met again as a new tide of passion washed over them.

"Lovie, lovie, heh, heh, heh," Clown sneered as he peered through the blinds of the master bedroom. "Enjoy yourself there, Simmons," he said to himself. "I know I'm enjoying it."

The rotund dwarf with the permanent blue grin tattooed on his face reached down between his legs to the bag of deep-fried whole crabs. He pulled one out and munched on it, the shell and all, as the grease dripped from his fingers to the ground. "Lovie, lovie, heh, heh, heh."

The shower was running and Simmons could hear Wanda's melodic voice rising above the pounding water. Lying on the bed in his boxer shorts, Simmons aimed the remote control at the television on the wall cabinet, turning on CNN.

He stretched his arms overhead and noticed a photo on the bedside table. It was from last New Year's Eve, and he was celebrating with Wanda and Terry Fitzgerald, his best friend. They were smiling and laughing amid a shower of colorful streamers. Next to the photo was a pendant attached to a gold chain. It was a locket with the word *Forever* inscribed on the back. He reached out and popped open the locket, which showed a photo of himself and Wanda smiling, eyes glistening in their mutual happiness.

Just then, Simmons's attention was drawn to the forty-inch television set, where the announcer led off a new update with a report from Hong Kong.

"Terrorists fired rockets at Kai Tak Airport last night, killing twenty-six people, including four children, three of whom were aboard a jet that had just landed. It is believed that the target of the attack was Josef As-Amifar, leader of the Algerian Revolutionary Front. Investigators so far have made no arrests and have few clues to the identity of the attackers."

As the anchorman spoke, the screen filled with flames and smoke and the ruins of the jumbo jet as firemen poured water onto the burning hulk. Simmons shook his head in disgust and turned off the television. He felt heavy with sadness, but also flushed with anger. That plane was supposed to be empty, except for As-Amifar and his men. He'd been betrayed.

He shut the locket, slipped the chain over his head. "Think it's time for a change, Baby. A big change." He was dedicated and professional, but he had his limits and he'd just overstepped them. "Four kids," he murmured under his breath.

Killing people—especially kids—was hardly the sort of career his mother had envisioned for him. She had raised him on her own, working full-time in a legal office and saving money for his education. He'd excelled in sports in high school and had the potential to be either a professional football or baseball player. But he'd surprised his coaches and friends when he'd accepted a scholastic scholarship to Antioch.

Simmons had been recruited by the CIA during his senior year at the college. His mother had said that somehow she wasn't surprised. His father, a man she rarely mentioned, had something to do with secret matters. She never knew what and he wouldn't talk about it. About all Simmons knew of him was that he was white and he had disappeared without a trace when Simmons was three. He had no recollection of the man, but he often wondered what happened to him. His mother had lived to see Simmons graduate from college, but she had died of cancer a short time later.

As part of his preparation for the CIA, Simmons had enlisted in the marines as soon as he graduated. He'd proved himself in the Gulf War when he and several others were captured. Within twenty-four hours, Simmons had not only engineered a breakout, but he and the men captured the commanding officer. After he'd sent out a secret signal, allied troops poured across the desert and into the encampment, and the entire unit surrendered without firing a shot.

After that, Simmons moved rapidly through the ranks and gained a place on a special elite presidential guard. While on duty, he saved the president from an assassin's bullet—sometimes he still felt a twinge in his arm—and was promoted to a lieutenant colonel. That incident caught the attention of an intelligence officer named Jason Wynn, and as a result Simmons's career shifted gears.

Instead of leaving the military for the CIA, Wynn guided him into the A-6, considered the most secretive and powerful intelligence organization in the world. It was so secretive that most Americans had never heard of it, even though it was appropriated two billion dollars a year in a black-bag budget that never came under public scrutiny and was rarely seen by any elected officials.

Within weeks of moving from the military to the A-6, Wynn became Simmons's mentor and the two got along well. Wynn admired Simmons's combat skills and aptitude for quick learning as well as his physical prowess. For his part, Simmons was in awe of Wynn's background and experience. Wynn was a supervisor of clandestine operations and was considered a prime candidate to eventually rise to the top of the A-6.

At first, his missions for A-6 had a clear purpose and were for the good of American security. But gradually the assignments became more and more bloody, with fewer and fewer rational explanations. Now the Kai Tak Airport attack had made it abundantly clear that he would resign as soon as he had a chance to talk to Wynn.

Just then, a three-year-old wire-haired terrier leaped onto his lap. "Spaz! How ya been ya knucklehead?"

Simmons grinned like a kid as he rubbed and patted his excited little dog. Spaz loved the attention, and his entire body wagged back and forth as he inundated his owner with sloppy licks.

"I swear, sometimes I think you love that dog more than me," Wanda said as she emerged from the shower with a towel wrapped around her.

"Well, I've known him longer. What did you expect?" he said in mock seriousness.

Wanda's towel hit him in the face, covering his head. He ripped it off, feigning anger, and scowled at Wanda. Then his expression shifted as he scrutinized the sight in front of him.

"But then again, Spaz doesn't look nearly as good in wet hair."

Simmons reached up, grabbing for Wanda. He pulled her toward him.

"Don't you dare kiss me with that dog tongue all over your face."

Simmons woofed at Wanda and started to lick her face, Spaz-style, ignoring her pleas for him to let go of her. Spaz barked excitedly, jumping up and down until Simmons flung his boxer shorts over the dog's head.

The lure of the flames held his attention firmly. The orange and red, green and blue flames danced and lapped hungrily at the air. He imagined the fireplace as a doorway; beyond it the flames grew larger and larger.

He seemed to hear voices calling out from that place, yelling: "Leap, leap, leap!" The words turned gradually more and more menacing. Behind them were other sounds, the rantings, squeals, and cries of the condemned, and the insidious laughter of their masters.

"Well, are you just going to sit there or are you going to help me?"

Simmons snapped out of his uneasy reverie and looked up at Wanda. She held out a bottle of champagne wrapped in a cloth. He smiled and took the bottle. He dropped the cloth over the top of the bottle and popped the cork; Wanda sank onto the thick rug next to him, produced a pair of glasses, and he filled them.

"A toast," she said. They raised their glasses, clicked them together. "Congratulations, Al Simmons."

Simmons sipped his drink as the fizzing champagne shot liquid sparks against his cheeks. *Drink well while you can.* His gaze darted to the fire, as if the odd thought had leaped from the flames into his head. He pushed the notion away and turned his attention fully to Wanda.

"So what are you congratulating me for? What did I do, anyhow?" Simmons asked.

Wanda lowered her glass. "We've managed to spend an entire evening alone and uninterrupted. That's quite a feat."

Simmons's hand stroked her hair. He leaned forward and kissed her lightly on the lips. "Baby, I'm just getting started."

He pushed her back onto the rug, tickling and kissing her. She laughed and protested, trying to push him away. The flames seemed to grow in intensity and lap at Simmons's leg. For a moment, he thought he heard a strange crunching noise beyond the flames.

He needed a rest, he thought, and he needed a lot more of Wanda. He nuzzled her neck, ran his hands over the length of her body. They rolled from side to side, toward the fire, then away from it, then back again.

THREE

JASON WYNN leaned back in his chair, feet propped up on his desk and cigar in hand, as he watched the latest CNN report on the rocket assault at Kai Tak Airport. He smiled, visibly enjoying the detailed description of the deadly havoc and all the speculation on who was responsible. In his eyes, the Hong Kong operation had been an unqualified success, and he liked to think that what he thought was what counted.

At fifty-seven, Jason Wynn was an established figure in A-6, a secret umbrella organization that included the CIA, NSA, NRC, and NSC. He was a man with considerable clout. He tutored master killers, like Al Simmons, but was free from their taint. When a secret operation was carried out, with or without congressional approval, he was the one who approved it.

Yet his greatest ambitions had yet to be realized. Simply put, he wanted to be the most powerful man alive. He was intent on achieving his goals within five years. His advice would be sought by presidents and foreign leaders on major foreign policy decisions, but he would be beholden to no one. They would respect and fear him, because they would know he had the power to unleash a plague in virtually any and every city of the world.

To the public, he would be a mythical figure, the invisible power behind the world powers. Even among high-level intelligence personnel, he would be the subject of rumors whispered over drinks late at night in colonial mansions. He would be a legend and a reality.

"Cut out the mental masturbation, Jason," a voice said from a corner of the room. "You'll get ugly warts on your brain."

Wynn turned his chair and peered at the loathsome dwarf seated on a black leather couch in the shadows. Clown grinned as he puffed on one of Wynn's stogies and spun a large globe with his foot.

"North Africa is ready to burn, Jason. I think you know that."

"Simmons does good work," Wynn said as he knocked the ash on the end of his cigar into an ashtray. "He's helped me start more conflict than this world has ever seen. Almost every country has a bone or two to pick with one of its neighbors, and most of them are ready to fight. All we have to do is fire the first shot."

"That's fine and dandy, Doctor Doom, but this five-year plan of yours is way too long," Clown responded from a cloud of smoke.

Wynn's gaze speared Clown. "This isn't a game we're playing. Engineering a viral weapon is an exact science. If you want it done right, you have to do it my way."

Wynn didn't like dealing with the insidious demon-dwarf, but he endured it for his own dark reasons. With Clown on his side, his powers were potentially more enormous than even he had ever hoped possible. His concessions to the tasteless cretin were simply his way of taking advantage of Clown's considerable powers to manipulate the everyday world.

"I'm giving you a guarantee." Wynn leaned toward Clown and jabbed his glowing cigar at him. "All you have to do is keep certain agencies off my back and make damn sure I get what I've been promised."

Clown stared at Wynn's burning cigar in fascination. "Don't worry, Jason baby, we'll make sure you're running this outfit in no time." He spun the globe again as if to emphasize the potential of what he was talking about. This time its pedestal toppled over and the globe rolled over to Wynn's feet.

"And after that, when the big cookie crumbles, you'll get it all." Then Clown's voice turned deeper and darker. "Just don't forget who's boss."

Wynn let the threat pass—this time. He noticed that his cigar had gone out, but made no effort to relight it. He would use Clown for all he was worth. Then he would get rid of the imp and form a direct alliance with his boss. It was just the sort of tactic that had gotten Wynn where he was today.

From the very start, Wynn had been overly ambitious. In high school, he was captain of the ROTC, defensive tackle for the football squad, and number one on the karate team. He went to West Point, graduated cum laude. However, instead of pursuing a promising career in the army, he went into government service, where he was recruited by the CIA, and eventually moved to the A-6.

In his initial CIA assignment, he served as a vice-presidential aide for Richard Nixon from 1958–1960, advising him on National Security issues from the agency's point of view. Many assignments followed, from Dallas in November 1963 to the Gulf of Tonkin the following year. Wynn skyrocketed in the ranks of the intelligence community, helped along by a photographic memory and access to Hoover's files at the FBI.

But serving the country was not enough. He had inhaled the rarefied air of true power, and he liked it. He was instantly addicted to it. He wanted the country to serve him—not only this country, but many other countries as well. That was why he was dealing with the likes of Clown. The dwarf recognized his cravings and offered him a short-cut to the realm where power flowed like water.

Clown slid down off the couch, but stayed in the shadows. "There's one more item on today's 'to-do' list. You're going to recruit someone very special for us—your personal protégé and all-around favorite killer—Mr. Al Simmons.

Wynn dropped his cigar into the ashtray as he considered what he'd just heard. "Simmons? I told you, he's doing a great job right where he is. I don't want to give him up. Not yet."

"Fine, fine," Clown growled. "Then, instead, let's discuss that pretty wife of yours and those two lovely daughters. They spend so much time doing services for the community and the church. I was thinking maybe they could service us now. What do you think? We could make this operation a family affair."

"Keep them out of the picture," Wynn said, rising to his feet. "They've got nothing to do with any of this. Do you hear me?" He was seething now. Barely able to control himself. What the hell was he getting himself into dealing with this creep?

"Did you hear *me*?" Clown replied. "That's the point here."

Wynn lowered himself back into his chair, seeming to sink deeper into his cushion than ever before. "So why Simmons? Tell me that."

Clown chuckled softly as he walked over to the door. " 'Why' doesn't matter, Jason. Doesn't matter at all. 'How' is what's so much fun."

An hour before dawn, Al Simmons was awakened by a vibrating sensation on his left wrist. He rolled over and saw his watch blinking red and felt a slight charge pulsing into his arm. He grimaced and slapped the face of the watch. The light and pulsations stopped. He rolled over to go back to sleep. Fuck Wynn. He could wait until morning. After all, he'd just gotten home, for chrissakes. He'd call him in a few hours.

Five minutes later, he was zapped again. He muttered a string of curses and rolled out of bed. He groped his way to the kitchen, picked up the phone, and punched Wynn's number.

"I need you right away."

Wynn's voice was crisp, as if he'd been up for hours. Knowing Wynn, he probably hadn't gone to bed. Staying up two or even three days with only an hour nap every eight hours was common for Wynn, who probably had invented the term *workaholic*. As Wynn once told him, he could work eighty-hour weeks and still spend "quality time" with his wife and kids.

"Damn it, Wynn. I just got here. I need a couple of days with Wanda." What he really wanted to tell him was that he didn't want to go back at all, but he would resign in person.

"If it weren't important, I wouldn't be calling you. I'll give you until ten-thirty. Be here by then."

Simmons felt like throwing the phone across the room, but he didn't want to wake up Wanda. Instead, he went back to bed and stared at the ceiling as the first hints of dawn crept through the window.

Bright sunshine filtered into the kitchen as Simmons flipped a pancake into the air and expertly caught it with his spatula. He whistled as he cooked, acting as if nothing were wrong, as if he'd already left the agency and didn't have a care in the world.

He flipped the pancake again, but missed on his second try. The pancake flopped onto the floor. His momentary frown shifted into a smile as he pulled a dog biscuit from a cookie jar and dropped it on the center of the pancake.

He called out to Spaz, who charged into the kitchen with a ball in his mouth.

"Look what I made for you, Spazzy. Just like Mama Spaz used to make. A yummy dog-cake and it's all yours."

As Spaz dropped the ball, Simmons scooped up the pancake and biscuit and carefully balanced it on Spaz's nose. "Okay, are you ready?"

Spaz whined.

"Good."

Simmons released his hand from the treat and Spaz flipped his head up, chomping at the flying pancake and biscuit. He caught the biscuit, but the pancake flopped to the floor.

"I'll give you an 8.2 on that one, Spaz, but the two European judges only gave you a 6.3 and 6.5. You've got to work on your technique."

Wanda stopped at the doorway to the kitchen. "What's going on here?"

"Well, well, the ravishing princess has finally arrived," Simmons said, saluting her with the spatula. "Breakfast is now being served."

Wanda looked down at Spaz. "Yum, yum. My favorite. Maybe you can toss mine over here where the floor's a little cleaner."

Wanda smiled seductively, then raised her hands in surprise as a pancake flipped twice through the air and landed at her feet.

"With or without the dog-biscuit béarnaise?" Simmons teased. They both laughed as Spaz eyed the new pancake on the floor.

They ate breakfast in the small nook overlooking the backyard. Simmons wished their time together could extend on and on, that the morning would never end. He was all too aware that his gesture to partake in domestic life would be short-lived, but he kept putting off telling Wanda that he had to leave again.

"Seeing how it's Friday and you just got back from who knows where, how about if you and I head up to the coast tonight? You know, get a room at one of those cozy bed-and-breakfasts . . . a bottle of champagne . . . moonlight walk in the sand."

Wanda looked up expectantly. Simmons finished his juice and avoided Wanda's gaze. When he didn't respond, she quickly interpreted his silence. "Al, no. Not again. You just got back."

A car honked from the front of the house. Simmons knew it was Terry Fitzgerald, who Wynn had sent over to pick him up.

"I'm sorry."

Wanda sadly shook her head. "Can't they give you at least a few days off?"

Simmons sighed. "I'd hoped for some downtime." He was about to tell her his plans to leave the agency, but Wanda abruptly stood up.

"But duty calls. Right, Al?" She walked across the kitchen.

Simmons set down the fork on his plate. He was unhappy with the turn of events, but how else could he expect her to react? "Wanda, you know there's nothing more I'd like to do than take off with you, but . . ."

"Yeah, I know . . . the job. The job you can never talk about, the job that takes you away to who knows where. It's like this thing that has taken over your life. We don't have a life anymore. At least, not much of one."

Simmons, feeling guilty, responded weakly. "Something important has come up or Jason wouldn't call me."

"I believe you, Al, but I never know when, or *if* you are coming back. And I'll tell you, I'll be frank, it's hard on me. It really is. And I can tell it's not what you want, either.''

Fitzgerald honked again in the driveway.

''I don't have a choice.''

''Yes you *do*, Al. I just want you to make the right choice. For yourself.''

Wanda moved closer to him. ''Each time you go out there, you come back a little more *dead* inside. And I don't want to lose you, Baby, but I don't know if I can take much more. Besides, I have a really bad feeling about whatever you're doing.''

Simmons went over to Wanda and took her hand. He knew he couldn't walk out with her asking questions about the future of their relationship. ''Listen, Wanda, this isn't how I wanted the morning to turn out. I got up early and cooked our favorite breakfast because I've been thinking about us. About our future.''

Wanda met his gaze. She looked guarded, but hopeful. ''Yeah? And what kind of future are you talking about, Mr. Simmons?''

Simmons squeezed her hands. ''I've decided to find a new line of work, something closer to home.''

Wanda's smile brightened the darkness within Simmons, then she hugged him tightly. ''You don't know how long I've been waiting for you to say that.''

''And vice versa. Just one last piece of business and we can get down to the Wanda-and-Al thing.''

She ran a hand through his hair. ''Promise you'll come back in one piece?''

Fitzgerald honked again, this time more insistently, as if he were concerned that Simmons didn't hear him.

''Count on it. There isn't anything that could stop me. Hell or high water. You won't ever lose me again. I promise.''

As they kissed, Spaz pawed at Simmons's leg, his

ball locked between his jaw. Simmons broke the kiss and looked down. ''You wait your turn, buster.''

He returned to the embrace and the kiss, confident now that he wouldn't lose her and that their new life was about to happen. Just the way he had always pictured it.

FOUR

TERRY FITZGERALD leaned against the door of his gray sedan, sipping his coffee, and reading *USA Today*. He knew that Simmons hadn't even been home a full day and he didn't blame him for taking his time. He was expecting Simmons to grumble the entire way. But Jason Wynn had been insistent that he make sure that he and Simmons report promptly at 10:30. It was quarter after now and even with light traffic, they were going to be ten minutes late by the time they parked and walked into headquarters.

He tapped his horn again.

Fitzgerald had known Simmons since Antioch, when they'd crammed together for tests. They were roommates, best friends, and often double-dated on weekends. They were both on the baseball team. Fitzgerald was the lead-off hitter and played second base, while Simmons batted cleanup and roamed center field. Simmons studied hard and so did well in all his academic courses, but Fitzgerald was a natural. He breezed through the four years, earned straight A's and rarely lost any sleep over his studies.

After college, Terry's excellent academic skills landed him in a bidding war with five different government agencies. At first, he opted for the FBI, but the training at

Quantico proved too exhaustive. So he accepted a position with the CIA. There, he interpreted data from the Soviet bloc and kept current by taking additional training courses. He ran into his old buddy Simmons during one of those excursions, a language immersion school in Monterey, California. They lived close to each other in New York and became inseparable.

Wanda walked out the front door, dressed in dark slacks and a red sweater with her purse slung over her shoulder. She opened the iron gate and waved. "Morning, Terry. He'll be right out."

She headed for her Mercedes, which he knew was ten years old but looked as if it had just come off the showroom floor. She kept the convertible in storage every winter and drove Simmons's Explorer. He figured she kept herself in fine form for Simmons, too, but he didn't want to pursue that line of thinking too long. Simmons was his best friend, after all.

"Hey, do me a favor, Wanda. Buy your man a watch. We're running late."

She looked up at him and smiled as she unlocked the Mercedes. "You make sure he's back for dinner tonight. I haven't seen much of him lately."

"Do my best!" He saluted her. He didn't know what Wynn was up to, but Fitzgerald had the feeling that Simmons was not going to be home this evening.

Wanda started to drive away but stopped next to his car and rolled down the passenger window. "Say, Terry, is this your idea of a joke?"

He walked over and leaned down, looking in the passenger window. She was pointing at a clown air freshener hanging from the mirror. On it was an inscription that said: "Love and Bandages."

He frowned. "No way. Remember, I'm a clean-cut, straight-shooter. I don't do practical jokes. Don't even have much of a sense of humor."

Terry watched her go, then got into his car when he saw Simmons. Spaz barked at Simmons's feet and followed him all the way to the gate. The dog knew his master was leaving and he wasn't happy about it.

Simmons knelt down and Spaz cocked his head. "Okay, Spaz. Usual routine. Guard Wanda and the house until I get back."

Spaz barked and leaped into the air as Simmons climbed into the sedan. The dog raised its head and watched as the car pulled out into the street, then he retreated to the front stoop and lay down to patiently await his master's return. Even if it took twenty years.

As they drove off, Fitzgerald handed Simmons a file with CHAPEL written on it. "The morning briefing. You read while I speed."

Simmons sighed and unsealed the file. "I'm gonna get married, Terry."

Fitzgerald slammed on the brakes. "What? Is she pregnant?"

Simmons shrugged. "Wanda's the best thing that ever happened to me."

"Al, think about it. In your line of work, you don't get married. Wives are not happy with guys who are never home, who can never tell them anything about what they do all day and all night."

"I know, Terry. That's why this one is gonna be my last op."

Fitzgerald shook his head. "Man!" He stepped on the accelerator again and turned onto Rhode Island Avenue. "Wynn's gonna hit the roof. You know, he considers you the best."

"I don't care about Wynn," Simmons answered. "How're you gonna handle it?"

"Hey, whatever makes you happy. I'm there for you, man. You can count on me. Congratulations." He reached over and they shook hands.

"Just be there with the ring."

Fitzgerald shot him a look. "Now don't you start going to church on me."

They both laughed and Fitzgerald noticed that they were passing the old gothic-style church that was now the Emergency Deliverance Church. In front of it stood a bearded old man in a long coat and a wide-brimmed hat who seemed to watching them as they passed.

"Did you see that guy?" Simmons yelped, excitedly. "Stop. Go back."

Simmons pulled over to the side of the road. "What guy? What are you talking about?"

"Where'd he go?" Simmons sounded perplexed. "He was just there. Standing in front of the church. Didn't you see him?"

"We gotta get going, Al. We're already running late. It was just an old guy, probably a derelict. Lot of them hang out around that church."

"Okay. Go on. It couldn't have been the same guy, anyhow."

Fitzgerald started to ask what guy he meant, but thought better of it. He pulled away and was relieved when he turned left on Sixteenth Street and saw that traffic was moving at full speed. Simmons was silent, mulling over something.

"Okay, so who did you think the old fellow looked like?"

"An old man I saw in Hong Kong."

"That guy didn't look exactly like a jet-setter." Fitzgerald laughed. "I really doubt that he was in Hong Kong yesterday."

"Maybe it's just a disguise."

Fitzgerald thought about that. In spite of his job as an analyst for A-6, he tried not to think about the world in terms of conspiracies, spies, and counterspies. That was for the movies. He thought of his work as a good government job, one with increasingly generous benefits for those who stuck with it. But then, Simmons was a field operative and his work was was more closely related to the great game of spy novels and lore.

"It's kind of an obvious disguise, isn't it? He attracts your attention. He doesn't blend in very well with that hat, even among the homeless crowd."

"Yeah, you're right. Forget it."

Fitzgerald picked up the newspaper from next to his seat and held it out to Simmons as he shifted lanes and accelerated past three cars that were all exceeding the forty-five mile an hour speed limit.

Such is Washington traffic, Simmons thought. *Even on the roads, it was kill or be killed.*

"Take a look at the top story. Did you hear anything about it, Al?"

Simmons scanned the paper and saw the headline about terrorists knocking a commercial airliner, with three hundred and sixty passengers, out of the sky off the coast of Miami Beach. As he read the article the pain showed on his face.

"Jesus, I intentionally avoided the television this morning and didn't look at the paper. This must be the reason."

Terrorists from the same group that he supposedly exterminated had retaliated for the killing on their leader in Hong Kong. A hand-held missile launcher, similar to the one that he had used, had been responsible. It was speculated that the missile was launched from a yacht in Biscayne Bay.

"That airport op was supposed to stop the terrorists," Fitzgerald said. "We end up killing two dozen bystanders, and they come back and kill a planeload of innocent people. Another Jason Wynn special."

"What do you mean?" Simmons asked the question even though he thought he knew the answer. But he wanted to find out what his friend would say about Wynn.

Fitzgerald chose his words carefully. He knew that Wynn had a vindictive streak and was especially suspicious of analysts. "Seems to me like most of Wynn's ops have screwed the pooch lately."

Simmons was quiet for a couple of beats. "Well, I'm glad I'm not the only one who's been suspicious. I don't know what the hell's going on. We're supposed to follow orders with the idea that everything is for the greater good. But frankly, I don't see it. We seem to be creating problems, not solving them."

"You got it. Lucky for you, Al, you'll be out of here in no time at all. If I had any guts, I'd do the same thing."

Fitzgerald approached a massive complex of fortress-like buildings a few blocks from the White House and drove up to the main gate of the A-6 headquarters. He glanced over at Simmons and instantly recognized the intense expression on his face. He was seething inside like a slow-burning stick of dynamite that could explode at any time. Even though he usually didn't have access to details of specific missions, he knew from what Simmons had said that he was the gunman in the Hong Kong operation.

"Don't worry, Al," he said. "I'm going to keep an eye on Wynn. If he's abusing his power, I'll see that he gets nailed."

Fitzgerald leaned out the window, slid a card into the security machine, and entered a code. On the other side of the vehicle, a guard in an enclosed booth read the security data on a monitor.

A large scanner was turned on below the car and everything inside the vehicle, including Fitzgerald and Simmons, was analyzed. Fitzgerald grabbed his crotch, smiled, and in a Conehead voice, said: "Protect the seed pods from the evil eye."

Simmons stared straight ahead. He didn't laugh, didn't say anything.

A green light flashed on the guard's screen as the car cleared. The gate opened and Terry drove in. Three A-6 Suburbans and an armored urban transport were parked near the main entrance. Several men and women employees in suits were coming and going through the darkly tinted double doors.

Fitzgerald pulled into his personal parking spot. "Are you okay, Al?"

"Listen, let me go in first. I want to talk to Wynn alone."

Before Fitzgerald could reply, Simmons strode purposefully across the lot toward the door. "Uh-oh. Wynn's got one mad operative on his hands."

Wynn glanced at his watch, wondering how much longer he would have to wait for Simmons and Fitzgerald. He leaned back in his chair and turned to Jessica Chapel, who was seated on the black leather couch where Clown had sat the night before.

He smiled at the seductive blond. Chapel was like a sleek fighter jet: appealing to look at—if you liked a streamlined body—but also a death machine when it delivered its payload. She was beautiful, cool-eyed, sensuous; a mixture of allure and arrogance in a stunning and lethal package. She was one of Wynn's most efficient tools, especially with difficult targets.

At least a dozen enemies had met their end in bed with Chapel. If they appealed to her, she would satisfy them and herself first, then dispatch them when they were most vulnerable. Others would die before they had a chance to fulfill their desires. Chapel could never decide which fate was more exquisite to deal out.

Wynn knew all about Chapel's charms. They'd carried on a secret relationship for more than two years. He loved his wife, but Chapel was special. The erotic pleasures she provided were unequaled, and he sometimes had trouble separating Chapel as operative from Chapel as lover. Oddly, he even felt a measure of jealously toward the men she befriended as part of her work, even though they all died at her hands.

"Have you made up your mind?"

"You mean, will I do it?" She smiled seductively, brushing the tip of her tongue over ruby lips. "Of course, I will, Wynn." She winked. "You know that I'm here for you, any time."

"That's good. I knew I could count on you." His gaze trailed down to her breasts as she leaned toward him. "You'll be working with me on this one. I'll give you all the details later."

Suddenly the door burst open and Simmons walked directly over to Wynn and dropped a newspaper on his desk. He stepped back and glared at him.

Wynn glanced at the newspaper. "Thanks," he said, coolly. "But I've already read it." Simmons was out of control and Wynn knew that he had made the right decision.

Simmons hovered over him, his big hands propped on his desk. "So explain to me how a group of terrorists that I just vaporized managed to blow a plane full of people out of the sky."

Wynn turned his chair so he faced Simmons. "Listen, Al, I wish things had gone down differently just as much as you do, but the airport op had to happen when it did, the way it did."

"What do you mean by that? The airport kill zone was supposed to be clear of civilians."

Wynn casually reached for a cigar and lit it, ignoring the operative. He wasn't going to let Simmons intimidate him, especially not in front of Chapel.

"An unfortunate but necessary sacrifice," he finally responded.

"Right. If you want somebody filling body bags with kids, send someone else." He looked over at Chapel as if challenging her to say something.

"If you can't handle your assignments, I'll fill your boots," she answered with pouty lips.

Simmons glared at her.

"I'll send whoever, wherever I want," Wynn interceded. "You follow orders and do your job. You don't question the order because you are only seeing part of the picture. We can't and won't tell you everything. Nor do we want you to know everything. Got a problem with that, soldier?"

"I do. And I want out. I resign."

Chapel stood up. She wore a tight, low-cut dress. She smiled, throwing her shoulders back. "I always knew you'd lose your nerve, Simmons." She smirked with a sensual derision.

Wynn was taken aback. He hadn't expected him to quit. Simmons was a fighter, a competitor, who refused to accept defeat. He had been motivated to achieve, to fight back and win since he was a kid.

Wynn realized, though, that his new tactics were going to cause problems for operatives, like Simmons, who wanted clear justifications of their actions. He would have to weed them out, too.

"You don't quit us," Wynn said, stiffly. "We're not the Post Office."

"I'm getting married."

Now it was Wynn's turn to smirk. "Wanda." A beat passed. "I should've seen it coming."

He laughed and exchanged a look with Chapel, who knew Simmons's future definitely didn't include marriage. "Haven't you read your own profile? You're a borderline psychopath. Perfect for certain field operations. But you're not family material. No way."

Simmons met his gaze. He wasn't backing down. "I'm out."

"Have you ever considered that you won't be happy doing anything else?"

"You're *wrong* about me," Simmons retorted. "I can walk away and forget."

"Are you sure there's nothing I can do to change your mind?"

"Nothing."

Wynn leaned back in his chair, appraising Simmons. He bit off the end of the cigar but didn't light it. Then he stood up and smiled. He offered his hand. Simmons seemed surprised but shook hands with him as if they were parting as friends.

"Congratulations, Al. I'm not sure how we're going to replace you." Wynn turned serious and businesslike. "I'll sign your transfer . . . *after* we've run this op. It'll be your last one."

"Are you sure you still want me on board?" Simmons looked baffled and uneasy.

"No hard feelings."

Before Simmons could say anything more, Wynn grabbed his remote-control device and hit a button. An image of North Korea and surveillance photos of a manufacturing facility appeared on a monitor mounted on the wall. The photos were progressively magnified until the structure came fully into view.

"We've got a North Korean refinery here that is producing biochemical weapons. Enough product is being produced each month to wipe out the population of Los Angeles if it were strategically released throughout the city. We've recently learned that the weapon is being sold to our enemies in the Mideast, who are intent on getting it into this country."

Wynn paused to let Simmons digest the enormity of the situation and the importance of the mission. "It's up to us to destroy the manufacturing equipment and *carefully* neutralize the biochemical toxins. With an expert like you, Al, I think we can accomplish our goals with a minimum loss of life. But keep in mind that anyone working at that plant is associated with a type of weapon that has been outlawed by the civilized world.''

''I guess I'm not going to make it home for dinner tonight.''

Wynn smiled. ''I'm afraid not. Your plane leaves within the hour.''

Simmons nodded. ''So let's get it over with.''

FIVE

NORTH KOREA

The late-night ride north from Pyongyang went on relentlessly, hour after hour through the night. Simmons was attached to the bottom of an armored vehicle that he knew was destined for the plant. Rocks flew up from the road, striking his back and legs. Dust billowed over his face, clogging his nostrils. The cold air numbed him, even though he was well protected by insulated coveralls. Finally, the truck reached the biochemical plant and rolled to a stop at the gate.

Fortunately, the North Korean guards were not as technologically sophisticated as the folks at the A-6 headquarters. The vehicle was inspected, but from the tone of the exchanges, the guards seemed to know the driver and trusted him. After a couple of minutes, the truck moved through the gate and stopped a hundred yards inside the compound.

Simmons was set to carry out the mission, but once again Wynn had misinformed him. The truck had passed a village less than a mile away from the plant. He couldn't detonate the chemicals without killing everyone in the village. Instead, he would have to find a way to put the plant out of commission without the use of explosives. He cursed Wynn and waited for the the guards to move away from the truck.

He realized now that he should've refused to take this final assignment, in spite of its serious nature. He'd considered it the honorable thing to do at the time, but Wynn was no longer an honorable man. Not only had Wynn misled him again, but now Simmons realized something else. Wynn probably considered Simmons expendable. He knew too much. He would be dangerous on the outside.

Three days had passed since he'd left home and now he hoped he could finish the task in the next two or three hours and make his escape to South Korea. He'd crossed into North Korea with the help of South Koreans who had led him through a mountainous region to a hideout fifteen kilometers into North Korea. There he was met by a North Korean spy who transported him to the capital city of Pyongyang.

He'd traveled in a tiny hollow space beneath the backseat of the truck for twelve hours. North Korea was far more dangerous than Hong Kong, where foreigners were just part of the background of daily life. In North Korea, however, the mere sight of a Westerner was likely to attract attention and lead to incarceration.

Simmons had been relieved when he finally straightened his limbs again after the truck had arrived at its destination, a warehouse where the armored truck was preparing for its monthly trek to the plant. Even though the truck driver was involved in the scheme, Simmons was forced to travel in the only safe spot—the bottom of the armored vehicle. Very soon the cramped compartment under the seat had seemed like a comfortable haven compared to dangling several inches above the road.

He passed some of the time recalling statistical information he'd memorized about North Korea. Terrain: mostly hills and mountains separated by deep, narrow valleys; coastal plains wide in west, discontinuous in east. Natural resources: coal, lead, tungsten, zinc, graphite, magnesite, iron ore, copper, gold, pyrites, salt, fluorspar, hydropower.

Environment, current issues: localized air pollution attributable to inadequate industrial controls; water pollution; inadequate supplies of potable water. Natural hazards: late spring droughts often followed by severe flooding; occasional typhoons during the late summer and early fall.

Population growth-rate estimates (1995): 1.78%. Birth rate: 23.31 births/1,000 population. Death rate: 5.47 deaths/1,000 population. Infant mortality rate: 26.8 deaths/1,000 live births.

Net migration rate: 0 migrants/1,000 population.

Zero plus one, Simmons had thought. But he wasn't planning on staying.

Finally, the guards and the driver walked away from the truck. Simmons disengaged the electromagnet that held him to the chassis and dropped to the ground. He rolled to the edge of the truck, peered through an infrared viewer, and inspected the area, first on one side of the truck, then the other. He counted half a dozen sentries, then he spotted a darkened catwalk high on the plant wall where several more armed guards patrolled. Reaching the main building was going to take some finesse, but no more than usual.

The closest sentry was less than a hundred feet away, guarding a refinery tower. After Simmons watched him for a few minutes, the sentry moved to the far side of the tower and lit a cigarette. That was when Simmons made his move, dashing toward the tower. The sentry had just crushed out the cigarette with the heel of his boot when Simmons dropped from above and snapped his neck with a quick turn of his hands.

He'd once heard a chiropractor say that it was extremely difficult to break a man's neck with your hands, like you saw in the movies. He figured it was the man's way of appeasing Simmons's concern about getting his neck adjusted. Either that or the chiropractor didn't know the technique. It was all in the visualization and the follow-through. You saw it happening; it happened.

Snap!

Simmons moved toward the plant, stealthily avoiding other guards. But as he turned a corner near an elevator shaft, he nearly walked right into one. He quickly delivered a blow that knocked the guard's gun away, but the man instantly retaliated with a side kick that knocked Simmons against the wall, where he smacked his head.

His knees buckled for a couple of seconds, but then he stuttered back to his feet, clearing his head. The guard assumed a martial-arts stance, then kicked hard and high. But this time Simmons ducked, avoiding the blow, and tumbled forward and up onto his feet. The guard charged, leaped, and drove his heel toward the bridge of Simmons's nose.

Simmons instantly ducked and spun around, catching the guard off-balance. His swing-kick struck the side of the man's head. The powerful blow flipped him over a railing, where he landed on his back and didn't get up. Simmons checked for other activity, then moved on. He pulled open the gate to the industrial elevator and descended to a lower level.

When the elevator stopped, he cautiously pushed open the gate. According to the plans he'd studied, the entrance of the wing to the biochemical processing plant was just around the corner to his right. He turned the corner and saw the double doors to the processing area. Just like the plan, except for one thing. There was no guard at the entrance as he'd expected.

The unoccupied entrance puzzled him. He knew that anything that varied from the prescribed game plan might signal trouble. He sensed a trap and hesitated. Finally, he moved ahead, edging toward the door, his smart-gun in hand, his mind alert, his muscles tensed.

He pushed open one of the double doors, stepped through the doorway, and stopped. A body lay on the floor, a puddle of fresh blood under its head. He crouched low and moved forward, expecting trouble at any moment. He glimpsed a second body lying a few feet away. Someone had gotten there ahead of him. He didn't like it; that wasn't part of the plan.

He continued forward, more cautious than ever. The large core-processing area contained several hi-tech tanks and other apparatus. His attention was immediately drawn to a pair of huge tanks, which were labeled Level 4 Biohazard in Korean script. Explosive charges were attached to each of the tanks.

Simmons was concerned and confused. It was as if someone else was doing his job. He had no idea what was going on, and he had to get some answers fast before he, or someone else, made a serious mistake.

A man wearing a biohazard suit appeared between the two tanks and waved to him. Simmons aimed his weapon at the man, who moved toward him seemingly unconcerned. As he neared Simmons, the man pulled off his protective hood as if he'd just walked inside from the cold. Simmon was momentarily stunned at the sight of Jason Wynn.

"What the hell are you doing here?"

"Priorities have changed," Wynn snapped. "I'm taking over here."

"There are people living less than a mile from here," Simmons responded. "We can't detonate these tanks. We'll wipe out the entire town."

Wynn smiled. "Yes, I know about Lichon. Eight thousand experimental hosts. Now we'll find out how effective the toxins are that they've developed."

Anger rippled through Simmons. His hands curled into fists. His shoulders tensed. "What are you talking about?" He aimed the smart-gun at Wynn. "Get out of my way. I'm not gonna let you do it."

He brushed past Wynn and headed to the tanks, intent on disarming them. But as he approached the tanks, another figure, also garbed in protective gear, stepped between the tanks. The hood was pulled back, and with a sinking feeling he recognized Chapel. She was armed with her own smart-gun with laser sights and a silencer.

"Hold it, Simmons!"

He hesitated and that was all she needed. She fired and the first volley struck his weapon, knocking it from his hands. The next shots hit him in the leg and shoulder and sent him sprawling.

"Looks like I'm up for a promotion," she said, standing over him.

Simmons gritted his teeth, trying to push away the pain. "Do you wipe Jason's ass, too? Or do you just lick it clean?"

He tried to grab his smart-gun, but Chapel kicked it out of his reach, then stomped on his hand. "Oh, does that hurt? Try this?" She kicked him brutally in the head and he dropped flat to the floor.

Simmons tried to raise his head. When his vision cleared, he was staring up at Wynn. "Is this another necessary sacrifice, Jason? You knew exactly what was going down all along."

Wynn took out a silver cigarette case and lit a Dunhill. "You know, Chapel, I do believe he's starting to catch on." He snapped his lighter shut and slipped it into the pocket of his protective suit. "Time for Al's big send-off."

Chapel engaged a special function of her smart-gun. A nozzle emerged and sprayed a clear gelatin over Simmons's face and down his body. Then she sprayed the area around Simmons.

"What are you doing?" he yelled, but he already guessed their plans.

The gelatin burned his skin, especially over his wounds, where the gelatin and blood mixed in a sickly solution. Whatever she'd sprayed on him, Simmons guessed that it was highly flammable. He tried to stand up, but his wounds were too serious and he fell back to the floor, coughing and gagging.

Wynn took a drag on his cigarette and held the glowing tip over Simmons. "So, enjoy your retirement. Oh, and don't worry about Wanda. I'll take good care of her."

"Touch Wanda and you're a dead man!" Simmons shouted, angrily.

"Correction. You're a dead man."

Simmons realized that he'd been working for a sadist, a sick, cruel man whose actions had nothing to do with patriotism and the defense of the country. He'd once admired Wynn and considered him his teacher, his general. But Wynn had sold his soul to something dark and evil, that was all he could figure.

Wynn took another deep drag from his cigarette. The ash glowed bright red. "I really should cut down. It's a terrible habit."

Wynn flicked the cigarette and it twisted through the air. Simmons strained to knock it away with his good arm. He managed to hit the cigarette and smother it in the gel with his hand. It smoldered and went out. But then he noticed a thin stream of smoke curling up from his arm where a part of the burning ash had landed. He swatted at it, but the rush of air ignited the tiny coal, and before he struck it, the gelatin ignited, sending flames racing up his arm and over his neck and face.

He frantically batted at the flames, but they quickly rushed over his chest and abdomen. Within seconds, he was entirely engulfed, the flames spreading now in a circle around him. His arms flailed as his skin bubbled and popped. He tried to stand up and fell over. He rolled and rolled, but the flames burned hotter and brighter. Then he could feel nothing, his nerve endings gone, and Simmons knew he was doomed.

"See you in Hell," Wynn yelled. His laughter trailed after him as he and Chapel dashed away. Amid the horrific smell of his burning flesh, he saw Wanda standing in front of him. She was smiling, playing with Spaz. They were at home waiting for him to return.

"Wanda! Wanda!"

Then an enormous explosion rocked the building.

Wynn and Chapel pulled on their their protective headgear and turned on the internal air tanks as they raced out of the plant. Three guards were positioned between them and the waiting truck, but Chapel brought down all three with a flurry of gunfire. A couple of the guards on the catwalk shouted and fired in their direction, but at that moment Wynn hit the button on the remote detonator. The tanks exploded, sending multiple fireballs through the roof of the plant. Guards tumbled from the catwalks, yelling in surprise.

The driver of the truck who had taken Simmons to the plant was wearing a gas mask and waiting for them. They leaped in the front seat and roared off. The flames spread out from the plant, and the deadly gas was dispersed over the land. A few miles away, a chopper was waiting, manned by a North Korean pilot who was ready to defect. He'd picked them up after they'd crossed the border and had flown them here. After their arrival, another truck driver smuggled them into the plant. Everything had gone without a hitch, except that they'd had to remain in hiding for three hours while they'd waited for the truck carrying Simmons to arrive. But that didn't matter now.

Wynn patted Chapel on the thigh. The first part of the mission was complete.

Al Simmons's burnt corpse spiraled down, down, down, trailing flames like a dying meteor. Then he was sucked into a swirling, tunnel-shaped firestorm, and Hell's welcome wagon rose up to greet him: the sound of countless wailing, laughing, screaming, tortured souls roiling through the inferno. The pain had returned a thousand-fold more agonizing.

Simmons smashed into a lake of hellfire, a landscape of blue and crimson flames where he sizzled, dried, and hardened like a piece of meat abandoned on a charcoal grill. A titanic beast, so tall he seemed to curve as he rose over Simmons, thundered through curtains of magma flames to greet him. Its crimson-yellow eyes flared a moment at the sight of the new arrival, then it let loose a concussive volley of laughter.

Nearby, Clown gleefully howled, delighted by his success.

Simmons struggled in pain to stand up. Clown multiplied and rippled like a mirage, and the pain intensified. He heard a woman's voice crying out and turned to see Wanda's face through the flames. She was screaming and crying at the bad news. His own anguished cry melded with the scream, and the flames rose around him.

"No rush, fellow," Clown chortled, "the nightmare is just beginning. Gotta go now. Got another appointment back where you came from."

Wynn checked his watch. Five after four. He'd rested for about three hours. He felt groggy and sore, but he was alive, and that was the first good sign of the day.

He shook Chapel's shoulder and gave the helicopter pilot a brisk shove. They'd spent the night on the floor of a barren hideout on the far side of a small mountain range.

Wynn had figured that the mountains and the favorable wind direction would keep the drifting biochemical death away from them, and it looked like he was right. He checked the air with his particle detector gauge and was relieved to find no trace of the deadly airborne weapon.

"Let's go and get it over with."

They put on the biohazard suits, and a few minutes later climbed into the chopper. Before taking off, they tightened the head shields and turned on the oxygen.

They arrived on the outskirts of Lichon twenty minutes later. A gray, ominous dawn crept over the countryside, barely illuminating the dense overcast sky. It was a dawn without hope, one that brought no promises of a fine day.

Their suits' two internal oxygen tanks fit neatly around their bodies. They would have approximately forty more minutes on the first tank, then to be safe, just half an hour longer on the second one before they would leave.

That should be plenty of time to accomplish their objective. Besides, the longer they stayed, the greater the likelihood soldiers would arrive. Reports of the explosion and deaths had probably escaped the town during the night. The remote location of Lichon and the nature of the disaster had given them several hours, but Wynn knew the window of opportunity was closing.

The pilot powered down the engine and Wynn and Chapel climbed out. But when Wynn signaled the pilot to come with them, he shook his head and pointed down, indicating he wanted to remain behind. Wynn hurried around to the other side of the chopper and jerked the pilot out. He wasn't about to give the guy a chance to change his mind and fly off without them.

"Hey, if you want your defection to be taken seriously, you do what I say."

As soon as they entered the main street, it was obvious that the wind had swept the toxic fumes from the explosion over the town. Dozens of people lay dead on the street. Their faces were twisted in horrid death masks, indicating that their deaths had been excruciatingly painful. Not a pleasant way to go. But Wynn was impressed that death had come so quickly for so many.

Others weren't so lucky. They were crawling, gagging, weeping. Some barely alive. He would be interested in finding out how many survived, and why they survived. He knew the North Vietnamese were experimenting with a weapon that combined deadly gases with an even more deadly viral strain.

He wanted to refine the weapon, then begin manufacturing and selling it abroad. It was all part of his master plan. But first he needed to obtain blood samples from the victims here in Lichon.

He checked his gauge and saw that the fumes were almost gone, but that didn't mean anything. He couldn't detect the presence of a deadly virus, and that was what would eventually take the lives of the majority of the hapless victims.

As they continued down the narrow side streets, the body count increased with every step. There was no need to go into any buildings to search for victims. Hundreds, maybe thousands, had fled their homes, trying to escape whatever was consuming their lungs.

He noticed that the pilot was sobbing behind his mask. Once they were safe in South Korea, they would take care of him. No need to have any witnesses around to talk about what happened here.

At the next corner, they came upon a military Jeep. One soldier was hanging over the steering wheel, the other had dropped his head against the dashboard. They both looked up at the white suits and helmets, held out their hands, and jabbered for help. Chapel quickly dispatched them with shots to the head. They'd probably been sent to see what they'd find and had reported back on their radio.

Now the other soldiers were staying out of the town until they were properly equipped.

Wynn glanced at his watch. "Let's get busy."

He opened the Velcro pocket on his leg and carefully took out one of several hypodermic needles. He found a boy of six nearby, jabbed the needle into his neck, and took a blood sample. "Try to find little kids and babies," he told Chapel. "The concentration will be higher in their blood."

They finished in twenty minutes and headed back to the chopper. The quicker he was out of here, the better. He was feeling weak and worried that he had punctured his suit somewhere. He asked Chapel to look it over. To his relief, she didn't find any rips.

He tried not to look at any more bodies. Instead, he thought about the rest of the day, and how he hoped it would turn out. By evening, he and Chapel would be safe in their luxury suite in Seoul. They would clean up, rest a while, then enjoy a champagne dinner, toasting their success. And of course Chapel would be ravenous for him, out of her mind with desire. She was always that way after the most dangerous and deadly assignments. Somehow death and sex went well together.

He heard coughing down an alleyway to his right. He didn't want to look, didn't want to see another dying Korean. But something made him stop and turn. He couldn't believe it. Clown was leaning against a wall with no protective suit, without even any warm clothing on. His arms were wrapped around one another over his belly, and he gagged and choked.

Then he looked up and motioned to Wynn, then bent over and started coughing again. Chapel and the pilot had walked on ahead of him, hurrying to the chopper, unaware of the intruder.

Wynn moved cautiously over to him. He had no idea how Clown had gotten here, and he didn't really want to know. Clown was a necessary evil, a power that he only faintly comprehended. "What are you doing here?" he asked.

Clown stopped coughing and looked up. "I'm a tourist, here for the fresh mountain air. But I don't feel so good now."

He wretched suddenly and spewed a vile green liquid. "Ah, that feels better."

Wynn stepped back, not knowing what to expect next. "Aren't you concerned about the gas that's killing these people?"

He grinned. "I'm never concerned myself about the competition." He laughed. "Hey, better catch your chopper. The bad guys are on their way. Or . . ." He scratched his head. "Are we the bad guys?"

Wynn turned away, disgusted. Maybe the biochemical weapon wouldn't kill him, but there were other ways. When the time was right, he'd rid himself of the dwarf.

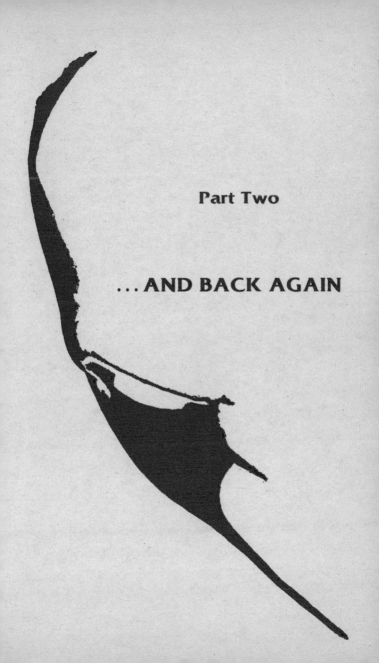

Part Two

...AND BACK AGAIN

SIX

HIS SCREAM faded back into the depth of his lost soul; his eyes snapped open. He had no sense of time, no sense of place, only a vague notion that something horrendous had happened to him, that something overpowering and ominous had overtaken his body and drained him of all that he had once been.

Lightning flashed above him, illuminating his seared torso. The sight of it sent Simmons twisting and convulsing as if he were still on fire. Thunder clapped like cymbals striking either side of his head. Pigeons took flight and another flash of lightning reconfirmed what he'd seen. Again he writhed and twitched, as if trying to escape the sight of his toasted body.

When he finally calmed down, he realized he was lying on the slanted roof of a building. A steeple grew from the peak of the roof and atop it was a huge gray, weather-beaten cross. Lightning zigzagged across the sky, and the cross cast a shadow that fell over his ruined body.

He sucked in a painful breath and rolled onto his side. Less than a foot from his leg, a black cat hissed, and the hair stood up on its arched back. It spat angrily and fled across the edge of the roof as Simmons tried to push himself to a sitting position.

Somehow he knew he was on top of the old Gothic cathedral, the one he passed everyday on his way to the

A-6 headquarters. He recalled that it had been abandoned years ago, then turned into a street mission. At first, the mission had been controversial. Residents and business owners didn't want to believe that there were many home-less people in the city or that they needed some source of support. But gradually the reality of the situation had set in and the mission and its homeless clients had become a part of the neighborhood.

He remembered details about the neighborhood; he re-membered his childhood and his life with Wanda. But what had happened to him, and how had he gotten on the roof? He tried to concentrate on the recent past, but all that came to mind were some strange statistics.

The numbers and facts ran rampant through his head: total area: 120,540 square kilometers; land area: 120,410 square kilometers; comparative area: slightly smaller than Mississippi; strategic location bordering China, South Ko-rea, and Russia; mountainous interior is isolated, nearly inaccessible, and sparsely populated.

Religions: Buddhism and Confucianism, some Christi-anity and syncretic Chondogyo. Autonomous religious ac-tivities now almost nonexistent; government-sponsored religious groups exist to provide illusion of religious free-dom.

He struggled to push away the surging flow of facts and figures. He had a vague recollection of being some-where in North Korea, of seeing Wynn and Chapel. Slowly, the memories returned. He'd been torched by Wynn. He was dead, burned to death beyond recognition. He couldn't have survived. But why was he here and in so much pain?

A squealing, snorting mix of chuckles and guffaws and the clapping of hands redirected Simmons's attention. He turned to the source and saw a short round figure with stubby legs and arms. The shadowy figure waved, and as lightning illuminated the roof again, he saw a monstrous grinning clown face, a nightmare image from child-hood.

The figure was standing at the far side of the roof be-tween two partially disintegrated gargoyles. He wore grimy, mismatched, undersized clothes. Its eerie, neon-blue clown grin leered at Simmons. As he chortled, flies swarmed around him, buzzing.

The longer he stared at the creature, the more Simmons knew about him. Sickeningly self-absorbed, malicious, perverse, arrogant and insecure, emotionally volatile, ver-min that saw himself as superior, even as royalty from a dark kingdom. A clown who distorted and twisted the term clown, unless he was understood for who he was—the Clown Prince of Hell.

The clown creature snorted and snickered, and his grin exposed a dental graveyard of rotting teeth. He licked his lips and Simmons tried to look away. But it was as if his gaze were permanently attached to the disgusting being.

"Hmm, look who was left in the oven too long." His voice was deep and sarcastic. He laughed, flapped his arms like wings, and scuttled away beyond the spires and gables and out of sight.

I'm hallucinating. That must be it, Simmons thought. He tried to clear his head and gazed out over the rooftops and brick walls of the dark urban sprawl. The stench of slums, squalor, and decay wafted toward him from all directions.

Slowly, painfully, he raised himself from the roof. He wobbled on his feet like a drunk and did his best not to look at himself. Every fiber of his body ached, and the smell of burned flesh filled his nostrils, overwhelming the other acrid odors. He glimpsed his charred, twisted hands and then felt his hideously scorch-scarred face. His hands shook and the world suddenly began to spin. He clattered back down, dropping to one knee, then the other as his hands smacked the roof.

He crawled clumsily toward the edge of the roof, intent on throwing himself over the edge and ending the pain and confusion. He lifted up into a half-crouch and noticed that he was dressed like a wino in old tattered clothing and old boots with holes in the toes.

What the hell? How long have I been here? Why don't I remember anything?

When he reached the edge of the roof, he saw a decrepit fire escape. His preference was to simply roll over the side and end his misery, but something inside told him it wouldn't work, that there was no easy way out, that the fall would just result in more pain. He didn't want to believe it, but the thought was simply too frightening to find out if it were true.

He climbed down the fire escape and dropped to the alley floor, falling into several battered trash cans. The shadowy alleyway was one of many that twisted through this downtrodden part of the city that had changed so much in recent years. He crawled out of the cans and stopped at the edge of a stagnant, smelly puddle. Another bolt of lightning ripped the black sky, making a mirror of the puddle, and forced Simmons to glimpse his . . . *remains,* he thought. His face was covered with grotesquely healed burn wounds. He touched his fingers to his face, confirming what he saw in the puddle. He didn't recognize himself.

No way that he was looking at Al Simmons. He slammed his ruined hand against the puddle and bellowed out his pain and confusion. "No! no! no!"

He was not just burned; he was changed, altered somehow. He realized that his body was too large. His shoulders were wider, his chest broader than he remembered. He was taller and thicker than the old Al Simmons. Even his voice was deeper, more menacing. He curled his fingers into fists, his raw anger swelled.

A kid wearing worn sneakers splashed into the puddle

and stopped in front of him. Simmons looked up to see a boy of about ten. He was wiry, with mussed hair that hadn't seen a comb in a long time. He wore layers of dingy clothing, the uniform of the homeless.

"Hey, mister, you don't look so good."

Simmons staggered to his feet and the boy helped to steady him. Simmons brushed the kid away and turned his back to him.

"I'm Zack, Zack Webb. You thirsty, mister?" He pulled out a half-empty bottle of Coke from inside his coat pocket and held it up to Simmons.

"Get lost, kid."

When he didn't move, Simmons slapped the bottle from his grasp.

Instantly, with startling swiftness, another hand snatched the bottle in midair. Simmons looked up and saw someone standing in the shadows behind the boy. He was about to walk away, but something drew his attention back to the man.

He wore a threadbare olive drab greatcoat dating back to the First World War. He had long silver-gray hair, a matching beard that rippled over his chest, and harsh, angular features. He looked to be in his early sixties, and there was a strangely commanding presence about him.

His hard, dark eyes held Simmons's gaze. Vaguely familiar eyes. Simmons recognized him but couldn't place him. Where had he seen him? A flash of an explosion, an airport, soldiers and the old man passed before his inner gaze. Hong Kong. It seemed so long ago. But his sense of time, like his entire body, was distorted.

"Who are you, anyhow? What do you want?"

The bearded old man kept his gaze fixed on Simmons but said nothing.

"What are you looking at?" Simmons said in a low, forbidding voice.

"You tell me."

Simmons ignored the man and leaned heavily against the alley wall. He felt weak, felt himself spiraling again. He started to fall, but caught himself.

Simmons held his temples, groaning. ''Where am I, anyhow?''

''Rat City . . . heart of the alley,'' Zack answered. ''I sleep over there.''

He pointed past a pile of rotting trash to a clutter of cardboard condos. Legs protruded from a couple of the box houses. Beyond them, two men scrounged through a Dumpster, searching for something they could eat or make use of. Near the wall, a mother wearing a stocking cap, a heavy coat, and a skirt over ragged slacks huddled with her three children around a fire. Their faces were smeared with soot; their eyes dulled by the burden of poverty.

''That's my place,'' Zack said, pointing to an old doorless refrigerator that lay on its side. Dirty blankets and old clothing were piled across the bottom. ''It's a good home because it won't fall apart in the rain like those cardboard places.''

''This is a holy place, where anyone can find sanctuary,'' the old man said.

Simmons wasn't sure he was talking about the church or the alley. He looked around the rundown surroundings. ''Yeah, right.''

''You've been here three days,'' the old man said. ''On the roof. I found some clothes for you. You didn't have any.''

''Three days,'' he said, shaking his head. ''I don't remember that.''

''You weren't conscious. You weren't completely here with us.''

Zack looked up at him with a curious expression. ''I've seen worse faces, mister. My dad used to work for a mortician.''

''Thanks a lot, kid,'' Simmons muttered. ''I feel much

better now.'' He pushed away from the wall and shoved Zack and the old man. He wanted to get away from this place. He didn't belong here. He didn't *want* to belong here. He was a competitor, a winner who never accepted defeat. These people were losers, bottom feeders. He had nothing in common with them.

He stumbled down the alley, past several of the local residents, who looked at him as if they knew him, as if he were one of them, a regular among the down-and-out alley-dweller. No, he told himself. It wasn't true. It couldn't be true.

He staggered through the filth and detritus to the end of the alley. Rain was falling, glossing the night street. A helicopter buzzed overhead, its spotlight bouncing over the decrepit buildings. For a moment, it blinded Simmons, and he held his arm over his eyes, backing away.

Two men rushed by, knocking him aside and pushing past the others on the street. From the helicopter, a blaring voice ordered the men to stop immediately.

Simmons looked around, confused by the turmoil. The street didn't look much better than the alley. Things had definitely gotten worse than he remembered. It was dirtier, scarier, and there were more police patrolling in their vehicles behind closed windows.

He stepped into the street and people on the sidewalk reacted to him, pointing and hurrying away. He crossed the street and shouldered a woman as she stepped out of a doorway. The woman jerked back at the sight of his face. She screamed and ran from him as if she'd just bumped into a demon from Hell.

Simmons reeled backward and stumbled into a mound of broken crates containing rotting fruit. Slowly, he stood up and brushed himself off, but the odor of rot still clung to him tenaciously.

The old man appeared in front of him. He held a battered overcoat and with a swift, agile movement tossed it to Simmons. The former A-6 ace, the man who saved a president's life, looked up suspiciously at the bearded old man. Then, begrudgingly, he pulled on the huge overcoat that looked like it was made for an elephant. It fit surprisingly well. He pulled the hood up over his head and was glad that it hid his battered face.

"Thanks, old man."

He was still suspicious about him and wondered what he wanted from him. He steadied himself against the wall and started walking away. The old man suddenly was at his side, walking with him.

"You know, you're welcome to join us, if you choose. We'll be here."

Simmons looked over at the old man, then staggered on without answering him. He took several more steps, began to weave back and forth. He stumbled, but stayed on his feet as he disappeared into a crowd.

Behind him, the old man—Alessandro di Cogliostro—stopped and watched the confused and disoriented figure who still believed he was the old Al Simmons, risen from the dead. With a hunter's patient gaze, he followed Simmons's progress down the street as two Rollerbladers, girl-punks with crewcuts and multiple rings piercing their ears, noses, lips and tongues, cruised by.

One of them signaled the other, and they turned around and made a second pass by the hulking form of Simmons. Trouble, Cogliostro thought, but the new Simmons could handle it. It wouldn't be long before his full transformation would be completed and Al Simmons would vanish forever. That was when Cogliostro would face his ultimate challenge.

SEVEN

SIMMONS REACHED a stop sign and leaned heavily against it. The signpost bent under his weight. He was weary from the walk, but now he had an objective. He just wasn't sure how long it was going to take to get there.

He staggered into the street and suddenly a Rollerblader cruised by him and pulled a club from a sheath. She swung it in the air and it telescoped out into a weapon the size of a baseball bat. The young girl-punk darted behind him and slammed the club against the back of his legs.

"Take that, you creep."

But the baton shattered upon impact, as if she'd struck it against a concrete wall. She stopped in amazement and stared at the remains of the club.

Simmons turned around and angrily lurched toward the girl. She skated out of his reach and frantically signaled to her friend. "Let's cruise."

She tossed the broken stub over her shoulder, and the pair skated away at full speed.

Simmons reeled across the street as the skies opened up. He kept walking through the night, block after block. The rain finally let up, but dogs began howling and baying when they picked up his scent. He fell down at least a dozen times, and finally collapsed behind a hedge.

At midmorning, he was awakened by a growling cocker spaniel that had just been let outside. He stumbled to his feet; the dog snapped at his ankle and ripped his already tattered pant leg. Angrily, Simmons kicked at the dog. It yelped once and retreated to the safety of its house and pawed at the door.

He moved on and after a few minutes recognized the row houses of his old neighborhood. Now he was close. He blundered down the sidewalk for several blocks and stopped by the iron gate in front of his house. Something was wrong. The house looked different. The color was lighter and the landscaping now included neatly trimmed hedges. He ducked behind a tree as a neighborhood security patrol motored past. He didn't remember that, either.

"What's going on here? What happened to my house?" Simmons said aloud.

Then he noticed balloons tied to the gate. Children's laughter came from behind the house along with applause. A little girl, about five, ran along the side of the house, chased by another giggling girl.

"Cyan," a voice called. "C'mon. It's time for the piñata."

The voice was achingly familiar. Wanda.

The two girls ran to the back of the house and disappeared. Simmons opened the gate and walked around the side of the house. He had to see Wanda. Somehow seeing her again would end this nightmare. Everything would be all right.

He stopped at the corner of the house and saw more balloons, tables, a cake, colorfully wrapped presents, and a dozen kids. A clown was performing tricks for the kids and a banner read: HAPPY BIRTHDAY CYAN.

The clown pulled a dove from a hat. He snapped his fingers and the dove transformed into a blackbird, which flew off into a tree. The kids applauded and cheered the clown.

"Now, where's our birthday girl?"

The clown moved over to little Cyan and blindfolded her. She was given a stick and led over to a hanging papier-mâché donkey. She swung several times at the piñata. "Harder, hit it harder," the kids yelled.

Finally, it burst open, spilling a shower of candy. All the kids rushed for the sweets, diving and grabbing whatever they could get.

Cyan pulled off the blindfold and a man moved forward, picked her up, and kissed her on the cheek. Simmons gaped in astonishment. It was Terry Fitzgerald. Then Wanda stepped into view, kissed Cyan, then Fitzgerald.

"What the hell?" Simmons coughed.

He couldn't believe what he was seeing. None of it made sense. It was as if he'd returned to the wrong world. In this one, Wanda was with Fitzgerald and they had a kid. The closer he looked, the more he saw that didn't fit with what he remembered. Fitzgerald looked older and he was wearing a goatee. Wanda's hair was longer than he ever remembered it. And there was something else about her. She looked more settled, more at home, happy.

He wanted to shout and to wave his hands like a movie director. "Cut, cut, cut. This is all wrong." He wanted to start this scene all over again. He wanted to walk back here and find Wanda waiting for him, and he desperately wanted to be his old self.

"I wanna do that again, Mommy."

"Oh, I don't think so, sweetie. Not this year. It took Daddy a week just to make that one."

She looked disappointed, then she hugged Fitzgerald. "Thank you, Daddy."

"You're welcome, sweetheart. Now, go get some of those goodies."

Cyan rushed off to gather candy with her friends. "I'll get more lemonade for the troops." Wanda kissed Fitzgerald again and playfully slapped his rump as she headed back into the house.

How could Fitzgerald do this to him, Simmons wondered. *How did it all happen so fast?* He couldn't fathom any of it. His life, his world, everything he'd known and trusted was shattered. Wanda and Fitzgerald were clearly a loving and contented married couple with a beautiful daughter.

Fitzgerald had stolen his life. Simmons's body began to quake as he fully absorbed the shock of what he had witnessed. *It couldn't be,* he told himself over and over again. Yet he knew he couldn't deny what he had just seen. He dropped to one knee and held his head in his crusty hands. Pain ripped through his body, amplifying the weakness and confusion that was overwhelming him. He took a ragged breath and tumbled face-first into the grass.

Wanda refilled the pitcher of lemonade and thought how blessed she was. She had gone through some rough times, rougher than she deserved. It all began five and a half long years ago when she'd heard the news about Al. She'd lost control. She'd started drinking heavily; she'd quit her teaching job. Days went by when she never left the house, had never even gotten dressed. She thought the alcohol and the pills would help her forget.

But whenever she began to surface again, all the old memories of Simmons and her former life returned, and the cycle began all over again. One day she decided she'd had enough and she swallowed a dozen Quaaludes, washing them down with half a bottle of Wild Turkey. She would never wake up again to her memories.

The last thing she remembered was seeing Terry Fitzgerald standing over her, shaking her shoulders. She told him over and over to go away. But he wouldn't leave her alone.

She found herself in a hospital. Her stomach had been pumped and Terry was at her side. He said he wasn't going to leave her, and he didn't. That was when she found out she was four months pregnant with Simmons's baby. She stopped drinking and took care of herself. With Terry's help she recovered, and by some miracle she gave birth to a perfectly healthy baby girl. She and Terry were married a few weeks later, and she put her past behind her.

But for some reason, she couldn't get Simmons out of her mind today. She knew she could never return to the past, and she certainly didn't want to think about the pain and sorrow she'd experienced. So why was he on her mind, haunting her thoughts?

And just like that, she was weeping, her shoulders shaking. She gasped for breath, leaned against the counter, and finally steadied her breathing. She dabbed her eyes with a Kleenex. What in the world has gotten into her? she wondered.

Maybe it was because of the birthday and because she could see so much of Simmons in Cyan. *Okay, cheer up. Stay with the present,* she told herself, then picked up the pitcher of lemonade and carried it out to the table.

"There you are, Wanda. I was about to go looking for you. You ready to cut the cake?"

"I guess so."

She busied herself, refilling the glasses as the kids raced around the backyard playing tag with the funny-looking fat little clown. She spotted Cyan sitting in the grass, looking at the candy she'd picked up from the piñata. Spaz was next to her, eagerly sniffing the wrappers, looking for a dog treat, as usual. Then suddenly, the wire-haired terrier looked up and dashed off, as if on some special mission that only he knew about.

Terry came up beside her and encircled her waist with his arm. "You okay? You look like something's on your mind. Hey, what's wrong? Your eyes are all red. Have you been crying?"

She smiled. "Tears of joy, I guess. I'm fine." She set down the lemonade and hugged him. "Just don't ever leave me, Terry. Do you promise?"

He leaned back, held her by the shoulders, frowning as he stared into her eyes. "You know that nothing and no one could ever separate us. You're the best thing that ever happened to me."

She hugged him again. "Good."

"So what brought this on?"

She shrugged. "I was thinking about Al."

He nodded, watching her, but remained silent.

"I don't know what brought it up. Suddenly I was thinking about him and it all came back." She shook her head, frowning. "All the old stuff."

She glanced at the clown who was standing off to the side staring at her. There was something strange about that clown, but she couldn't put her finger on it. "Where did you get the clown from, Terry?"

"Me? You got him, I hope."

"He told me he was a surprise," Wanda said. "I assumed it was your surprise."

"Let's ask him."

Wanda looked around, suddenly concerned. "Terry, where's Cyan?"

"She probably snuck inside to go to the bathroom. You know how excited she is."

Wanda sensed that something was amiss. She glanced at the clown again and felt even more uneasy. He was still staring and grinning. The word pervert came to mind. "I'm going to find her."

*   *   *

Simmons heard a sniffing sound and felt a wet tongue lapping his cheek. He raised his head from the grass and saw Spaz, who jumped up and down excitedly, his rear end shaking. He had a little gray beard now, and his eyes looked gray and rheumy, but Spaz actually recognized him. Spaz nudged his nose against Simmons and licked his face again. He whined and whimpered and barked and danced on his hind feet, performing for his long-lost master.

Fighting against the burning agony that still racked his torso, Simmons reached up and petted Spaz. Then he saw Cyan approaching and quickly pulled his hood up to hide his face. His pain momentarily subsided as he saw Cyan smiling at him with genuine charm and innocence. She was curious about the stranger, but not the least bit repulsed or frightened.

"Do you want some candy, mister? It'll make you feel better. It does for me."

She crouched down and offered a lollipop. Simmons turned his head away, still trying not to reveal his distorted features to the little girl.

"Cyan! What are you doing over there?"

It was Wanda. Now she would see him and he didn't know how he was going to explain to her what happened to him. But would she even listen to him?

Wanda grabbed Cyan by the arm and backpedaled in horror as Simmons peered at the woman whose love had kept him alive. Momentary speechless, he tried to stand up, and the hood fell away from his burnt face. Wanda gasped as she caught sight of Simmons's repugnant, unrecognizable continence.

"Terry . . . Terry! Over here. Hurry!"

Wanda bent down. "Are you okay, Cyan? Did anything happen?"

Cyan was clearly puzzled by her mother's reaction. "I

was just going to give the man a lollipop, Mama. That's all.''

Simmons raised up, fighting back the pain, and stumbled several steps forward. He reached out a charred hand and touched Wanda's arm. His face was just inches away from hers. He whispered her name.

Wanda looked up and screamed and shouted again for Terry. She wrenched back, dragging Cyan with her. ''Go away. Leave us alone. You don't belong here.''

Simmons was crushed by Wanda's utter rejection of him. He was still reaching for her, but his hand dropped away. A wave of emotions washed over him; Wanda not only didn't know him, but she was repulsed by and frightened of him.

The terror in the sound of Wanda's voice sent a chill along Fitzgerald's spine. He couldn't imagine what had happened to Cyan. One moment she'd been playing with Spaz, then she was gone.

He bolted around the side of the house and saw Wanda and his daughter huddled together near a clump of something that he didn't recognize. He scooped up Cyan. ''What happened? What's wrong?''

Then he saw the man, an indigent, heaped pathetically on the ground. He looked closer and saw that his skin was burned, so badly burned and scarred that his face made Frankenstein look handsome.

''I came out,'' Wanda gasped. ''And this . . . this man was lying here next to Cyan.''

''What are you doing back here, fellow? I think you should be moving on now.''

The man struggled to stand upright, but his knees wobbled and he grabbed his stomach and grunted in pain, all the while trying to cover his face. Terry felt sorry for him, but he was in no position to take in every destitute character that wandered by, and there were more and more finding their way here.

He locked eyes with the stranger and for a moment sensed something familiar about him. The man looked at Wanda and held out a hand as if he wanted to say something to her. But she turned away in disgust.

"Listen, fella, beat it now before I call the police. I mean it."

The day had started out great with Cyan and Wanda all excited about the birthday party. But it suddenly was turning into something else, starting with Wanda mentioning Simmons after all these years of silence. Fitzgerald thought she'd gotten over him, but he was kidding himself. She and Simmons had had something special, something she would never quite get over. Then this homeless tramp showed up. And that clown. There was something off-beat about him.

As if in reaction to his thought, the clown bounded up to him. His beady eyes and ear-to-ear smile seemed to offer contrasting messages. He was both apologetic and bellicose.

"Sorry, sorry. There's no problem here folks. There really isn't. Everything's okay. My friend here lives at a halfway house where I perform regularly. My biggest fan, follows me everywhere. He's harmless, safe as milk, in spite of his looks. It was just a freak accident with some Jiffy-pop."

"Just get him outta here," Terry ordered. "He's upsetting my wife and daughter."

"A thousand pardons, terrible mistake, hot pokers through my eyes. Hey, nice shoes. Please, don't worry about my fee. It's all covered. Enjoy the rest of the day with your adorable little girl."

"Hey, who sent you here, anyhow?"

The clown's face loomed close to Terry, and as he backed away, he caught a whiff of the clown's breath;

it smelled like a combination of rotten fish and garlic.

"Oh that. You didn't know? It was your friend and boss, Jason Wynn."

The clown turned to Cyan, slipped his hand up his sleeve, and presented her with a bouquet of flowers. Then he reached inside his jacket and pulled out a red balloon, which inflated by itself and floated at the end of a blue ribbon.

"Look at that," he said, pointing at the smiling clown face on the balloon as he handed it to her.

"That's you!" Cyan shouted, gleefully.

"You got it!" The clown patted her on the head.

Then he pulled the big derelict roughly to his feet and hauled him toward the street with surprising ease. They moved around a line of hedges and out of sight. Spaz whimpered and tried to follow the pair, but Cyan held on to his collar.

"That's odd. Really odd," Wanda said.

"What's that?" Terry asked, knowing that Wanda was still thinking about the derelict.

"He knew my name."

"Are you sure?" Terry felt more and more uneasy about both the clown and the burned man.

The balloon farted. Cyan looked up and now the balloon's clown face looked embarrassed. "That clown had funny eyes, Daddy. I didn't like him much."

"Let's get the kids inside," Terry said, herding his family to the backyard.

EIGHT

"OKAY, TIME for a break," Clown said, as he dragged Simmons into the parking lot of a gas station mini-mart. He shoved him into the wall on the backside of the building and kicked him in the knee, knocking him to the ground.

"You sit here like a good crispy critter and I'll get us some treats from inside. We'll party back here, and then we'll see what happens."

He cackled and slapped his knee. "You ain't seen nothing yet. You just wait."

Clown sauntered off to the front door of the quick stop. Simmons was barely aware of what Clown said. He had lost all hope since Wanda had rejected him. He didn't care what happened. He was a burnt shell. He had no purpose. Yet, in spite of these thoughts, deep inside he knew that he was here for some reason. He had no idea what it was, but he had a sickening feeling that it had something to do with Clown.

He tried to stand up but fell back down. He felt as if he were being pulled down by invisible weights. He looked down at the ragged, filthy clothing beneath his overcoat. His shirt was so threadbare that it barely hung onto his charred frame. His pants were ripped at the seams. He'd once been proud of his muscular torso, but now he just wished he could vacate it. He smelled like burnt toast and looked like he'd been dug up from a grave.

Three punks on Harleys revved their engines as they circled the station. They spotted him, stopped, and stared. They wore black leather jackets with chains, World War II German helmets, leather chaps, and oily engineer boots. They climbed off their bikes and ambled over toward Simmons as if they were approaching a beached whale.

Punk-1 was tall and thin with long arms and a short ponytail. Punk-2 left his jacket unzipped, displaying a bare chest covered with snake tattoos. His hair fell loosely to the middle of his back. Punk-3 had a belly that fell over his belt and a frizzy beard that reached his chest. All three wore wraparound sunglasses.

"Looks like scum to me," Punk-1 said, his arm dangling nearly to his knees.

"Burnt offerings," Punk-2 said. "Reminds me of when we torched the church over on Elmwood Street with the altar boys inside."

"Hey, I told you not to brag about that," Punk-3 said. "Cops are still looking for us on that one." He took a closer look at Simmons and wrinkled his nose. "This one smells like he's still smoldering." He scratched his belly. "Why don't we put out his fire, man."

"Good idea," Punk-2 said.

The three biker-punks moved closer to Simmons, and a moment later doused him with three streams of urine. Simmons sputtered and tried to get up, but Punk-3 kicked him in the chest knocking him back down.

"Oh, so you don't like the smell," Punk-2 said, zipping up his pants. "Is that it?" He grinned at his buddies. "Well, I think we can take care of that problem. A little high-octane gasoline should do the trick."

Simmons growled in protest, his voice deep, hoarse,

and unintelligible. He tried to climb to his feet but fell back down.

Punk-1 grabbed a hose from the nearest pump and stretched it as far as he could. He squeezed the handle and gasoline squirted out, reaching Simmons's feet but no further.

The other two punks rolled him over until he was close enough so that the gasoline poured over his entire body. Simmons sputtered and raised up on his hands until Punk-3 kicked his arms out from under him.

"Good enough," Punk-2 shouted. "Now, maybe we should just haul this big turd over to the Dumpster, where he belongs."

The three of them picked Simmons up; gasoline dripped from his soaked clothing and body. "You should've thought about this first, before we doused him," Punk-1 muttered. "I'm getting the damn gas all over my new boots."

"This guy must be full of rocks," Punk-3 groused. "He shouldn't be so heavy."

They shoved him over the top of the Dumpster and Simmons sank into the rotting garbage.

"Dumpster's kind of full," Punk-2 said as he tried to wipe the gasoline from his chest where the snake tattoos were shining like serpents that had just shed their old skins. "Maybe we oughta toss a match in there to burn it down some."

"We love to burn 'em, don't we boys," Punk-1 said, taking out a small box of wood matches. He struck one against the side of the Dumpster and was about to toss it on top of Simmons when Punk-3 knocked his arm away.

"Cop car just pulled in," he hissed. "Let's split before it gets too hot."

The police car cruised past slowly. The bikers mounted their hogs and roared away.

*   *   *

Clown slurped noisily from a sixty-four-ounce Super Frosty and hugged a box of doughnuts as he headed around the building. A kid inside a station wagon pounded on the window and waved. Clown stuck out his tongue. "I'm off duty, you little rug rat."

When he reached the back of the store, he stopped in his tracks. The spot where he'd left Simmons was now occupied by a puddle of gasoline. "Hm, is that you, Al? Returning to your roots? Naw, I don't think so."

He scanned the area, twitched his nose, and hummed as he walked over to the Dumpster. "Dump-ditty-dump-dump. Dump-ditty-dump." He flung back the top on the Dumpster. "And what do we have here? Al Simmons napping in the garbage. Tsk! Tsk! Not good hygiene."

He sniffed Simmons's soaked clothes. "You're a gas, Al. Super unleaded, right?" He laughed at his joke. "Just clowning around."

He opened the box of doughnuts and stuffed one after another into his mouth. "I just love the chocolate sprinkles. How about you, Al?" He picked another doughnut from the box, jammed it into his mouth, then ate a couple more in rapid succession. He held out one to Simmons. "How about jelly-filled powdered or do you prefer glazed? It'll sweeten your temperament."

Clown guffawed, spewing bits of half-chewed doughnut. He guzzled the Super Frosty, then dropped the box and paper cup outside the Dumpster. "That's better. Now, time for us to get real."

He ripped off his clown costume, revealing his old grimy duds. He wiped the circus-clown makeup off his face with the sleeve of his gaudy shirt.

"God, I hate clowns. Bozo, Ronald McDonald, corny freakin' Chuckles. All those stupid red noses and lousy squirtin' flowers. I hate 'em all." He grinned, wiping more makeup off his face with the palm of his hand, leaving behind his permanent neon-blue grin. "I just wanted to set you straight on that matter."

He farted and leaped forward. "Jeez, think that one left skidmarks." Clown reached into his pants, pulled out his underwear with a tear, and tossed them into the Dumpster.

"You don't want to be in there with those things." He grabbed Simmons by the arm and, with amazing ease, jerked him out of the Dumpster. Simmons wobbled on his feet like a giant marionette, then grabbed the side of the Dumpster as he dropped to one knee.

"No time for any praying, Al."

Clown wrinkled his nose. "We gotta do something about that smell. I don't care what you paid a gallon, fellow. You ask me, somebody pissed in your tank when you weren't looking."

Clown skipped over to the water hose, turned it on, and dragged the hoses over to Simmons. "Next time we'll take you through the car wash."

Simmons sputtered and waved a hand as the water struck him in the face. "Don't worry, Al. You'll be a new man soon enough." He tossed the hose aside.

"Okay, let's march, soldier. The break is over." He shoved Simmons ahead of him.

Simmons staggered ahead, groaning with each step. He lost track of time, of direction, of place. He was a zombie without any control of body or mind. It was dark again when he began to itch all over. He felt as if he were overheating, that his scorch-scarred flesh was about to burst open. He struggled to take control of his mind to overcome the pain.

Clown pushed him and Simmons stumbled, then took a swipe at him with his arm. "Get away from me, you fat little freak."

"Oh, my, my," Clown said. "Aren't we choosy now about our friends."

Simmons staggered onward down the sidewalk. He turned a corner and leaned against the wall of a building. He couldn't go a step farther. The itching tormented him, and the pain in his gut was unbearable. He doubled over and nearly collapsed.

"What the problem, Al?" Clown asked, trying to straighten him up.

"It feels like my skin is about to explode. I can't take it anymore."

Clown chuckled. His laughter grew louder and collapsed into a high-pitched howl. "You're at that awkward age. Soon you'll get hair in funny places, then you'll start thinkin' about girls." His expression turned serious. "I got news for you. You don't have any skin. That's just your armor going through the larval stage and, oh boy . . ." He smiled broadly. "Is it ever going to hurt!"

At that moment, Simmons buckled over again and let out a sharp, anguished cry; a wave of pain swept over him. "Just get me to a hospital. Fast."

He pulled off his coat and opened his shirt, trying to cool off.

Now Clown was laughing hysterically. "A hospital! Heh-heh-heh! How about a deep fryer?" He rapped Simmons on the head with his knuckles. "Hello in there. You're dead, pushing up daisies, taking a dirt-nap. Five years feeding earthworms has turned that little brain of yours into a ball of mush."

Clown suddenly grabbed hold of Simmons's head. His beady eyes became pinpoints filled with soulless glee. "Allow me to kick-start your memory. Hang on, these flashbacks are killers."

Simmons's eyes rolled back and a green energy consumed his head. He no longer felt any pain. He no longer felt his body at all. He was separate from it, floating in a space devoid of description that was neither pleasant nor unpleasant—a neutral zone. He just wanted to disappear into this place of nonexistence, to never feel the pain or see Clown again.

Then Wynn was standing in front of him, holding a cigarette and grinning, and Simmons was lying on the floor of the biochemical plant with two bullets in him and a liquid gel covering his body. Wynn smiled and flipped the cigarette at him.

This already happened, Simmons told himself as he struggled to put out the smoldering fire. Then flames engulfed him, a living-dying human torch. And he screamed out Wanda's name.

A flaming, screaming meteor spiraled down through darkness, and for a moment he watched in awe. Then he realized that he was the meteor, and he was falling through a flaming tunnel into an inferno. It was exactly as before. Even though he knew he was reliving his death, it was still happening, and he felt all the same horrifying sensations in explicit detail.

His wretched, burnt corpse shambled aimlessly through flaming passageways—the corridors of Hell, in and out of arenas where lost souls tortured, murdered, and raped each other over and over in an unending, joyless orgy of the damned. Repeatedly, he was clubbed and maimed, torn limb from limb, eaten alive, sacrificed to the Evil Lord, only to walk away into another godless feast of debauchery and mayhem.

Then he was standing above a pool of viral necroplasm and for the first time he felt a sense of hope in a place where there was no hope. He was being given an offer, a chance to do what he had done best in his life, to go back and kill.

"Yes! I'll do it! I'll gladly kill Wynn and lead your army."

Thunderous laughter greeted Simmons and his torched corpse was dipped into the viral necroplasm. Then he was raised above the Hell's assembled army and greeted by a roaring, bellicose ovation as the horrific deeds of his life-time were graphically reviewed. He wanted to call out that he killed for a reason, but no one cared. Instead, they worshipped him for slaughtering innocent children as well as other killers.

But those were accidents.

No one listened. They only believed what they wanted to believe. That he was a ruthless killer. He loved to torture and maim. He was worthy.

The same hideous laughter resounded through the corridors of Hell. Malebolgia, the enormous demon-ruler, tromped through walls of flames. Its gigantic, malevolent presence terrified him. Pure evil stretched into malignant bone and diseased flesh. Its mocking, pupilless eyes were the color of fouled blood and infected urine. Malebolgia spewed hatred for all that was not part of its world, while he controlled and manipulated those who were among his legions.

Simmons could only think of one thing. Anything for Wanda. He would be back again in her world with another chance.

Malebolgia grinned at the thought that his evil would now spread throughout physical existence, that Earth would finally become his personal toy, that Simmons would be the one to lead the spiteful battle for control of all existence, for the union of Hell and Heaven. Simmons would lead the charge and Malebolgia's army would do the rest.

"No mercy, no mercy, no mercy," the horde from Hell would chant as they marched on, destroying everything and everyone in its wake.

All Simmons could think about was getting his revenge against Wynn and returning to Wanda. If there was a bigger picture involved, a picture that encompassed Heaven and Hell, he didn't want to know about it.

He was coming back. That was all that mattered.

NINE

CLOWN STOOD nearby watching Simmons with naked envy. "All you've got to do is take care of Wynn, then you and the army can go kick some angelic butt." Then he muttered, "It *should* be me . . . not some pussy-whipped twit."

An enormous hand clamped Clown by the scruff of the neck. Talons lifted him high into the air, and Clown wriggled under the demonic gaze of eyes that pierced his heartless carapace like hot coals.

"Don't worry, boss," Clown sputtered. "I'm with the program. I'll be there to keep him on track. That's a promise."

A whirlwind of laughing, screeching, keening voices rose at once as Malebolgia let go of Clown's neck and Clown simultaneously released his grip on Simmons's head. Simmons fell heavily against the brick wall, panting. He was disoriented for a few moments, but then realized he was back in the world.

Clown's shadow grew and consumed him. "And so here I am. Or, I should say, here we are."

"Why me?" Simmons muttered, gasping for breath. He looked weak and helpless from the experience, hardly like the leader of anyone's army.

"For reasons known only to His Highness, Malebolgia decided to overlook his most loyal and brutal lieutenant, namely *me,* and chose you to be the general of the Army from Hell—ain't that a kick in the 'nads. And you, being the ambitious type, went right ahead and signed on the dotted line."

Simmons pressed his back against the brick wall, steadying himself. His head hung to one side as if it were too heavy to lift. "I don't remember doing anything like that."

"You don't need to remember. I witnessed the whole wonderful and disgusting thing, and you're the number one man. Numero Uno." Clown frowned and blabbered on to himself. "Malebolgia moves in mysterious ways and sometimes he moves his bowels right over your head. Where do you think he got that stupid name, anyway?"

Clown looked around nervously as Simmons slid to the sidewalk. "So, it took more than five years to get the Earth ready for your arrival. You know, death and destruction on every corner. Corruption in high places. Wars on every continent. More people living on the streets. Bombs on school buses. All that stuff that gets shown over and over again, day after day, on the new in case anyone tries to forget."

He kicked Simmons in the side, a gentle love tap to the ribs. "Are you paying attention, Al, baby? Anyhow, who knew that in your absence Wanda'd go and marry Terry Fitzgerald, your best friend from the good ol' days."

Clown thrust his hips forward and back several times. "Doin' the nasty, and doin' it and doin' it over and over with your old buddy, Fitz. Humping up a storm. Hey, nice girlfriend, buddy."

Simmons, trying to stand, reeled back and forth in anger and frustration. "You . . . You," he croaked, reaching for Clown's feet.

Clown tiptoed out of his reach, then bent forward and

spoke in a confidential tone. "All you've gotta do is take care of Wynn, then you and the army can go kick some angelic butt. And in return for your services, you get your Wanda back."

Clown smiled. "Now doesn't that make you feel better? Heck, you can have every Wanda on the friggin' planet. Why settle for Fitzy's leftovers? Not to mention the fact that the entire earthly domain is yours to do with as you please."

He cupped his hands on either side of his mouth. "You don't deserve it, pal."

Simmons lunged and snagged Clown's ankle. "This is all some sort of sadistic game Wynn is playing with me. When I find him, he's gonna wish he'd really killed me when he had the chance."

He let go of Clown and grabbed his gut, cringing in pain.

"That's the spirit." Clown rubbed his hands together. "Get good and mad at him. Pay him back big-time. Revenge-revenge-revenge!"

Simmons crawled closer to Clown. Seething in anger, he tried once again to stand up. Clown grabbed his arm and jerked him to his feet. "You and me are a team now. Think of me as your fallen angel . . . the guardian-clown from Hell! You're Jimmy Stewart and I'm Clarence."

Clown arched his back, raising his butt. "Every time someone farts, a demon gets his wings." He backfired twice. "Hey! Twins."

Simmons tried to stumble away.

"Hey, where do you think you're going? Still don't get it do you, amnesia boy? Maybe we'll just have to *dig* a little deeper. Let's take a little trip, you and me. But we'll go my way. You're too slow."

Clown grabbed Simmons by the back of his neck and a flash of green consumed them both.

*   *   *

Smoke wafted upward as a vicious-looking dagger, gripped by two hands, hung in the air against the night sky. A voice chanted: "Hail, Satan! Lord of all that we see. Lord of all that we be. I command the forces of Darkness to bestow their powers upon me!"

The dagger hung a second longer, then slammed downward into a skull that rested on an overturned, graffiti-covered gravestone. Incense curled skyward from a pair of censers that had been placed at the ends of two of the points of a black pentagram scrawled on the diabolical altar.

Simmons found himself standing by an oak tree. Next to him, Clown leaned against the trunk, his arms crossed, looking bored. "Pay attention," he whispered. "It's amateur hour."

Simmons turned his focus back to the gravestone and saw three punks in leather jackets. As one of them turned, he realized they were the same ones who had tormented him earlier at the gas station.

Punk-1, the tall, gangly kid, looked around nervously, waiting for something to happen.

Nearby, Punk-2 stripped off his jacket, baring his tattooed torso. He rippled his muscles and the purple snakes seemed to dance across his skin. "I don't feel anything happening."

Punk-3 patted his gut. He looked bored, as if he'd seen it all before. He guzzled from his forty-ounce bottle of Colt-45, then belched loudly. "Yeah, well, maybe we need a bigger pentagram."

"We made it just like the cover of the Black Sabbath album," Punk-2 replied.

Clown elbowed Simmons in the ribs. "Good album. I play it all the time."

Punk-3 turned to his companions with an evil look on his face. "Maybe we need to use a live skull!" He looked over at Punk-1, who seemed more wary than his two companions. "Any volunteers?"

Punk-1 ignored him and the burly punk grabbed him by the arm and wrestled him down to the gravestone. "I call upon the Dark Lord to devour the wretched soul of this sorry excuse for a human being right now."

Punk-1 reached up to protect his head as Punk-3 poured beer on his head and laughed hysterically.

"Knock it off," Punk-1 yelled.

Punk-2 joined the laughter. Heat lightning streaked across the sky, casting harsh shadows across the length of the gravestone.

Punk-1 struggled to escape. "No, no, no! Let me go!" he screamed.

"Yeah, I like it!" Punk-2 called, flashing the horned-hand sign toward the sky.

"Cool. Way cool," Punk-3 called out. He pulled his frightened buddy off the gravestone. He finished his brew and tossed the bottle at another gravestone. He motioned for the other two to follow him.

Punk-1 looked around warily, his anger overcome by his fear. He hurried after the other two, dodging clumsily between gravestones.

"Well, they've got the right idea," Clown snorted as he pushed away from the oak tree. "But who needs 'em? We've got more converts than enemies around here."

He grabbed Simmons and pulled him over to the gravestone where the punks had performed their satanic rites. "Take a real close look."

Simmons stepped closer and peered at the gravestone, which read: "Allan Simmons," followed by an epitaph: "A True Patriot."

"What's this?"

"Hm, let's see, it's cold, gray, and in granite," Clown mused. "And it got Al Simmons written all over it. Could it be—YOUR GRAVE?"

Simmons backed away, shaking his head in disbelief. But Clown shoved him forward onto the grave. "Don't take my word for it. Let's dig it up and see what the hell's inside."

Clown laughed, his whole body shaking as he pulled a shovel, seemingly from his pocket. Its handle telescoped out and he tossed it in front of Simmons. "Get to work, Dig-meister."

Simmons stared at him, uncertain what to do.

"Now chop-chop, pal. Your corpse ain't getting any fresher."

Simmons remained dumbfound, but slowly and tediously he began digging into the grave, tossing one shovelful of earth after another to one side, then the other. As the coffin was exposed, his digging turned more frantic. Finally, he clawed at the top of the coffin with his bare hands. He found the latch, flipped it open, pulled open the lid, and pushed it back until the interior of the coffin was exposed.

Inside was a body bag. Next to it was a neatly folded marine uniform with lieutenant colonel stripes and Simmons's silver nameplate on the breast pocket.

Simmons froze as he stared at the uniform and the bagged remains. *It must be a fake,* he told himself. He wanted proof. He had to see the body. He reached carefully into the coffin and tore open the body bag. Roaches spilled out, and Simmons shrank back as a dozen of them climbed over his hands and up his arms. If what Clown was saying was true, the roaches had survived for five years inside the coffin, generation after generation, living on his remains. He pushed away that thought as he frantically brushed them away and shook them from his hands.

He could see the top of a bone-dry skull. It could be anybody's skull, he told himself. It didn't mean anything. He was still certain that Wynn and this creepy Clown were pulling some sort of demented trick on him. Sure, that had to be it. Wynn was pissed because he'd challenged his authority.

He pulled the bag open wider, hoping somehow to prove that it wasn't his body. He saw the upper part of a skeleton. A gold locket was fused to the skeleton's sternum. The locket looked vaguely familiar, like the one with a picture of him and Wanda. It couldn't be. He ripped the locket and chain loose. He wiped away the black soot and popped open the locket.

He gaped at the photo in the silvery moonlight that filtered into the grave. The photo had been singed around the edges and a scorch mark cut through the word, "Forever." But it was clearly the same photo he remembered of him and Wanda smiling and happy together.

He shook his head in disbelief. "Nooo! Noooo! I don't believe it! It can't be!"

He squeezed the locket shut in his fist, dropped his head back, and howled in misery. His scream seemed to carry to the clouds and beyond. Lightning flashed and dead leaves swirled and eddied as he thrashed about inside his own grave. He knew it was true. He sensed it in every fiber of his being.

At the edge of the grave, Clown rubbed the corner of his eyes with his fists and mockingly cried like a baby. "Ah wee, ah wee. Poor Simmons died and went to Hell." He turned solemn. "I think we should take a moment to remember the deceased. I'm done."

Simmons climbed out of the grave and angrily charged toward Clown. But he was immediately struck by a tidal wave of naked, excruciating pain. He crumpled into a fetal ball and screamed.

Clown licked his fingers and giggled expectantly. He was pleased with himself and waiting for the next stage to begin. "I told you it was gonna hurt."

He enjoyed every second of Simmons's anguish. Let him suffer. He deserved it. "Too bad. Too bad," he laughed. "It's going to take awhile, too."

"Hey, did Satan send you guys?"

"Huh?"

Clown spun around to see the tall, lanky punk who had stabbed the skull. "Are you kidding? You think there are clowns in Hell? You think it's a funny ha-ha sort of place? Do ya, do ya?"

Punk-2 looked nervous and zipped up his jacket, covering his tattoos. But the beer-belly punk shoved Simmons with the heel of his boot. "What's this ugly creep's problem?"

Simmons, still writhing in pain, knocked the boot to one side, nearly toppling the punk. "Get away from me," he rasped. "Just get away."

Punk-2 moved closer for a better look. "Hey, aren't you the dude we hosed at the gas station?"

Punk-3 pushed his tattooed buddy aside. "That's him. That's the same crispy freak." He bent down to Simmons. "Why are you following us, scumbag?"

Simmons reared up and smashed the punk in the teeth, catapulting his huge frame through the air and into Punk-1. They both tumbled over twice and into another gravestone. Punk-2 was frozen with fear, stunned by the feat of strength he'd just witnessed.

Simmons himself seemed surprised by the power of his punch. But Clown wasn't. He knew all about the making of Hellspawn.

Then Simmons wailed in agony as something horrendous and totally unexpected happened. Living, pulsing, viscid Hellspawn armor spread across his hands like a runaway virus. He screamed, louder than any previous howl, as spikes burst out of the backs of his hands.

He groaned in pain as the armor pulsed along his body, beneath his tattered clothing, and streamed up his chest and out the back of his neck and shoulders, creeping over his skull. Spikes and blades burst out of his upper arms and thighs, ripping his clothes. Simmons wailed, moaned, and cursed. He fought fiercely, but without effect, against the continuing storm of transmutation. Without a doubt, he was being savagely transformed into a new being.

The punks were like deer caught in headlights. The rapid flashes of lightning illuminated their stunned faces. They dropped to their knees, folded their hands, prayed to God and begged for mercy.

Clown loved every minute of it. He bounced up and down, excited and curious by what he was witnessing. He'd never watched a transformation quite so dramatic, and he couldn't wait to see the completed Hellspawn product. All were different and interesting in their own way, but this one was special.

The wet, necroplasmic armor grew over Simmons's face, and he howled and clawed at the spreading cancer. It covered his mouth, his nose, his eyes. It quivered and thickened and locked itself directly to his nervous system. He collapsed to the ground. The armor breathed with him as he gasped for breath. It throbbed and chewed at Simmons like a parasite overcoming its host, sucking its life.

The tall, gangly punk stared in slack-jawed wonder and awe at Simmons, who was no longer Simmons.

Clown leaned down near the punk's head, licked his rotted fangs, and dribbled saliva from his chin. He ran a talonlike finger across the punk's throat. "Shocked and amazed by the wonders of necroflesh, are we? You ain't seen nothin' yet. Your model is fully loaded." He grinned and exhaled his fetid breath into the punk's face. "Eerie, ain't it?"

The punk began shaking; his teeth chattered. Clown leaned closer, sniffed. "What's that smell? Something warm and wet running down your leg and into your boot? Forget your diapers?"

He cackled madly, spun around, and flung his hands in the air. "Get lost. All of ya."

The punks dashed away, fleeing for their lives, stumbling over tombstones, scrambling to escape. None of them dared look back. All their silly childhood fears returned, but this nightmare was real and they couldn't wake up no matter how much they wanted to.

"Run on home to Mommy, you littler wankers," Clown called after them. "Nothing I hate more than weekend Satanists."

The punks kept running, racing blindly ahead. They were so frightened, they didn't notice the hooded old man with the long silver beard who stood like a statue next to an ancient oak tree.

Cogliostro watched and waited. The creation of a new Hellspawn was always reason for concern and for hope. This one, though, he had known from the start, actually from before the start, would be more powerful, more deadly, and more dangerous than any others. He'd seen it coming long before Al Simmons went to Hong Kong. He'd sensed the man would soon be consumed by Hell fires and returned. He knew there was no way for the man to avoid his destiny. He'd been chosen long ago by Malebolgia. He was fated to become Hellspawn, but what he did from this point on was another matter. There was still hope, no matter how slim the chances, that he would reject Malebolgia's scheme.

Cogliostro moved closer. Very close. The dwarf, who had once been his partner in debauchery, deceit, and destruction, was too busy enjoying the transformation to notice his presence.

Now was the time to act. He needed to get Simmons's attention.

*   *   *

Clown inspected the freshly armored Spawn and examined him from all sides, nodding approvingly. "The devil, you say. From Spawn-larva to full-fledged Hellspawn in record time. I'm impressed; and believe me, it takes some doing to impress me."

He moved closer and grinned as he spoke in a confidential tone. "So tell me, Big Guy, was it as good for you as it was for me?"

Simmons ignored Clown. All of his attention was focused on the imprisoning armor. He ripped away the last shred of his filthy, tattered clothes. The pain was sharp and cruel; he was weak and gasping for breath. He tried to pry away the slick, wet, hardening armor, but it was part of him. Like it or not, he was Hellspawn. Whatever that was.

Clown swatted at his hand. "Uh-uh, Big Guy, don't pick at your armor until it hardens. You want it to get infected?"

"What is it? Get it off me."

"It's your armor, numbnuts. Love that new leather smell. Made from the finest necroplasm this side of Purgatory."

Simmons looked down at himself and shivered. The forbidding armor was dark and ominous. There was a beauty to it, too, but Spawn didn't appreciate it. He stared at his new self, still groaning in agony.

"Congratulations, *Spawn*. That's your new name, kid. You are the man, the general of Hell's army. Knight of the living dead. He-he-he."

Clown walked around Spawn and sniffed at him. He touched his fresh, sticky armor. "I don't know," he said, a bit disappointed. "You don't look so special to me."

Spawn's body was weighed down under the cumbersome armor. He felt as immobilized as if the mere act of walking had to be relearned. The armor was shrinking against him. But at the same time his torso seemed to be expanding, and the result was relentless pain that consumed all of his strength. He didn't care what Clown said. He barely heard him talking.

Clown bent down close to Spawn and grinned inches from his eyes to get his attention. "And if it turns out you can't hack it, then I'll gladly send your worthless carcass back down to the fiery abyss. And this time, Malebolgia ain't gonna roll out no welcome mat." His clown features contorted into a twisted, pained expression. "Not to mention what would happen to my sorry ass."

Spawn pushed to his feet again and turned away, refusing to believe any of what he was hearing. That was when he saw the bearded old man. The man who had haunted his life. But the life now seemed like a dream, like someone else's life.

There was some reason the old man was here. He didn't know how he knew that, he just did. But what could be so important about an old man staring at him?

"Hey, what's going on?" Clown looked around suspiciously. "You see something out there? Spooks?" He chuckled maniacally. "Naw, I don't think so. We'd scare them off."

Spawn realized the old man was gone. He couldn't have taken his eyes off him for more than a second, but somehow he'd vanished.

Clown looked around again, uneasily. He was still trying to convince himself they were alone. "Nope. Nobody here but us dead guys. Right, Spawnzy, ol' buddy."

The comment annoyed Spawn and reminded him of what he'd found in his grave. His gaze fell on the headstone again. He still found it hard to believe that he was dead. Dead people didn't feel pain as far as he knew, and he'd felt plenty of it.

He raised his fist, lurched forward, and tried to strike Clown, but the dwarf expertly dodged the blow. Spawn's fist smashed into his gravestone, breaking it into pieces. Spawn was startled by his strength. How could he feel so weak and be so strong at the same time? He didn't understand any of it.

In a rage, he ripped a large brass cross off the splintered lid of his coffin. He drove it viciously through his newly armored thigh, penetrating almost to the bone. Spawn screamed in pain, then watched in amazement as the cross was forced out of his body. The wound that was left behind started to heal instantly. Within seconds, all traces of it had vanished. In frustration, Spawn hurled the cross across the cemetery, and with a clang it skipped off another headstone and planted itself in the ground.

"Aahhh!"

"Calm down now," Clown told him. "You should be pleased to see how well your armor takes care of itself. You're virtually impermeable. Believe me, you're gonna need the protection."

"I thought I was dead. What do I need armor for? Tell me that."

"For your information, Spawnzy, dead people can still die. Being a beginner, I guess you didn't know that. The point is, you wouldn't want to miss all that painful pleasure you've been enjoying, would ya?"

"Oh God," Spawn screamed.

"Did you have to use the *G* word?"

Spawn dropped his head back and yelled in despair, "Wanda, what have I done?"

He picked up the locket from the ground, again feeling the loss and sadness. He held it to his chest. To his surprise, the armor surrounded the locket and incorporated it into his chest, placing it where it would normally hang. Spawn looked down at it, then collapsed to the ground.

TEN

"**ALL RIGHT,** all right. Enough of the sentimental crap," Clown said. "Heart lockets and sweetheart pictures. Oh, puke!"

He grabbed Spawn's foot, pulled, and the green energy surrounded them again. When he let go, the graveyard vanished and they stood in a wet, filthy alley cluttered with garbage. Spawn wobbled from side to side and finally hobbled over to the wall. He pressed his back against it and slid down to the ground.

"That's good. You stay there, like a good Spawnzy. I've got some business to take care of."

Clown started to walk away but stopped and turned back to Spawn. "I'll be back when your armor hardens. Don't play with it too much or you'll go blind." His exaggerated eyebrows moved up and down, then they shifted into a frown. "You better be ready to party, 'cause I don't want to have to get nasty with you."

Clown snorted a loud guffaw and strutted away, his blue grin spread from ear to ear. His teeth were huge and gleaming wet. He stepped on top of a battered garbage can cover and performed a jaded pirouette, twirling his short plump body on tiptoes. Moving on, he kicked over a stack of garbage cans and grabbed a rotten pizza

slice covered with maggots. He looked at it in disgust.
"Yuck! I hate anchovies!"

He picked off a small bit of anchovy, tossed it aside,
then slid the rest of the slimy, maggot infested slice into
his mouth as he stepped into the street. "Yum, I needed
that protein."

Jason Wynn relaxed on a reclining chair by his pool
as he soaked in the sun's late morning rays. Next
to him, Muriel, his wife of twenty-three years, read a
novel. She was an attractive blonde who still turned heads.
He could hear the chatter of his two teenage daughters
coming from the house, where they were making brownies. It was one of those rare days for Wynn when he could
put everything aside and enjoy life on his ten-acre wooded
estate.

He wasn't taking any phone calls, wasn't going to any
meetings, wasn't going anywhere, at least not until this
evening, when he and Muriel would dine with several
heads of state, the finale of a three-day summit in Washington. He had met with the leaders for four hours yesterday and they had listened very closely to him.

Later this evening, he would go alone to a formal black-
tie affair at the Swiss embassy, where many of the enemies of the Western democratic nations would be
gathering. He had more business to attend to at that party.

In the last five years, he'd moved up from a middle-
level field supervisor at A-6 to the director's position. His
goals had all been realized. The president and other heads
of state called him up whenever an important decision
needed to be made.

Wynn was quickly becoming the legendary figure that
he had always aspired to become. His name was whispered in the White House, the halls of Congress, and the
chambers of the Supreme Court. He was a man of vast
power who was ruthless and gutsy and solved world prob-

lems in his own way. The legends of his successful missions pleased him. But he often thought that if the full truth were known, the stories would be even more dramatic.

His swift rise had been accompanied by early retirements and the "accidental" deaths of several people who blocked his way. He had received help from certain unscrupulous quarters, but now his power was so great that he was feared by all—even the ones who had opened the way for him.

All, that is, except for the nefarious Clown, who taunted him every chance he got. He recognized that Clown was a powerful force, an ally whose recommendations on field operations against friends and foes had succeeded grandly. The same could be said about his suggestions for cutthroat political maneuvers against opponents in Congress. They were strokes of genius that had ended the careers of more than one powerful senator.

But now he was ready to dump the nasty dwarf. He no longer needed the annoyance.

Of course, the state of the world had not improved any in recent years. To the contrary, it was generally conceded that the rich were richer, the poor were poorer. The cities were rotting, crime was over the top, diseases were spreading. Life for ninety percent of the world's population was at best uncertain; at worst, abysmal.

For the vast majority, it was going to get worse, far worse. Just the way he wanted it. Secret government operations thrived during times of instability and discontent.

For the other ten percent, life was better than ever within the confines of their secure homes and retreats. Within that elite set were the ones who made all the important decisions, the people who needed Jason Wynn and his expertise.

"Excuse me, Mr. Wynn."

He looked up to see that the housekeeper had led Marcus, his bodyguard and assistant, to the pool. The uniformed woman disappeared and the guard moved forward.

"I assume everything went well." Wynn always turned his questions into statements when he was worried about something. In this case, the matter was so serious that if it hadn't gone well, Marcus might not want to be here.

"No problem, sir."

The bodyguard glanced up at Muriel, who was reading her book and paying no attention. But he still lowered his voice as he continued. "The boat is expected to be in port on schedule, and everyone is happy on the docks. Thanks to your kindness and generosity."

"Good. You can take the rest of the day off," Wynn said.

"What about this evening?"

Wynn thought a moment, then shrugged. "That too. I won't be needing you." He released Marcus as a gesture to Muriel. She hated having bodyguards around the house. Marcus, in particular, made her nervous.

Marcus left and Wynn settled back in his lounge chair, satisfied that everything was set for the big send-off of the operation that would catapult him to a greatness few imagined, few still aspired to. He would no longer be a trusted advisor to world leaders. He would *be* the world leader.

But five minutes later, Marcus was back. "What is it now?" Wynn asked.

Muriel looked up and frowned.

He apologized for the interruption. "I was leaving when I found a man on the property. He says he knows you. He's a . . . a strange fellow."

Wynn looked annoyed. He was about to tell Marcus to get rid of him. But his curiosity got the better of him. "A strange fellow wandering around who says he knows me? What's this man's name?"

The guard hesitated as if he didn't want to say any more in front of Muriel. But finally he answered. "That's the odd thing. He says you know him as Clown. And he looks like a clown, sort of."

Wynn bolted upright and grabbed his silk robe. "Get him into my office, right away."

"A clown?" Muriel looked up from her book.

He waved a hand, stood up, and quickly put on the robe and tied the belt. "Just a nickname for one of the operatives."

How dare that little monster show up at his door. He would see what he wanted and send him on his way with a warning never to bother him at home again.

"A clown is a strange nickname for someone in *your* business," Muriel said.

"I know It's really a code name. You know, stuff I can't talk about."

For her protection, and that of their girls, he kept Muriel in the dark about most of his dealings, and she'd learned not to ask. Like most everyone else in America, she hadn't even known the A-6 existed until a series of reports in the *Washington Herald* had recently brought Wynn and the agency into the media spotlight. Before that she assumed he was a ranking CIA officer.

"I'll be right back," he said and walked inside. He stopped in the kitchen, chatted casually with his two daughters, Tina and Terri, who were sixteen and fourteen. Slender, long-legged blondes, they reminded him more and more of Muriel every day. "Those brownies smell good. Make sure you save a couple for me."

"If you were home more, Daddy, you'd get lots of brownies," Terri, the older one, said.

"Maybe I will be, very soon."

"Who was that funny-looking man Marcus brought in the house, Daddy?" Tina asked. "He looked at me in a strange kind of way when I opened the door."

"Never mind him, darling. I'm going to take care of him right now."

As he walked through the house on his way to his office, he thought with dismay about the wretched state of the world and wondered how his daughters would fare in it. Fortunately, he had provided well for them and they would never want for anything in their lives. That was all that mattered. They were safe, even if the rest of the world wasn't.

Marcus was standing by his office door with his arms folded. "He's inside, sir. As you requested."

Wynn nodded and motioned for Marcus by the door. He walked into the office and looked around. At first he didn't see anyone, but then the chair behind his desk spun around and Clown grinned at him.

"Get out my chair!" Wynn slammed the door and walked over to his desk.

"Oh, Papa Bear is angry about Little Red Riding Clown sitting in his chair."

Wynn leaned menacingly over the desk. "I'm warning you . . ."

"I was just admiring the family photo." Clown held up a framed picture of Wynn, his wife, and daughters. "Such an attractive family. My, my, if they only knew what Papa Bear did when he went out to work."

"What are you doing here? I could have you arrested for trespassing."

Clown stood up, kissed the photo, then placed it back on Wynn's desk. "Jason, Jason. You're threatening the hand that feeds you."

"What do you want?"

"Your cooperation." Clown moved around the desk and eyed Wynn's silk robe. "I need you to do something very important for me."

Wynn stepped back from Dwarf as he caught a whiff of breath that smelled like rotted garbage. He crossed his arms, leaned his head back, and waited for Clown to continue.

"You've got to kill her."

"Who?"

"Chapel, of course."

Wynn's body tensed. "What are you talking about? This is nonsense."

"No it's not. You do it or else."

"Or else, what?" Wynn snapped. He was losing his patience with the dwarf and was ready to kick him out of the house.

"Or else . . ." Clown grinned. "Let's look at my pictures now." He pulled a sheath of eight-by-ten photos from his sleeve and dropped them on the desk.

Wynn leaned over and saw a photograph of himself and Chapel in bed together with no covers. He quickly scooped up the photos and flipped through them. They were all of him and Chapel together in bed in various poses that left nothing to the imagination.

"Where did you get these from?"

Clown grinned broadly and rubbed his knuckles against his chest. "I took them myself. Good shots, don't you think? I like the way you're both arching your backs in that one. Dynamic. Graceful. Symmetrical."

Livid, Wynn ripped the photos in half. "You're disgusting. Get out of my house."

Clown's wide blue grin plunged downward. "That wasn't nice, Jason." Then he smiled and pulled another set from his sleeve. "Ah, but there's more where those came from. In fact, I have matching sets for your beautiful wife and each of your lovely daughters."

"You wouldn't dare."

Wynn knew that Muriel would leave him if he she saw the photos. He had no doubt in his mind about that. Several years ago, she had caught him with another woman and she'd vowed that if it happened again, the marriage was over, and he believed her.

He'd been caught after she'd overheard a phone conversation that he'd accidentally taped. It was sloppy, very sloppy, for someone in his business, and he still cursed himself for the mistake. In spite of his dalliances, he loved Muriel and didn't know what he would do without her. He needed the family life to balance the cutthroat activities that took up the rest of his time. And if his daughters saw those photos . . .

"You do that and I'll have you killed," Wynn said. "I'm through with you."

"Ah, gee. Do we have to get down and dirty? What a shame. Well, if Chapel means that much to you . . ."

Clown pulled out an oversized pocketwatch with his own features on the face. Wings sprouted from either side of the watch and flapped up and down. "Oh, how time flies, Jason. Gotta go."

He headed for the door, but Wynn called out to him. "Wait a minute. Why is getting rid of Chapel so damned important?"

"First of all, Wynn ol' buddy, you can't trust her. I'd have told you that sooner, but you were too blinded by whatever it is you see in her. But now she's getting dangerous, out of control. Believe me, you don't need her any longer."

Wynn didn't answer. He trusted Chapel like no other operative.

"Besides," Clown continued, "I've got a friend coming back to town, and I don't want any trouble from Chapel. She doesn't like him. She'll try to kill him and I don't want her to interfere. He's got some important business to take care of."

"Who is he?"

Clown's grin seemed to stretch to the wrinkled corners

of his eyes. "Oh, that's a surprise. But don't worry, you'll find out soon enough."

Spawn rested against the wall, his armored mask peeled back, exposing his charred necroflesh. He felt his face and puzzled over the nature of the armor. Maybe it would all retract or even disappear. He tried to stand up but slid back down the wall. He lay there for a moment, then rolled onto his knees, using the wall for support. Slowly, gripping the wall, he pulled himself upright to his full height. To his amazement, he stood at least seven feet tall and his chest easily spanned seventy inches.

He took a few tentative steps, staggered, tripped, and crushed the corner of a Dumpster. His forearm struck the wall and shattered several bricks. Smiling, Spawn swung and smashed his arm right through the wall, pulverizing the bricks with ease.

"When I get my hands on Wynn, this freak stuff is gonna come in handy," he said to himself.

He started to stagger away. He didn't know how he was going to get to Wynn. He just knew that he had to find him. But before he reached the end of the alley, he plowed headlong into someone and nearly fell over. The man offered a steadying hand.

"Need some help?"

Spawn shrugged him off, keeping his head down. He just wanted to get past the man and on his way.

"Easy friend. Each choice we make has its consequences," the man said. "Please keep that in mind as you go about your business."

Spawn raised his gaze and saw the bearded old man who had been in the cemetery. "Out of my way, old man. Stop following me."

"Don't you want to know who I am?"

Spawn brushed off the question with a flick of his hand,

as if he were swatting a fly, and moved on down the alley and out into the street.

Cogliostro watched in disappointment as Simmons disappeared around the corner. He could see that the transformation into Hellspawn was completed. He had expected as much. The only surprise was the swiftness of the change. It had come quicker than he had ever seen before. He had hoped to have a long talk with Simmons before it happened, but Clown's presence had prevented it.

Even though Clown was gone for the time being, it was obvious that his influence had been left behind. Simmons was intent on carrying out the will of the Dark Lord. He seemed to have no interest in anything else and that included Cogliostro. Clown was guiding the new Hellspawn and he would be back to direct Simmons on whatever malevolent deed Malebolgia had proposed.

Cogliostro suspected the worst. He took out an ancient iron spearhead and ran his hand over it, as if to gather power from it. Then he slipped it into the sleeve of his greatcoat and followed Simmons at a distance. He didn't have to worry about losing him. He knew right where he was headed.

ELEVEN

THE A-6 compound seemed more militaristic and fortified than Spawn remembered it. There were not only barbed-wire fences now but automated cameras and sentry lights that washed back and forth across the compound's manicured grounds. In addition, there were guards stationed on the grounds, as if the place were a fort on the frontier of the wilderness. In a way, there was some truth to that analogy. The city was truly becoming a jungle.

Spawn wasn't sure how he'd gotten here, but it had taken a long time. He remembered cars honking at him and he'd heard a few screams and shouts. He tried to avoid any confrontations by focusing on his intent to find the headquarters and track down Wynn. So when several kids pelted him with rocks, he just kept going. Besides avoiding people on the street, he also had to watch out for police cars. Once he'd ducked into an alley. Another time when he saw a police cruiser, he pushed through a door and found himself in a Chinese restaurant, towering over a frightened hostess, who asked him if he wanted takeout. Then she took a second look at him and fled to the back of the restaurant, shouting in Chinese.

When he'd reached the outskirts of the A-6 compound, he hid behind a vacant building between two Dumpsters until well after dark. Finally, he crawled out of his hiding place and crept along the barbed fence. After resting for hours, he felt charged with energy, as if he were plugged into an enormous battery. The sensation buoyed his spirits.

His armor had hardened now and actually felt light and flexible, a natural part of his body. But best of all, the pain had subsided. He still felt an occasional dull throb here and there, but for the most part he was healed and free of the excruciating stabbing sensations that had racked his body.

Now he was ready to test himself, to see if his new armored body could meet the demands that he required. He made sure no guards were in sight. He climbed up the fence, hand over hand, then vaulted over the barbed wire with an agility that surprised him and landed on his feet in a crouch. He wasn't winded in the least. In fact, he felt stronger and ready for more.

Spawn was eager to find Jason Wynn. Eager and set to strike, to repay him for what he'd done. He sensed Wynn was here inside his well-guarded office, or that he would be soon. He climbed up to a catwalk, moved swiftly ahead. He stopped at a corner, peered warily around it. He saw the gates opening and a black limo easing through the entrance. It stopped in front of the main gate. Wynn never drove around in limos when Simmons had worked for him, but times had certainly changed since then.

A man dressed in a tuxedo stepped out of the limo, accompanied by a bodyguard. They moved quickly into the building. Tux Man was too far away to recognize, but Spawn was almost certain that it was Wynn. His jaunty gait was the same as Wynn's, and so was the way he tossed his head from side to side. The sight of him brought back memories and made him all the more anxious to catch up to him and do what he'd come back to do. It would be easy to finish him off quickly, but he wanted to make sure that Wynn knew who was killing him. He wanted that to be his former boss's last horrifying thought as he died.

He heard voices somewhere below him and tensed. He moved ahead on the catwalk, then leaped over the side and onto a flat roof. He hurried to the edge, and looked down. Two guards stood in front of heavy metal doors. Above the doors was a sign that read ARMORY.

One of the guards was talking on a two-way radio. "Will do. Over."

He turned to the other guard. "The director is on his way to his office."

"I wonder what he's doing here tonight?" the second guard asked.

"Don't know," the first guard replied. "He was at a state dinner with his wife. He's probably meeting Chapel now." He flicked on his radio again. "Is Church Girl on premise? Over."

"Affirmative. She's waiting for the director in his office. Over."

The first guard smiled at his companion. "See what I told ya."

The second guard laughed. "Gotcha."

Spawn silently leaped down on the two men and smashed their heads together. They crumpled to the ground and never saw what hit them. Spawn found the keys to the armory in one of the men's pockets and quickly opened a heavy metal door. He dragged the bodies inside and closed the doors behind him.

"Just like old times," he murmured, moving through the armory.

He looked around the dimly lit room, then went to a wire cage with a padlock on the door. He ripped open the wire mesh as if it were made of thread. Once inside, he tore apart crates, bins, and canisters containing state-of-the-art firepower. Cold joy washed over him.

"Looks like I've found some old friends," he said, scooping up weapon after weapon until he'd completed his arsenal.

He checked each weapon with a familiar smile. He snapped the clips into two smart-guns and cocked them. "Okay, Jason, ol' pal, it's time for you and I to get reacquainted."

Jason Wynn paced across his sleek, luxurious hi-tech office in his tailored tux. The office was equipped with thin, flat-panel displays, touch-screens, and a situation wall. The situation wall currently contained newscasts from the U.S. and different countries broadcasting the latest mayhem around the world.

On one of the screens, Terry Fitzgerald, acting A-6 spokesman, was being interviewed by Natalie Ford of CNN. She was one of the reporters who had been keeping close tabs on the A-6 during the past few months. He pressed a button and the image grew to fill most of the screen as the other broadcasts disappeared.

"Director Wynn has been meeting with several world leaders in an attempt to quell the proliferation of global conflict," Fitzgerald exclaimed in a firm, sincere tone. The voice of understanding. "He is doing everything in his capacity to come up with a solution that will satisfy all of the parties involved."

Wynn muted the set. He turned to Jessica Chapel, who was sitting on a black leather couch in a corner of the office. One knee was crossed over the other, and she was smoking a long, thin cigarette. Her hair was shorter than in years past, and she wore a black op outfit made of molded ultralight Kevlar, a corseted exo-skin that outlined every curve of her body.

"Fitzgerald may be a spineless bureaucrat, but he's doing a great PR job for me." He nodded toward the situation wall where Fitzgerald was still talking. "The world's going to hell in a handbasket, and it's just another story on the five o'clock news.''

"Like lambs to the slaughter," Chapel said in a soft, sexy tone. "Are we still set for the delivery?"

"Of course. Everything is ready."

She stabbed out her cigarette and stretched her shoulders back. Wynn admired her body. He could never get enough of her. *So beautiful, yet so deadly,* he thought. How could he have her extinguished when she was so good in so many ways?

The answer was that he couldn't, that he wouldn't do it. He wanted Clown put down, not Chapel. But his people had never been able to track him down. It was as if Clown didn't live anywhere. He just appeared as he had appeared at Wynn's house this morning, as he had appeared that day in Lichon when Wynn and Chapel had been collecting their blood samples from the victims.

Clown had been useful, especially in predicting where the next hot spot would arise. The information had made Wynn appear to be prophetic and had contributed to the legends surrounding him. That was all fine, but Clown's usefulness had effectively ended.

Wynn refused to believe what he said about Chapel. The little freak was jealous of her because she and Wynn got along so well. His accusations were just one more of his dirty tricks. He couldn't be trusted.

Wynn still wondered if it had been a mistake eliminating Al Simmons five years ago, as Clown had recommended. No, he'd demanded it. Even though Simmons had gotten suspicious about Wynn's motives and tactics, he had been his best field technician. He'd also felt a certain sense of responsibility and pride. After all, he had discovered Simmons, trained him, and been his mentor in his early years. He often used Simmons's work as a comparison when he talked with his operatives. Simmons had handled missions alone that now required five or six highly skilled operatives. Wynn could use someone like Simmons again. It would allow him to put his new plans into effect a lot easier.

And now Clown wanted him to eliminate Chapel. No, he wouldn't do it. He already had a plan to counteract the damning photographs. If he couldn't eliminate Clown before he sent the pictures to Muriel, he would tell her about them.

He would say that the whole thing had been staged to expose a treacherous colleague who had been leaking important documents to the press. Nothing had actually happened between him and Chapel; it was just part of another operation. It was an off-the-wall story; but she just might fall for it, because she knew about the exposés on the A-6 in the press and she'd heard him complaining about a betrayer. He didn't talk much about his work with Muriel, but she certainly knew the nature of it, if not the specifics.

She would understand, he told himself.

He turned his thoughts back to matters at hand. He clicked a remote-control device for the touch-screen. A bio-matrix materialized on the wall. It showed a rotating 3-D molecular structure, a supervirus code-named HEAT-16.

"Look at it, Jess! It's finally ready. HEAT-16 makes the Ebola virus look like a skin rash. That Korean biochem op really paid off. We harvested the raw materials for the ultimate weapon from those wretched bodies."

He walked over to the refrigerator built into the wall behind his desk, opened the door, and took out a sealed vial. "And we have the only supply of vaccine if we're ever exposed."

He returned the precious vial back to the refrigerator, then turned to the touch-screen. He clicked the remote again. This time a world map appeared with more than two dozen red dots indicating where the viral weapons were headed.

"Very impressive, Jason," Chapel said, moving to his side.

"Now that we're ready to disperse our HEAT-16 over half the godforsaken planet, anyone who refuses to join my consortium won't be around to argue," Wynn said, jutting out his chin.

"They won't know what hit them," Chapel said as she took Wynn's hand.

He smiled and squeezed her hand.

"Jason, you went to that dinner this evening with Muriel, didn't you?"

"Of course. You know I have to keep up the appearances."

She let go of his hand. "For how long? You've told me over and over that you don't love her. I'm wondering if that's really true."

"Chapel, I've told you that I want to wait a few more years until my daughters are out of high school. I'll divorce her and then we won't have to hide anything longer." It was a promise that he had made without any sense that it would ever be fulfilled. Chapel was a great lay and a savvy operative, but as a wife he had serious doubts about her.

"A few more years is a long, long time," she said in a moody tone. "Can't we speed things up?"

He didn't like being pressured by her. After all, she was still his employee. A buzz saved him from responding. He touched the panel display on his desk and a female voice addressed him.

"Mr. Fitzgerald is here to see you."

"Send him in. We'll talk later. Just remember that you're always on my mind, even when we aren't together." He returned the wall screen to the newscasts just as Fitzgerald walked in.

"Director."

Wynn turned to Fitzgerald, who stood in the office doorway in his black tux. "Well, speak of the devil. Come in, Terry."

"The car's waiting downstairs." He glanced at Chapel, then back again to Wynn. "Could we speak for a moment, sir, in private?"

"Of course."

Wynn nodded to Chapel. She glided out of the room, giving Fitzgerald an icy smile as she passed him. Wynn knew that Chapel would kill Fitzgerald in a heartbeat, if she wanted. He moved across the room and selected a bottle of aged Scotch from a concealed wetbar on the wall behind his desk.

"I've been meaning to commend you on the way you've handled the media. Those rumors about me were becoming a real headache." The rumors were generated from secret documents leaked to a well-known investigative reporter. While the betrayer was yet to be found, the reporter with the *Washington Herald* had an unfortunate fatal accident that ended his series on Wynn and the A-6.

"Thank you. I did my best." Fitzgerald was clearly uncomfortable. He couldn't figure out what to do with his hands, and his shoulders kept twitching. "I know we're covering up problems with our missions overseas. I can't keep lying like this."

Wynn's look hardened as he poured the drinks. He offered Fitzgerald a shot of Scotch. "Oh, really? Drink, Terry?"

"No thanks." A beat passed. "I'd like to put a team together to analyze the field op data and find out what's really going on."

"You're not an analyst anymore, Terry. There's no need for you to be concerned about precise details of field operations."

"There's no reason not to look," Fitzgerald responded. "I think it would be a good idea, in fact. If we find some problems, we could take care of them before they get any worse. No sense overlooking something, then getting caught with our pants down later."

Wynn sat down at his desk and motioned Fitzgerald to sit. He sipped his drink and turned the full weight of his sinister gaze on his subordinate. "How are Wanda and Cyan? She just had a birthday, didn't she? How old is she, five now?"

Fitzgerald stared across the desk. Wynn could see the understanding slowly dawning. "Yes, she's five. They're both fine. Just fine. Thanks for sending the clown to the party. He was a—a surprise."

Wynn was about to deny that he'd sent a clown, but he caught himself. He knew immediately which clown had shown up at the party and wondered what it meant. Clown didn't act like a clown just for the fun of it. Everything had a purpose with him. "You're welcome. I hope he was good."

"He was astonishingly good."

"I'm glad to hear that."

In spite of the seemingly friendly exchange, Wynn sensed that Fitzgerald understood that he was not to interfere with any secret operations. But just to make it clear, he spelled it out. "I run this place the way I see fit, and I do whatever is necessary to keep it that way. Your job is to make sure the public agrees with me. Is that clear enough?"

Their gazes locked for a heartbeat, then they looked away. Wynn set down his glass and stood up. "Good. I'm glad we understand each other." He headed toward door. "Let's go. The car's waiting, as you said."

TWELVE

SPAWN WAS armed and armored, ready to make the assault. He knew the layout of the A-6 headquarters well, but he guessed that Wynn was no longer in his old office. He would be housed in the director's office, if that indeed was his new position. That office was more difficult to attack with more guards to overcome.

His concern was that by the time he reached the office, Wynn might already have fled. There were hidden passageways built into the A-6 building, and Wynn would certainly know where they were located. Meanwhile, Spawn would face a militia of firepower. He would be trapped inside the building with little chance of escaping a barrage of gunfire.

But what were his choices?

Just as he was about to make his move, a party of several people exited the building. They headed directly to the limo and Spawn glimpsed Wynn and Terry Fitzgerald, surrounded by bodyguards. He was about to leap out, but the limo pulled away.

He moved through the shadows and crept toward the security gate as the limo passed through. As soon as it disappeared, Spawn crashed into the guardhouse and grabbed the guard by the neck, lifting him off the floor.

The guard glimpsed him for a moment before Spawn turned his head away. But it was long enough for the guard to see that there was no use fighting the creature that held him.

"Where was that limo with Jason Wynn going?" Spawn demanded, squeezing the guard's neck.

"I don't know. They don't tell me."

"You're lying," Spawn seethed. "You guys know what's going on. You used to clue me in all the time to the whereabouts of the director."

"Who are you?" The guard tried to look at him again, but Spawn held his head in place.

"Never mind. Just answer my question." He squeezed harder on the guard's neck.

"Okay. Okay. The Swiss embassy. Some sort of formal party."

"Thanks." He smashed his head against the wall and the guard slithered to the floor. "Sorry about that."

Spawn bounded up and over the fence and made his way through the darkness toward Embassy Row. The Swiss would have a surprise visitor this evening.

Wynn called Muriel at home as they motored toward the embassy. Muriel was in a good mood, chatting about the dinner party they attended. She'd gotten along well with a wife of a minister from one of the former Soviet nations. They'd talked about travel and art, while her husband had talked to Wynn in veiled terms about how he could gain the ability to destroy his neighbors on all three sides. The minister was especially interested since two of his neighbors already had the ability to destroy his country. Wynn, for his part, was ready to accommodate him with several canisters of HEAT-16.

"Don't wait up for me, dear," he told Muriel. "I'll be out late at another function."

"At the Swiss embassy, right? You already told me."

She sounded suspicious as she added: "Since when do you report your whereabouts to me, Jason?"

"I just didn't want you to worry. I have a special task to handle tonight. Something unusual has come up. I'll tell you about it later."

"Now you're going to tell me about your work? Jason, how many drinks have you had?"

He chuckled. "You'll understand better when I tell you about it."

He hung up with a smug smile. She hadn't received the photos from Clown. That was a good sign. Now she was set up for his explanation.

He looked over at Fitzgerald, who was twitching nervously and tapping his fingers against his knees. Fitzgerald would be the one who would be discovered as the betrayer in Wynn's little setup, the one who sent the photos to Muriel. Wynn laughed to himself again.

If Clown carried out his threat in his effort to destroy his marriage, Wynn would not only head him off but take advantage of the situation by exposing Fitzgerald as the betrayer who was leaking important documents. For all he knew, it was true. He'd suspected Fitzgerald from the start, but all his efforts to catch him at it or in possession of the documents in question had utterly failed. If nothing else, Fitzgerald was clever.

Chapel paced angrily up and down the third-floor corridor outside of her office. She would've paced inside the office, but as a field operative her space in the building was limited to a cubicle, which she rarely used, and didn't really need. More important was her locker, which was nearly the size of the cubicle, where she kept an array of outfits for all occasions and a selection of her personal weapons.

She was miffed that Wynn had left for the Swiss embassy without her. She could understand the state dinner, that it was still prudent for the director to take his wife. Showing up with Chapel certainly would have raised eyebrows in some quarters. But she knew that Wynn was more concerned about what his wife and kids would think if they found out than what the power brokers and world leaders thought about his private life. After all, he held his family on a pedestal, as if they made up for his sins. The others were no more than wooden pieces on a game board.

Wynn's professional image already had been tarnished more than once, yet nothing seemed to faze him. No one tried to stop him anymore. They were afraid of him, afraid he knew their secrets and would expose them, or worse. As a result, Wynn was amassing more and more power so that now he made even J. Edgar Hoover, the notorious collector of files on politicians and criminals alike, look like a small-time operator.

But Chapel was offended that Wynn hadn't taken her to the Swiss embassy. She wasn't going to hang on him. She just wanted to get inside, to move around, to be seen, and to make her own contacts. She had her own career to consider, and sometimes she felt that Wynn hindered as well as helped her. She wanted to advance from a mere precision-killing machine, one who literally caught her victims with their pants down, to a power broker in her own right. She could be deadly at both games.

That was where Clown came in. He had offered more than she had imagined possible. She was playing along with Clown to see what would come of it, but she wasn't relying completely on him, either. Not by any means.

Her immediate concern was talking to a certain international terrorist, known as the Hyena, who Wynn considered a competitor. Chapel had become closely acquainted with him during the past couple of weeks. He was at the party, and it was the perfect place to casually pass information. She was working with him completely on her own. Neither Wynn nor Clown knew about it.

Two nights ago, they'd struck a deal over crepes in a Georgetown restaurant. But now she had to renegotiate and had hoped to contact him at the embassy party. Wynn must have gotten worried about the security of the HEAT-16. He'd moved it from the warehouse in Baltimore to God knows where. He'd done it without telling her, which made her even more concerned. So now she was unable to keep her side of the bargain with the Hyena. She needed to delay the delivery until she could get her hands on the product.

She knew Wynn well, probably even better than his wife, and she knew that he was acting oddly toward her tonight. But then again, if Wynn suspected she was dealing HEAT-16 on her own, she was sure he would've called her on it. He wasn't one to tiptoe around his subordinates when he suspected misconduct. In spite of her relationship with him, she was also one of his subjects.

Then again, he'd left for the embassy party without her. She wondered if Fitzgerald had something to do with it. She knew the twerp didn't like her because of her relationship with Wynn. As far as she was concerned, Fitzgerald was on his way out, a step from the door. He definitely didn't fit in her game plan.

But he was smart. All of her efforts to expose him as a betrayer had failed. When she planted evidence showing how he had sabotaged an operation by informing the target in advance, he had taken the document in question immediately to Wynn, thus defusing the suspicions against him before she could ignite them.

Then she had released three embarrassing documents to her secret contact at the *Herald*. They were highly classified internal memoranda that showed how Wynn had personally taken down two members of Congress by exposing their bad habits to the public. But the third document was the killer. It revealed how Wynn was unable to find anything on a special prosecutor who was attempting to link him with the execution of an Asian head of state. Wynn had said that "other means" would be used to silence him. Three days after he'd written the memorandum, the prosecutor had disappeared without a trace.

Chapel was certain that Fitzgerald would fall hard. She'd even been concerned that she was taking Wynn down. She'd thought long and hard before releasing the third document, but then she'd decided that even if Wynn fell, she could capitalize on it. But to her chagrin, neither Wynn nor Fitzgerald had been seriously affected. The evidence showing that Fitzgerald had turned over the memoranda to the reporter had disappeared, and he'd gotten away again.

She felt a pulse against her wrist and glanced at her watch. It was throbbing red, indicating an emergency. She darted into her office and hit the security button. She identified herself with a code and was told that three guards were down—two at the armory, another at the gate—that an intruder might still be hiding somewhere on the premise.

She pulled out an automatic pistol from the drawer of her desk, then raced down the hall. She passed Wynn's office and saw that guards had already secured it. She headed down a back staircase, wondering if the attack was somehow related to the deal that she'd made. Maybe the Hyena already knew that she was reneging on it. Or maybe one of the Hyena's enemies had gotten wind of it.

By the time she reached the armory, the entire facility was secured. There was no sign of an intruder. But once she inspected the armory, Chapel knew that the incident was only beginning. Whoever had broken in knew what he was doing. He knew right where to look and what he wanted. It could've been the Hyena, except he already had easy access to the kind of weapons that had been stolen. So why would he bother? It didn't make any sense to her.

She talked with the two guards who had been knocked out, but they were useless. They hadn't seen anything. The guard at the gate was more helpful.

He had briefly seen a distorted figure who looked as if he'd been covered with leathery armor. His face looked badly burned. That was disturbing enough, but then the guard had said that the man knew about the inner workings of the A-6 security system.

She didn't know what it meant. But she didn't like the sound of it.

Wynn glanced out the window as they passed through one the capital's more decrepit neighborhoods. Layers of graffiti covered the walls. The storefronts looked fortified enough to withstand a direct missile attack. At one corner, several police were pounding on a man with billy clubs. *The best sort of therapy available for all of them,* Wynn thought without a moment's concern for the battered man.

The Emergency Deliverance Church came into view and in front of it, a bearded old man in a hooded cape stood by a fire burning in a trash can. The flames illuminated his eyes; they seemed to stare directly into the limo, as if he could see through the tinted windows. The old man looked familiar, but Wynn pushed that thought aside when the limo turned and the downtrodden neighborhood disappeared in favor of national monuments and wide, landscaped boulevards. From deterioration to preservation in the blink of an eye.

A minute later, they turned into the embassy. Security vehicles with spotlights and armed guards gave the place the feel of a bastion under siege. Two color guards and two plainclothes security guards were stationed at the entrance where the limo stopped. Wynn's driver emerged from the limo and handed a pass to a guard, then he opened the back door for Wynn and Fitzgerald.

They walked into the lobby together, talking amiably

as if there was nothing wrong between them. A light came on and a television cameraman and a reporter stepped out from an alcove. A bright light flooded Wynn's face; a microphone was shoved under his nose.

"Mr. Wynn, can you tell me your reaction to the rumor that you are planning a major event that will shock the world?"

Wynn laughed. "I only react to events, I don't plan them. But I do try to solve problems and make things simpler."

The reporter started to ask another question, but Fitzgerald stepped in front of him. "That's all. You can call us at our offices tomorrow morning for a statement." He put on his professional smile, handed the reporter a card, and he and Wynn moved on.

A doorman showed them to the bank of elevators where a valet held a door open for them, then pressed the button for the thirteenth-floor ballroom. The black-tie affair was in full swing when they arrived. The leaders of several nations, revolutionary groups, and international crime cartels were present, and Wynn quickly picked out several of them. The event was being held in the Swiss embassy, because it was considered neutral territory.

Wynn ambled among the foreign leaders and liaisons with confidence. He was at ease with both esteemed statesmen and criminal figures. He was recognized as a major international powerbroker with a prominent place on the world stage, and received icy respect from these influential men and women. He saw the notorious terrorist, the Hyena, but stayed clear of him. He wasn't afraid of the man, but several of the deals he'd made were contingent on his promise not to supply the Hyena with HEAT-16.

A group of African liaisons were drinking wine and smiling graciously as Wynn approached. "Gentlemen, have you made a decision?"

One of the liaisons, a man in his fifties who wore colorful native attire, including a brimless, flat-topped hat, stepped forward. "I found your HEAT-16 test very impressive. Tell me, how do you control delivery of the weapon?"

"An important question," Wynn responded. "The answer is the latest in nanotechnology. Problem free I assure you. We've already placed orders with several of your neighboring nations. I hope you will join us."

"You're becoming quite a powerful man, Mr. Wynn," said a second member of the group, a man in his thirties, who wore similar clothing. "Your consortium will soon rival the UN."

Wynn smiled and lifted a glass of champagne from a passing tray. "I'm just a facilitator. My partners are the beneficiaries."

Clown wore heavy makeup to disguise the permanent smile tattooed to his face. He was garbed in a white waiter's uniform and worked his way through the crowd, carrying a tray of hors d'oeuvres. He paused near Wynn as he discussed HEAT-16 with the African liaisons. No one seemed to notice him, so he held the tray higher.

Clown was enjoying himself at the affair. He reveled in all the deceit and treachery that was taking place or being planned by these tuxedos and gowns. More and more of them were sensing the ultimate plan that Malebolgia was preparing—and they would be useful allies, if they were still alive when their help was needed.

Wynn reached over and picked a canapé off the tray. To his surprise, the topping on the piece of quiche resembled a clown face. He looked around, but the waiter had disappeared.

Fitzgerald approached, his expression limned with concern. He signaled discreetly to his boss, who excused him-

self from the African liaisons. He turned to Fitzgerald.
"So what is it now?"

"There's been a break-in at headquarters. The armory
was hit and three guards were hurt. There's some serious
firepower missing."

"Any ideas who it was?" Wynn asked.

"We don't know. Chapel's out front with a security
detail. She thinks we should leave right away. It's not
safe."

Wynn looked around uneasily. "I agree with her. Let's
get out of here."

THIRTEEN

THE EMBASSY looked impenetrable. All the entrances were guarded and the windows were covered with decorative, but protective, steel shields. He moved through the shadows near the surrounding buildings, surveying the structure from every side. Guards were also stationed behind the building, even though there were no entrances or even any first-floor windows there.

Just as he was about to give up any hope of finding a way inside, the guards were distracted by a Jeep that pulled to the front entrance. A blonde in a tight-fitting outfit leaped out and began shouting orders. Even the guards in the rear moved forward to see what was going on. When they saw Chapel, they forgot about their posts.

"Thanks, Chapel," Spawn said as he saw a slender chance open in front of him.

He pushed through a thick hedge, creating a ragged tear in the shrubbery. Then he stole quickly over to the back wall. The guards assigned to either corner would return momentarily. He knew he couldn't stay there long before he was detected. But how was he going to climb the sheer wall? His fingers and feet were too large to fit between the bricks.

He'd no sooner registered the thought when he felt a

peculiar tingling sensation, as if his hands and feet had fallen asleep. When he opened his massive pawlike appendages, claw hooks sprang from each hand. He stared in amazement as matching claws spread from the armor that covered his ragged boots. The tingling sensation vanished as he reached for the wall.

He began to climb, hooking the claws expertly into the space between the bricks. Within seconds, he had reached the level of the second floor. He continued on, floor after floor, until he was just below the roof. But now he was stuck. The roof jutted out three feet from the wall. He would have to spring up and out at the same time, and even if he could do that he would still have to catch the edge of the roof with his distorted hands.

He looked down and saw guards moving about directly below him, shining a searchlight on the damaged hedge and along the building. They already suspected something was amiss, and soon one of the guards would shine the light up the building and spot him. In a matter of seconds, they would alert the entire security force and he would be trapped like a fly on fly paper. He had no choice but to try.

Spawn crouched low, then leaped with all his strength, hoping to latch onto the eave with at least one hand. To his surprise, he vaulted several feet higher, and his knees struck the underside of the roof. He slapped his hands and arms down over the rooftop and pulled the top half of his body forward. His legs kicked over the side of the roof for a couple of seconds, then he pulled them up after him. He lay on the roof panting until he caught his breath.

He crawled away from the edge, then scrambled forward, across the roof toward a glass dome in the center. He peered through it, into a ballroom where formally dressed men and women were gathering. He knew that Jason Wynn was down there.

*   *   *

Wynn sensed that whatever had happened at headquarters was somehow related to HEAT-16. He suspected that the Hyena was behind it. He knew that the infamous terrorist was angry because he was being denied access to the viral weapon. Wynn once feared the terrorist and had made him an ally in a couple of his undercover plots.

He didn't fear him anymore, however. He knew the Hyena's power was waning, and after the delivery of the weapons, he would be effectively neutralized. But now he suspected the Hyena had attacked the armory, thinking that was where the weapon was being kept, and timed the attack to coincide with the embassy party.

As he and Fitzgerald stopped to wait for an elevator, he turned back and surveyed the crowd. He felt vulnerable and knew it was a mistake giving Marcus the night off. He spotted the Hyena, a handsome dark-haired man of Euro-Asian descent, standing off to one side, staring at him. To Wynn's surprise, he looked puzzled by Wynn's early departure, as if he had no idea what had motivated the A-6 director to leave.

Maybe his scenario was off-base, but who else would've dared to attack the A-6 armory?

He had no time to speculate further. Just as the elevator arrived, a metallic screech from high above ripped through the ballroom.

The crowd's attention turned upward; the dome suddenly exploded inward, showering bits of colored glass over the ballroom and the assembled guests. As everyone screamed and scrambled to the sides of the room, an enormous humanlike form crashed through the dome, a figure the likes of which Wynn had never seen. It was covered with armor, including its face, and a long cape trailed behind it, accompanied by chains that extended out to either side. The uninvited guest landed on his feet amid the scrambling of tuxes and gowns.

The menacing figure towered over everyone. A smart-gun was strapped to its back. Its chains and cape undulated with a sinister slowness, like a hissing snake. The armor looked impermeable, as if it were part of the being within. Wynn marveled at the beast, wondering if it were part human and part machine. But then the creature's dark eyes met his and held his gaze. Fear rippled up Wynn's spine as the beast charged toward him. He was so startled he couldn't move.

"You!" the beast roared as it collared Wynn and lifted him over its head. A woman screamed. Some of the guests dashed for exits. Others edged along the walls.

"Who are you?" Wynn managed to gasp.

"What's the matter, Wynn, don't you recognize your own handiwork?"

Wynn shuddered as the armor retracted from the creature's face; he stared at its charred flesh and angry eyes filled with hate. "You left me to die in that biochem plant, remember?"

"Simmons?"

"Why did you kill me?" He squeezed harder on Wynn's neck. "Why?"

"Clown. It was Clown," he sputtered. How could this be Simmons? It must be a Clown joke. Wynn was certain he was dead.

"That son-of-a-bitch. He's next." The Simmons-creature laughed. "You sent me to Hell, Jason. Now it's your turn to take that trip." He backhanded him across the room and Wynn crashed through a table covered with hors d'oeuvres. His legs swung out and tripped Fitzgerald, who was heading for an exit.

Until that moment, most of the guests had been frozen in stunned astonishment. Now the influential, international, crowd bolted for the exits like a spooked herd of sheep.

Chapel dragged on a cigarette as she waited outside the embassy for Wynn and Fitzgerald. From what she'd heard

from the guard at headquarters, the invader sounded like
Simmons. But she had seen him torched; he couldn't have
survived. Unless Simmons hadn't been alone. There was
the unlikely possibility that he had been accompanied by
a second operative—a freelancer he'd hired on his own.
Somehow the freelancer had saved Simmons, even though
he'd suffered terrible burns.

Now Simmons was back and on the attack. But who or
what was he after? Chapel guessed that he was out for
revenge and she and Wynn were the main targets. Wynn
had lit the fire and she had stood by, watching him.

Chapel tensed and jerked up her head at a sound like
a thousand wineglasses shattering. Security guards rushed
into the building. She crushed out her cigarette and turned
to the other A-6 agents standing near a Suburban, waiting
for directions.

"Must be a helluva party. Think I'll see what's going
on. Wait here."

She walked toward the embassy entrance, ducking inside in the confusion as several party-goers rushed outside, jabbering to the guards about an armored beast
who'd crashed the party.

"Sounds familiar," she said to herself and dashed for
the stairs.

Fitzgerald started to pick himself up from the splattered
canapés when a pair of massive hands pulled him upright
to his feet. He held up his hands and backed away from
the armored beast. He was about to make a run for it when
one of the big hands snagged him and pulled him so close
that their faces were just inches apart.

"You told me you were going to stop Wynn, Terry. I
trusted you."

Fitzgerald could hardly believe what he'd just heard,
let alone what he saw. "Al? No, it can't be."

"How could you marry Wanda?"

Fitzgerald shook his head. "I—I thought you were dead. So did Wanda. You were dead, but . . . Jesus, is that really you, Al?"

"Yes. But you can call me Spawn now."

"When Al died, Wanda needed help. She was in bad shape. I just tried to comfort her. One thing led to another . . . over time."

Fitzgerald felt the tight grip gradually loosen. He thought he saw tears forming in the corner of the beast's eyes. "Do you know about Cyan, our daughter? She just turned five."

Wynn started to crawl away, but Simmons saw him in the corner of his eye. He let go of Fitzgerald and grabbed his former boss by the thigh. He hoisted him easily, then kicked him like a big football, sending him tumbling through the air and onto a serving trolley on the other side of the room.

"All I know right now is that Wynn's about to die, Terry." Then he went after the director of A-6, who was crawling again.

"Time to kick some monster ass," Chapel said, clasping her smart-gun in both hands. She pushed open the balcony door and strutted into the ballroom. "Who said I need an invitation?"

She surveyed the chaos below, searching the floor for the invader. Impulsively, she squeezed off a couple dozen rounds over everyone's head. Bullets ripped across the ballroom, shattering lights and chandeliers and shredding the walls. Screaming guests dove for cover.

Chapel spotted the armored, caped creature and caught her breath. He was enormous, too big to be Simmons. *It must be a gimmick,* she thought. She fired another barrage of bullets at the beast.

"Nice outfit, asshole."

* * *

Spawn pulled out his smart-gun, rolled over a couple times, and returned fire. He strafed the balcony where Chapel had been standing and blew out a chandelier; shards of crystal shot out in all directions. Two other chandeliers swung from side to side, casting eerie shadows against the walls.

Chapel leaped to her feet and viciously fired across the ballroom, chasing Spawn as he sprinted for a door. Displays of food, ice sculptures, and trays of glasses exploded. Spawn screamed in pain as a half dozen bullets plugged his armor. But with a final burst of strength, he dove through a service door.

He rolled over and over, and smashed into a serving trolley, knocking a petrified waiter against a wall and sending a dozen bottles of champagne rolling in every direction. He looked down at himself, wincing in pain, and saw what he already knew. His armor was tough, but it didn't stop bullets.

Chapel cautiously surveyed the ruin of the ballroom. A couple of dozen people were huddled under overturned table, or crawling away. Some were wounded, others were lying still in expanding pools of blood, their bodies contorted in odd positions. One of them looked familiar—the Hyena. He lay, staring wide-eyed at the smashed dome. So much for her private deal.

But she had another concern right now. There was no sign of the armored giant. She climbed over the balcony and dropped to the floor. She spotted Wynn under a table and moved over to him. He was nursing an injured shoulder and battered ribs.

"What the hell was that?" she asked.

"It's Simmons."

"That? How could it be?" She'd suspected as much, but she hadn't truly believed it.

"I'm telling you, that thing is Simmons and I want you to nail him . . . now!"

One of the swinging doors suddenly crashed to the floor. Chapel cautiously moved toward the service entrance, certain she'd hit him several times. If the Simmons thing was still living, she probably had him cornered. But cornered creatures were the most dangerous kind.

Spawn slowly and painfully pulled himself beneath the stairwell. His final stand, he thought, and he'd failed to finish off Wynn. Chapel had interrupted him before he'd completed the payback. He was badly wounded and wouldn't last long. He knew his vital organs had been hit, and he was surprised he was still conscious.

Then, to his amazement, the bullets were pushed out as if the armor were somehow expelling them. One after another, chunks of lead dropped to the floor. Then, in a matter of seconds, the wounds closed and healed as the armor repaired the damage to his body.

"Damn!" He tried to shout his excitement, but his face armor suddenly closed into place and his exclamation was muted. He grabbed his weapon, stood up with barely a trace of pain, and bounded up the stairs as if he'd never been shot.

Chapel burst through the door into the service stairwell. She glimpsed Simmons just as he rounded the top of the stairs and opened fire. Bullets pinged off the steel railing and metal stairs and were buried in the walls. Just one bullet from her smart-gun should have been enough to stop an elephant in its tracks. Yet the Simmons creature was acting as if she'd missed.

She jumped over bottles of champagne and moved past a waiter who was shaking in fear. Warily, she mounted the stairs and climbed backed up to the balcony, her weapon at the ready. She paused beside the door, then kicked it open. She darted forward, turning one way, then the other, aiming the weapon along the balcony and then down to the ballroom floor. She nearly opened fire on the remaining guests, who raised their hands over their heads.

Where did he go? He'd come up here. There were no other possibilities. One of the guests motioned out past the balcony. She couldn't understand where he was pointing. She moved closer to the railing, her finger still tensed against the trigger. Suddenly, Simmons swung down on a chandelier from the interior of the dome and kicked her in the head. She sprayed gunfire into the remains of the dome, but the smart-gun slipped from her grasp as she smacked into the wall.

Chapel was stunned by the blow, but shook it off. She spun around and delivered a swift kick to Spawn's groin. To her astonishment, a skull emerged from his groin area and its jaw clamped down over her leg. She screamed in pain as its sharp fangs pierced her skin.

Spawn grabbed Chapel by the back of the neck, released her leg, and threw her brutally down against the balcony railing. He stood over her as his face armor retracted.

The gruesome, burned face terrified and appalled her, but she didn't let Simmons know it. "Well, it's a little early for Halloween, Al."

He leveled his smart-gun at her. "Where you're going, Chapel, everyday is Halloween, but it's all tricks and no treats."

She sneered at him. "You don't have the guts." She was trying to bluff him. But a sickening feeling suddenly overcame her. She sensed that all her schemes were coming to an abrupt end, that Wynn would never be all hers, that she would never see Fitzgerald beg for mercy as she killed him, that she would never seduce another victim.

She stared down into the dark barrel of the gun and glimpsed a flash, then nothing more.

Spawn didn't hesitate. He squeezed the trigger, firing point blank into Chapel's face. She broke through the balcony railing and crashed down on top of a pyramid of champagne glasses. Shards of glass and champagne sprayed everywhere.

Spawn leaned over the balcony and looked at her lifeless body lying amid the shattered glass. From under the balcony, he heard someone applauding. Then Clown walked out in his waiter outfit and stood over Chapel, munching on clown quiche. He looked up at Spawn and grinned.

"That was beautiful, just beautiful! Right as I'm thinking we got the wrong guy, you make us proud. Stay with that emotion."

The service doors burst open and two A-6 agents dashed into the ballroom, their smart-guns blazing up at the balcony. Spawn seemed to fly as he sprinted away. Bullets ricocheted off the railing and walls. They struck his arm, shoulder, and neck, and he felt a burning pain like wasp stings. Below him, the few remaining guests huddled together in a corner behind several tables.

Spawn returned the fire and hit both A-6 agents, who toppled to the floor a few feet from Chapel. He leaped off the balcony and crashed onto a table, which collapsed to the floor. Nearby, several guests shrank back toward the wall, shrieking in terror. Spawn ignored them and walked over to Clown. He knew now that the dwarf was the one responsible for his death at the biochem plant.

"What's the matter?" Clown asked. "You're fine. Just look at your armor."

The bullets that had hit him on the balcony clattered to the floor and again the wounds quickly healed. Before he could respond to Clown, two more A-6 agents bolted through the service door and fired on Spawn. He whirled around and returned the fire. Clown grabbed a couple of tuxedoed bodies and used them as shields.

Spawn fired wildly, but hit both agents. The bodies Clown hid behind were ripped apart in the crossfire. "Too bad about that," Clown said, brushing off his hands as he dropped the bodies. "I don't think it'll be an open casket for those two."

He laughed uproariously and clapped his hands, reveling in the violence. "Kill, kill, kill, and when they're dead, kill them some more." Clown looked down at one of the bodies. Guts spilled out of the front of the dead man's bloodied tuxedo shirt and onto the floor. "Oh, I think he had the veal for dinner."

Spawn turned on Clown, aiming the smart-gun at his head. "I've had enough of you."

Clown ignored his threat. "Congratulations on your first mission. The flames of chaos and destruction are gonna be seriously stoked by tonight's events. I do believe I'm getting a stiffy."

"You were the one who had me killed."

Clown grinned. "Yeah, but look at you now. You're a hunk."

Spawn was about to blast the dwarf to pieces when the ballroom was assaulted by a throng of security forces and A-6 agents who poured in at the same time through three doors. Spawn spun around, hopelessly outnumbered. Gunfire erupted from all directions. He leaped over Clown, who had dropped to the floor, and ran across the ballroom returning fire as he was struck over and over again.

A million scorpions seemed to sting him simultaneously. He spun around, firing wildly until he crashed through an enormous stained-glass window.

He fell backward and flipped over and over as he plunged down, down, down, thirteen stories, plummeting toward the parking lot and to extinction.

Part Three

AFTER THE FALL

FOURTEEN

THE STREET seemed to jump up to meet him, but then at the last instant Spawn's chains reacted instinctively and sent their hooked ends sailing outward. They snagged a hole worn in the mortar two floors above the ground. The chains tightened and Spawn's body jerked up just before he hit the pavement. He bounced twenty feet into the air, then dropped back down and swung toward the building, barely missing the pavement. He banged hard against the embassy wall and swung back out again, his back inches above the parking lot.

On the next pass, he reached out for the wall and the grappling claw hooks emerged again from the armor around his hands and feet. He latched onto the wall, steadied himself, the chains retracted into the armor. Bits of lead dropped to the ground as the armor healed itself and the sharp stinging sensations slowly faded.

Spawn spider-crawled along the wall, moving upward and toward the corner. He'd climbed the outside of a few buildings in his time with the A-6, but until today he'd never done it without climbing ropes, pitons, and a harness. Now he was doing it in the dark for the second time in an hour. But then, nothing was the same anymore. Although he still held his old memories and still thought of himself as human, he was starting to have a hard time holding on to the idea that he was still Al Simmons.

Every so often he caught vague glimpses of Hell, and he was reminded that he was here on a mission. He just couldn't remember what the mission was about—except to kill Wynn. On that count, he'd failed. Somehow Wynn had evaded him and escaped the final punishing blows.

Suddenly, several guards rushed into the street. They quickly spread out, searching for him. "I know we hit him," one of them yelled. "He couldn't have gone far." Spawn recognized the voice of an A-6 agent he'd worked with on a couple of missions.

"There he is," another guard yelled and pointed up at him. The rattle of gunfire greeted Spawn just as he reached the corner and slipped around to the dark side of the building. It only took a few moments for the guards to rush around the building and beam searchlights from the security vehicles onto the wall.

Spawn climbed upward to a ledge and pulled himself over it as a searchlight moved slowly in his direction. He ducked down behind a stone cherub, tucking himself behind it and crushing part of it in the process. He pulled in his cape, wrapping it around himself; and as he did so, the cape not only covered him but changed its shape and color so that Spawn was camouflaged as a second stone figure.

It seemed that with every desperate turn he took, his armor and the related appendages showed him a new trick. He had the feeling his protective shield and its accessories had even more capabilities that he had yet to discover. He just wished he knew what they were. He'd had enough surprises for one night.

The searchlight passed over him and drifted away. He needed to quickly get around the corner to the back wall and find a way down while the guards were focused on the searchlight's beam. As he began to move, the altered cape shifted to its normal appearance and retracted into the armor. But his foot pushed against the damaged cherub and it toppled off the ledge, landing a few feet from one of the guards.

"Oh, shit!"

Spawn had barely recovered from the last attack and now he knew that he would be on the receiving end of another assault.

The guard yelled out and pointed toward the ledge. Blinding white light washed over him. The guards opened fire, hitting him on the thighs, buttocks, back, and shoulders. He winced at the pain and started running along the ledge, toward the front of the building. He had no idea where he was going or what he was going to do. More bullets struck him and others pinged against the wall and ledge, chipping away brick and concrete.

Chased by gunfire, he reached the front of the building and was greeted with another swarm of stinging, piercing bullets. He wobbled on the ledge and it began to break away, falling in a hailstorm of chunks. Spawn lost his foothold and toppled off the ledge, tumbling out of control toward the heavily armed guards. This time his chains would do him no good. He would simply be a swinging target for a small army of sharpshooters.

Suddenly, his cape reemerged and formed into a huge gargoylesque wing spanning more than two dozen feet. The cape moved on its own and flipped him over so that he was facing down. He swooped low, just over the heads of the astonished guards, who ducked, then watched in amazement as he swept upward and soared down the street.

Spawn was as stunned as the guards as he stretched out his amazing wings, leaned to the right, swept down a cross street, and out of sight of the embassy.

"I could get used to this!"

He felt giddy from the new experience. He rose up above the buildings and quickly disappeared into the night.

* * *

The flashing lights of emergency medical service vehicles lit up the night outside the Swiss embassy as paramedics zipped body bags and attended to the wounded. Several police officers worked to control the crowd that had gathered on the sidewalk, and reporters moved about, searching for witnesses who could describe what had happened in the ballroom.

"Can you tell me what you saw take place in there, sir?" a young reporter asked the dwarf waiter who was standing behind an EMS vehicle, munching from a plate of clown quiches.

"Oh, it was horrible. This big ugly fellow, wearing black shiny armor, fell through the glass dome and started shooting at everyone. He was out of his mind. I'll never forget all those bloody tuxedos."

"Were there many killed?"

"Well, I was slipping on all the blood trying to get away and climbing over the bodies. Let me tell you, I've never worked a party like that one."

"I see," the reporter said, jotting down notes and nodding his head. "How did the killer get away when the embassy was so heavily guarded?"

"He came through the roof and left through a window. That's all I can tell you."

The reporter looked up from his notes. "From the thirteenth floor?"

Clown shrugged. "I didn't see him land."

The puzzled reporter shook his head, then took another look at Clown. "Were you injured?"

Clown's serious expression turned into a beaming smile. "Being short has certain advantages. The bullets all went over my head."

"Your name, sir?"

"Hm, name, name. Oh yes, I. M. Clown. With a *C*. It used to be a *K*, but we changed it." He handed the plate of clown quiche to the reporter and walked off as he spotted Wynn stepping out of the back of the EMS vehicle.

"How's the arm, Jason?" Clown reached up and rapped his knuckles against the field cast that was secured to Wynn's left arm.

Wynn looked confused. For a moment, he wasn't sure who was talking to him. Then he saw the dwarf. "You! Why didn't you warn me about Simmons?"

Clown raised both hands in exaggerated surprise. "Why didn't you warn me?"

Then, turning serious, he added: "Don't get your panties in a bunch, ya cheese weasel. I didn't think his armor would harden this quickly. Besides, surprises are always more fun. Don't ya think?"

"Fun?" Wynn fumed. "Does this look like Disneyland to you?" It didn't take long for the dwarf to start annoying him.

Clown looked around and scratched his head. "Um, no, it doesn't."

"He killed Chapel and almost killed me!"

"Such a shame about Chapel. Too bad. Too bad." He shook his head in a parody of sadness. "But on the other hand, you don't have to kill her for me now. I bet that makes you feel better."

"How could you bring Simmons back?"

"It wasn't exactly my idea. The boss had something to do with it. Spawn's just a little confused right now. He seems to remember that you killed him. But he'll come around." Clown slapped Wynn on the back. "Hey, give the guy a break, he's been through hell."

Frowning and crossing his arms, Clown continued: "And I mean Hell. Just as soon as he finishes one more little detail, his soul will be ours." Clown laughed as if his comment was hilarious.

Then in midcackle he abruptly stopped. His beady eyes focused on Wynn, as if he were looking right through him. "So, how are we doing on your front, turning the heat on high, are we?"

Wynn was more than slightly annoyed that he was still taking orders from Clown. But he was smart enough to acknowledge that the whole scenario about the evil, dark boss and Hell's Army was more than just talk. After all, Clown had power and he certainly was no angel from the heavens. As he figured it, the dark side was the way to get what you wanted fast. Suffering, sacrifice, and the pious crap wasn't for him. The same for peace and love. Sorry, but the weak and meek were never going to rule anything, much less the Earth.

If he could take advantage of the Dark Lord and his army, he'd do it, as long as the promised payoff came through. He knew that he had to keep his eye on these diabolical types. But if anyone could deal with them, it was him.

"HEAT-16 is ready to go," he said, looking Clown right in his shiny black eyes. "You can be sure that the results will be devastating."

"It better be . . . 'cause the army is just about at critical mass and Spawn is here to tip the scale. But without HEAT-16, this baby ain't gonna fly, and you won't get to reign supreme, not to mention named employee of the month."

Wynn peered darkly at Clown. "What's Simmons got to do with this? You never told me that he was still in the picture."

"He's the highest scoring killer of all times, kiddo. If we hadn't drafted him, the other side mighta picked him up. One of those oh-so-holy converts. You know the type, always preaching about their bad ways and how they found the light." Clown elbowed him in the ribs. "Don't go getting any ideas now."

Wynn ignored his chatter. He was still fuming about

Simmons. "So how am I supposed to work with him? He still wants to kill me!"

"You figure it out," Clown sneered and turned to go. "Oh yeah, I almost forgot. The boss figures you oughta have some kind of fancy-schmancy implant that connects your heartbeat to the HEAT-16 bombs. That way no smart-ass will dare to take you out."

What are you talking about?" This twist was news to him.

"You know, an insurance policy. Shoulda done it already. You're a very hot commodity, Mr. Bigshot. Wouldn't want to lose our point man just when the war's about to start."

Wynn nodded, impressed. The implant would make him more valuable and, best of all, would protect him from Simmons, once he found out about it. "It's a good idea. I'll take care of it."

"Glad it meets your approval," Clown said, sarcastically. "Now stay sharp; I'm gonna need your personal help dealing with Spawn."

"Looking forward to that." He still couldn't believe how close he'd come to death. And now he'd never see Chapel again. At least with her dead, he didn't have to worry about talking with Muriel about those pictures.

He wondered for a brief moment if Clown would give him a set—just for the memories. But he quickly pushed aside the thought. A door closed should stay closed.

As Clown walked out of earshot, Wynn offered a final comment. "When the world's mine, you get drawn and quartered, little fatboy."

An A-6 doctor fixed a sling over Wynn's cast and hooked it around his neck. "There you go. That should do for now. Let me check it next week. But the arm should heal without any problem."

"Good. But I'd like to make an appointment with you

about another matter. I need you do some special work on me."

Dr. Martin Vargas, a middle-aged man who had worked with A-6 employees for years, frowned. "What kind of work?"

"It has to do with my personal security."

Clown was pleased with the evening's developments. He'd enjoyed all the surprises, even though he was going to miss spying on Chapel and Wynn. Now he didn't have to send the nasty pictures to Muriel and the girls. Not as long as Wynn was cooperating so nicely. But what fun would that be. He laughed to himself.

"I'll send them, anyhow. Why not!" he shouted aloud to no one in particular.

He was about to pass by an unattended injured man lying on a gurney. But he felt so good about his decision to send the pictures that he kicked the gurney, spilling the man onto the ground. "Oh, sorry. I didn't see you lying there."

"Hey, I saw that," a paramedic shouted as he ran over to the fallen man and bent down to help him. "Why did you do that?"

" 'Cause that's what demons do!" He booted the paramedic in the jaw, sending him tumbling backward. His head cracked against the sidewalk and he didn't move.

"No more questions? Hm, guess he lost his curiosity."

Clown whistled merrily as he crossed the street. He pulled off his white waiter's uniform, uncovering his scruffy clown outfit. Then he wiped the makeup from his face, revealing his blue tattoo grin.

"Ah, that's better."

He walked down to the corner where he spotted a couple of scantily clad, over-the-hill, overweight ladies of the night standing in a doorway. He motioned them over to him. He needed some recreation after a night's work. After thousands of years of similar nights.

He'd nurtured one Hellspawn after another for the boss, who was always trying to convert pathetic humans, or rather pathetic has-been humans, into the real thing. He was tired of his baby-sitting chores, and more than slightly pissed off that the Dark Lord overlooked him for the job that he was made for. He was the true leader of Hell's Army.

Not Spawn.

The women moved out of the shadows and looked him over. "Hi-ya, little wanker-clown. What do you want?"

"Both of you. Of course."

"What sort of dude are you, anyhow?" the second one asked, then winked at her friend.

"Just the kind you've always been looking for. The one who will take you away from all of this." He grinned. "Come ladies, hearts of my heart, the night is still young and so am I."

They each took an arm as they wandered off. Clown looked up, beaming his big neon-blue grin at the women. "I want to show you two a couple of tricks of my own trade."

He laughed loudly. The fun was just beginning. By dawn, two more bodies would turn up on the street, increasing the night's carnage. These two would provide the police with a new mystery. Both women would be missing their hearts.

Moments before Spawn's fall from the thirteenth floor, Terry Fitzgerald escaped from the embassy. He saw none of the action outside the building. Instead, he was intent on returning to headquarters. He leaped into one of the standard-issue A-6 Suburbans and drove away.

When he reached headquarters, he flashed his ID to a guard at the gate. "Oh, Mr. Fitzgerald, so glad you're here. Have you heard what happened? We had some trouble with an intruder.''

He nodded. ''I heard. Hope everyone is okay.''

''We've got three injuries. But they're all doing fine now.''

''That's good.''

He drove through, parked, and approached the security desk as soon as he was inside the building. ''Harry, I'm going to check things out on the third floor. I'll be in my office. Can you ring me if the director arrives? I need to talk to him.''

He tried to sound as casual as he could so as not to arouse any suspicions. ''Of course. I'll let you know the minute I see him.''

''Thanks.''

Once Fitzgerald was on the third floor, he went directly to his office and his computer. He reached into his top drawer and up under his desktop to remove a mailing label. On it was a five-digit code that would allow Fitzgerald to get into Wynn's office, and a four-digit code that accessed his computer. He watched Wynn enter the numbers more than a year ago and had memorized them.

He just hoped Wynn hadn't changed the door lock since that time or implemented any new security devices on his computer software. At this point, Fitzgerald was more concerned about being denied access to the files he wanted than being caught in the act. As far as he was concerned, he was finished with the A-6. Unless he had a good reason to stay, he would tender his resignation in the morning.

But before he left, he intended to amass all the evidence he needed to prove that Wynn was guilty of mass murder, of genocide, and a variety of other crimes. But that wasn't all he wanted. Those crimes were in the past. He needed to uncover the details of Wynn's new mission. In spite of all the talk about peacemaking efforts, Fitzgerald was certain that Wynn's private talks with world leaders had involved some sort of secret new weapon.

He walked down the hall to Wynn's office and tapped out the access code on the door. He exhaled, relieved it worked. Inside, he moved over to the touch-screen built into Wynn's desk. He flattened the curling label with the code numbers onto Wynn's desk and entered the numbers for the computer. He smiled as the screen lit up with a message welcoming Director Wynn.

He moved through the project menu on the touch-screen and recognized many of the names. Wynn kept him apprised in varying degrees of depth about most of the operations. Some of them, Fitzgerald was certain, were diversions, operations that didn't really exist—like the plan to capture the major international drug lords and expose their associates in powerful government positions. Minor players had been taken into the custody, but nothing further had happened. Wynn liked to refer to it as one of his projects in development, but Fitzgerald was certain Wynn never intended to capture any of the drug lords. In truth, Wynn considered them valuable allies. Fitzgerald had figured that out by piecing together certain references Wynn had made to information that could only have been provided by the international outlaws.

He stopped when he saw the code name HEAT-16. He knew it as a South American operation that had been conducted three years before. It was a raid against a cocaine processing plant in the Amazon near Leticia, Colombia. But that mission was completed and a success, as far as Fitzgerald knew. There was no reason that it would be listed as an active operation.

He touched the name on the screen and the situation wall lit up, showing what looked like a rotating 3-D molecular structure. "What the hell is that?"

He touched a subdirectory called Intro. The graphic display vanished, replaced by a video of a jungle raid on the processing plant. It showed A-6 agents rushing into a concrete building with an aluminum roof. Shots were fired and several guards and scruffy chemists were dragged away, some dead, some wounded. *Nothing new,* Fitzgerald thought. He was look for something else related to HEAT-16 when the picture went black.

When it came back up, the camera moved through the jungle and the same building came into view. Fitzgerald recognized A-6 operatives with machine guns, but now they were standing guard rather than attacking. The camera moved through the door and into a surprisingly modern laboratory where chemists were working in sterile conditions wearing outfits like space suits, which covered them from the tops of their heads to the bottoms of their feet.

The camera pulled back into a wide-angle mode, and now, to Fitzgerald's surprise, he saw that the lab scene was being shown on Wynn's situation wall and being videotaped from inside the office. The camera panned across the office and settled on Wynn, who was seated behind his desk, where Fitzgerald now sat.

"That facility in the jungle was once used for processing bazuca, better known as crack cocaine, for consumption in North America. We took over the plant with little resistance and began processing our own formula that we had obtained with the help of the North Koreans. It is not a drug, but a weapon, a supervirus that will kill people quickly and in large numbers, but cause no property damage.

"We call it HEAT-16 and it will change the world. The haves and have-nots will be defined by which countries possess HEAT-16 and which ones don't. In other words, a new world order is coming into being."

With growing concern and a certainty that he had found Wynn's new mission, Fitzgerald tapped another file under HEAT-16 called North Korea, and saw several people in sterile space suits moving through the streets of a village where bodies lay by the roadside. Blood samples were being taken and stored in sealed containers.

He'd seen enough. He quickly copied all the files related to HEAT-16 onto a disk, then slipped it into his pocket.

He shifted menus to old operations in the hopes of finding more incriminating evidence linking Wynn to illegal activities. He had just touched the five-year-old Hong Kong project, involving Simmons, when he heard voices in the hallway. He tapped the touch-screen and the situation wall darkened. Wynn was at the door entering his code and talking with a guard. Fitzgerald raced toward Wynn's private bathroom, but then returned to Wynn's desk for the label with the code numbers that he'd left behind. He grabbed it and ducked into the bathroom just in time.

Wynn entered the office with a guard, who was describing what had happened in the armory. Fitzgerald knew he didn't have much time before either Wynn or the guard would look in the bathroom. He crept into the shower and reached up above the showerhead, where he found a tiny switch the size of a pencil lead. He flipped it forward, then pushed the tile wall at the rear of the shower. The right side of the wall rotated silently on its central axis.

He stepped through the opening and carefully closed the door behind him. Darkness closed around him. He found his key chain in his pocket and flipped on a tiny flashlight. A staircase led down and connected to a series of passageways. One route led out of the building, others led to various parts of the building and compound.

Just a year ago, he'd discovered the schematic of the building in a vault and found out that the rumored passageways were real. He'd explored them on his own and kept it to himself. One level down, he followed a passage that seemed to end in a wall. He touched a lever with his foot and the wall slid to the side. He stepped through it and into the handicapped toilet stall in the first-floor men's room.

A minute later, he walked out the front door and over to his car. He had what he was looking for. Now he needed to find a way of stopping Wynn.

FIFTEEN

"**WHERE WERE** you last night, Jason?"

Muriel Wynn was waiting for her husband when he walked into the house at five after nine, accompanied by Marcus, his bodyguard. She was seated at the kitchen counter wearing a robe. Her blond hair was tied back and she was drinking a cup of coffee.

"I was worried sick after I heard about that terrorist attack at the embassy. I tried calling you, but I just got your answering service. Why didn't you call me?"

Wynn didn't want to hear any nagging. Not this morning. "I'm sorry," he said tersely. "I was busy, okay? I didn't want to wake you up." He smiled, leaned down, and kissed her on the cheek. "We had a problem at the headquarters that I had take care of. That was after the trouble at the embassy."

He didn't like the way Muriel was looking at him. It was almost as if she were telling him with her expressions that she didn't believe a word he'd said. He hadn't seen that look on her face for a long time, not since she had caught him lying about that old flame of his several years ago.

"What happened to your arm?"

"It'll be okay. I was lucky."

She glanced at Marcus, then back to Wynn. She'd told him more than once what she thought of bodyguards. They were an unnecessary nuisance and belonged with presidents, celebrities, and drug-cartel leaders. Not someone like him. Muriel still didn't fully understand the extent of his power, and that was the way he liked it.

"Why didn't he stop you from getting hurt?"

"Because he wasn't on duty," he answered, annoyed by her question. "There were no bodyguards allowed in the ballroom. The embassy was supposedly impenetrable. So they said."

"I wonder about the people you do business with, Jason. The only one I've ever liked was Terry Fitzgerald."

It was ironic that she'd mentioned Fitzgerald, of all people. Fitzgerald, who was on his shit-list. He'd called him at five A.M. just to make sure he was coming into the office for a debriefing session on previous day's events. Fitzgerald had hesitated, almost as if he had intended to tell him no, but he'd shown up at the office at seven. At the end of the meeting, he sensed Fitzgerald wanted to say something to him. Whatever it was, he didn't say it. If Fitzgerald quit, which is what Wynn thought he was planning, he wouldn't be able to find another decent job anywhere. Wynn would make sure of that.

"I'm going upstairs to bed. I need some sleep. I'll be out late tonight."

"Late again?" Her voice was icy now. "There's something I need to talk to you about, Jason. Could you send him away?"

Wynn turned to Marcus, who left the room. "So what is it?"

Muriel's eyes turned dark. "You're not fooling me. You weren't working all night. You were with that woman, Chapel. You were playing with her all night, weren't you? And now you're tired."

"No, I wasn't. Whatever gave you that idea?" What was going on? Who had talked to her?

"Come here." Muriel walked into the library and over to a desk. She picked up a large manila envelope and tossed it to Wynn.

He opened it, but he already knew what was inside. He saw the first photo of him and Chapel together and pushed the photos back into the envelope.

"She's dead, Muriel. Don't worry about her."

"Dead, huh? She doesn't look dead in these picture, and neither do you. This hurts, Jason. It really does." She shook her head in disgust. "No wonder you're always so tired."

"Believe me. There's an explanation. When did you get them?"

"First thing this morning. There were two other copies for the girls, but fortunately I intercepted them."

"Look, it was a setup," he began. He realized his story would sound silly now, that it wouldn't work.

"A setup? Sure, Wynn." She moved closer, grabbed his belt, and poured her hot coffee down the front of his pants. "So was that."

He yelled out in pain and wriggled out of his pants as Marcus raced into the library. Muriel walked smugly away and kept walking.

In a darkened school auditorium, images of dying Korean villagers—children, women, and the elderly—flashed on a screen. They were followed by photographs of a deserted town. "Nearly three thousand people died in Lichon in one morning," a woman's voice said from the front of the auditorium.

"By the end of the week, more than five thousand of the town's eight thousand residents were dead. They are all innocent victims of an explosion five years ago at a plant where biochemical weapons were being made just one mile from Lichon. The faces you saw are some of the so-called lucky ones, the few hundred who managed to survive the disaster.''

Wanda Fitzgerald spoke with deep compassion for the victims as she described efforts to treat as many of the children as possible. Overwhelmed by the tragedy, the North Korean government belatedly sent out a call for foreign medical assistance, and some of the children were still being treated in other countries, including the United States.

''As you have seen, the terrible North Korean biochemical disaster unleashed a host of new diseases. And even now, five years later, the number of sick and dying children keeps growing and growing as latent affects of the chemicals take hold of their bodies.''

Wanda's interest in the North Korean disaster was directly related to the death of Al Simmons. She knew from the beginning that he had died on a mission in North Korea. But several months passed before she found out about the chemical plant explosion and the tragedy in Lichon. It didn't take long for her to link those events with Simmons's death.

She'd prodded Fitzgerald and he'd finally told her what he knew. Simmons had been trying to put the plant out of commission when the accident occurred. She suspected there was more to it, and she suspected it was something terrible, but that was all that Fitzgerald knew or all he would tell her.

As she continued talking, she noticed a shadow moving in the darkened rear of the auditorium balcony. She craned her neck, peering into the darkness, but couldn't see anyone on the balcony. She lowered her gaze to the foyer where Cyan who was playing quietly with Spaz, and was reassured to see that she was still there.

''The Children's Relief Fund needs your assistance. It

is up to us to end the suffering of these innocent children. Thank you.''

Wanda's talk was greeted by applause from the two dozen people in attendance. As several people approached the stage, Spawn watched, disturbed by what he'd heard. He knew that he was the one who had caused the death and disease that Wanda had been talking about.

''And I thought I was getting rid of the world's vermin,'' he said to himself. ''Now it turns out that I was one of them, on of the worst.'' He shook his head sadly. ''I'm sorry, Wanda.''

A day had passed since the encounter at the Swiss embassy. He'd remained in hiding on a fire escape in an empty alley less than a mile from the embassy. When he'd finally come down late in the afternoon, he had felt stronger than ever. There were no aftereffects from all the bullets his armor had eaten and then regurgitated. But he was still baffled by his armor, its cape and chains, and how everything worked. He'd tried to fly again, but his cape had just gotten tangled in his legs.

When he'd finally given up, he'd picked up the remains of the morning paper that was wrapped around chicken guts. The rotting organs had nauseated him. He had absolutely no interest in food. Not yet at least. Wherever his energy and power was coming from, it wasn't from ingesting animal or vegetable matter. The headlines on the paper read: ''23 Killed at Swiss Embassy Melee.'' The article attributed the attack to a terrorist named the Hyena, who was killed at the scene.

Very convenient. Spawn figured the Hyena was actually one of the guests, and the authorities had made the dead man the scapegoat to avoid explaining what really had happened. No doubt they didn't want to cause a panic in the city.

So, in spite of his public appearance, Spawn realized

he still didn't exist. No one had really seen him.

Then, as he'd paged through the newspaper, he'd spotted a short article about the Children's Relief Fund for the Korean victims of a chemical plant explosion. When he read that Wanda Fitzgerald would be speaking, he ripped out the article and immediately headed for the school where the event was taking place.

He took one more glance at Wanda, then turned and slipped out the back door of the auditorium. As he descended the stairs from the balcony, he felt overwhelmed by his loss. He knew he wasn't supposed to feel any love for anything anymore, but seeing Wanda again had incited the old buried sentiments.

He tried to hold on to the feeling. Even though it was painful, he knew it was important not to let it go. If he did, he would be no better than Clown or any of the lost souls of Hell. Somehow he knew that if he loved, no matter how much it hurt, he could recover his soul and be whole again. But as soon as his thoughts turned to Wynn, all those ideals about love disappeared, replaced by a deep longing for revenge.

He moved down a hallway that led to the foyer. He wanted to slip out into the darkness as quickly as possible so that no one would see him. But as he neared the foyer and moved from darkness to light, he heard a familiar bark, and stopped.

He peered around the corner. At first, all he saw were a couple of billboards with announcement about the ''The Tragedy of Lichon'' and displays of pictures of dying children. Then he saw Cyan sitting on the carpeted floor just outside the auditorium. Next to her was a little backpack with a doll lying on top of it; and nearby, watching closely, was Spaz.

Cyan bounced a red ball to the terrier. Spaz leaped up to snare it, but it bumped against his nose and then bounded off a wall, down the corridor past Spawn and into the gymnasium. Spaz barked and raced by Spawn into the gym, chasing the careening ball across the wood floor. Spawn pressed against the wall in the darkened corridor as Cyan ran into the gym after her dog.

"Where are you going, Spaz? Come back." Suddenly, Cyan screeched in pain and started crying.

Spawn hurried into the gym and found Cyan sitting on the floor by several basketballs as she nursed her bruised knee. "Ou-ey, ou-ey!" she cried out.

"What happened?" he asked.

"I fell on a big ball and hurt my knee," she whimpered without looking up to see who was talking to her. "It really hurts."

Spaz spotted Spawn and forgot about the ball, which had rolled under the bleachers. He trotted over to him, barking and growling softly. But then as he moved closer, he stopped and turned his head to the side, recognizing his old master. He barked excitedly, wagged his tail, and jumped up and down.

Spawn patted Spaz on the head, and then Cyan looked up and forgot all about her sore knee. She stared in fascination as Spawn bent down closer to her. She smiled with wide-eyed curiosity as she looked over his impressive armor. Spawn tried to avoid showing her his face, afraid of scaring her.

"Are you all right?" he asked.

"Yeah, I'm okay." She crawled around to his other side and stared at Spawn's face. "Wow, your face is really weird!"

Spawn looked deeply into Cyan's eyes, relieved that she didn't seem frightened by his appearance.

"I know you," Cyan said. "You were at my birthday party!"

Spawn smiled for the first time since he had found himself back in the world of the living. He was pleased that he didn't have to hide his charred features from the little girl.

"What's your name, mister?"

"Uhhh . . . Spawn."

"I'm Cyan."

"I know." Spawn was touched to be so close to a part of Wanda. "You're a very pretty little girl. You have your mother's eyes."

Cyan laughed. "No I don't, silly. These are my own eyes. If I had Mommy's eyes, she'd be blind. Anyway, I fell down on the big ball and hurt my knee."

Spawn slapped one of the basketballs and it bounced away. "Bad, dumb ball."

Cyan giggled, then she reached up and touched his scarred face, then his armor. "Cool!"

Spawn was enjoying the encounter with Cyan and wished he could stay longer, but he knew that Wanda would be looking for her at any moment. Spaz suddenly began to growl and bared his teeth. Spawn looked up and saw a balloon floating down from the bleachers. Inscribed on the balloon was Clown's grinning face. The balloon bobbed up and down for a few seconds, then popped.

"Bad, dumb balloon," Cyan said.

He scooped up Cyan and quickly carried her out of the gym. Spaz followed at his master's heels. Spawn glanced once over his shoulder and spotted the short, chubby silhouette of Clown, perched high in the bleachers. He kept going. Clown's malignant chortle drifted through the gymnasium like toxic fumes.

Clown clambered down the bleachers to the gym floor. He was wearing a bright yellow sweater with a megaphone design across the chest and a red pleated skirt. He was feeling particularly demonic today after trailing Spawn to the school and finding Wanda here. How wonderful it was that she was helping the little kiddies. Especially those kiddies.

As far as he was concerned, Wanda's pathetic attempt at helping them was a big, fat waste of time. He'd even told her as much on one of her posters in the lobby. "Wake up, Wanda!" he'd written in large black letters across the top of the poster by the door. Then in smaller print, he'd added: "You haven't seen nothing yet. It won't be long before you'll have more poisoned, diseased kiddies than you can handle."

He turned to the bleacher as if they were packed with fans. He adjusted the cheerleader's outfit he'd found in the girls' locker room while making nasty drawings on the walls. The outfit was tight in the belly, even though the elastic band at the waist stretched out more than a foot. These cheerleaders didn't eat enough.

He raised the pom-poms, shook them, and kicked his legs out to the side. "Spawny, Spawny, he's our man, if he can't kill them, no one can. Yaaay, Spawn."

He leaped high in the air, shaking the pom-poms, then made a face. "Uh-oh, I've wet my knickers.

Spawn set Cyan down at the edge of the foyer near a display about the relief fund. He took a closer look at the poster and saw the note scribbled to Wanda. He knew who had written it.

"Can you come over to my house and play, Mr. Spawn?" Cyan asked.

"Maybe."

"We'll have fun."

Spawn looked up as people began exiting the auditorium. He retreated to the hallway leading to the gym. A moment later, he heard Wanda call out for Cyan. He ducked back into the gym and searched for Clown. He found a cheerleader's outfit and pom-poms on the floor, but the dwarf-demon had disappeared.

* * *

"Cyan?"

"I'm here, Mommy."

Wanda rushed over and picked up Cyan, relieved that she was okay. "Oh, sweetie, I told you not to move out of my sight."

"I was playing with Spaz, but I fell down. I hurt my knee, and Mr. Spawn came and helped me." She turned around. "I don't know where he went."

Wanda frowned. "Mr. who?"

"Spawn. He's got a weird face, but he's really nice. I like him."

Wanda looked around, recalling the strange man who had known her name. "Cyan, I told you not to ever talk to strangers."

"Mr. Spawn's not a stranger, Mommy. He came to my birthday party."

"Wanda? What's going on? Is something wrong?" Fitzgerald rushed over to Wanda and Cyan.

"I don't know," she said, standing up and taking Cyan by the hand. "I guess everything is okay."

"Sorry I couldn't get here any earlier. Wynn was up all night and was like a madman carrying on about the break-in and the attack at the embassy. I finally got him to go home and get some sleep."

They headed outside, Cyan wearing her backpack and hugging her doll.

As they reached the car, Cyan tugged on her father's arm. "Daddy?"

"What, sweetie?"

"Can Mr. Spawn come over and play? I promise we won't be too noisy."

"What?" Fitzgerald looked from Cyan to Wanda, hardly believing what he heard.

* * *

Spawn crouched behind bushes near the school building and watched as Fitzgerald moved in his direction, whistling and calling for Spaz. The dog's ears were raised, but he stayed seated at Spawn's feet.

"Go on," Spawn whispered, but Spaz didn't budge. He kicked dirt on the dog, but Spaz held his ground.

He was tempted to pick the little dog up and toss him out into view, but that might just bring Fitzgerald over to investigate. He didn't want a confrontation, not with Wanda and Cyan in the car watching it all.

"Go on, Spaz," Spawn ordered.

The dog wagged his tail as Fitzgerald retreated to the Cherokee.

Spawn walked away into the night and Spaz followed close behind. The dog stopped when Spawn turned. "Go home, Spaz. You don't wanna be where I'm going."

But the dog barked defiantly, as if vowing to stay by his master's side. Spawn shook his head. "Okay, but it's your funeral."

SIXTEEN

THE A-6 doctor's face loomed over Wynn, and even though his words blurred together, his voice was reassuring. Something about the procedure. It wouldn't take long. Wouldn't hurt. He'd been given a local anesthetic for pain, but he'd also taken pain pills and aspirin for the burn on his groin. Now the combination was making him drowsy. He was having a difficult time keeping his eyelids open.

Dr. Vargas and the assistants lowered a complex surgical panel over his chest. A nurse wheeled over a small cart. The doctor popped open a panel revealing a hi-tech pacemaker. Tiny LEDs blinked as the thumb-sized electronic device was activated. A video monitor on the cart indicated that the heart monitor was on-line and ready for activation. Wynn had been shown all the equipment earlier, but now he was only vaguely aware of it.

Vargas nodded to the nurse, who used customized forceps to place the pacemaker into a mechanical arm that extended out from the surgical panel and over Wynn's chest. The arm had two mechanical hands, one that held the pacemaker and the other that grasped a surgical scalpel.

Wynn knew he should be more concerned about what

was going on around him, but he kept thinking of Muriel and the girls. They were gone now, and he wondered if all of his machinations to obtain power, prestige, and control were worthwhile. He couldn't escape the sad irony of his situation: he could control world politics, had done so for years, but he couldn't control his wife.

In the end, she'd poured hot coffee down his pants. The burns were minor, but his pride had been devastated. He'd treated himself, then taken a painkiller and gone to bed. When he'd awakened, he'd found a note from Muriel that she'd left with the girls for the country house, and that he would be hearing from her lawyer.

Vargas's face appeared above him again. This time it was blurry and Wynn couldn't focus. "I'm going to create a tiny incision and insert the heart monitor. You'll feel a slight pinch."

Vargas pushed a button and the mechanical arm disappeared into the surgical panel. As the doctor leaned into the surgical eyepiece, Wynn heard a mechanical hum and saw the arm moving. He winced in pain. He'd always feared being captured by a terrorist, like the Hyena, and being tortured. Even though the pain was minimal, he couldn't help thinking that he was helpless and that if he ever was captured, he'd probably start talking at the very suggestion of torture.

Vargas took the remote-control handgrips and performed a few more steps, then turned to look at a video monitor as a message appeared that read: HEART MONITOR UPLINK ACTIVATED.

Wynn was still conscious as Vargas leaned over. "The unit is locked into your circulatory system," he whispered. "If your vital signs flatline for any reason, the device will uplink and automatically detonate all of the HEAT-16 weapons."

Wynn blinked his eyes, coming fully alert. "Good work, Doctor."

"Also, no one will be able to remove the device without detonating it, unless they know the code. Now, do you want to know it?"

Wynn was still groggy, but he understood Vargas clearly. He shook his head. "No, keep it in the vault and don't you memorize it, either. If someone tortures me, or you, I don't want them getting the code." What they didn't know, they couldn't reveal.

Vargas seemed nervous. He was well aware of the consequences of what he was doing. When Wynn had told him what he wanted done, Vargas had silently pondered the matter. But only for several seconds. He'd asked Wynn one question. What if he died accidentally, as in a traffic accident?

"I guess I'm going to be very careful about who's driving my vehicle," Wynn had responded.

Vargas hadn't pursued the matter further. After all, he was an A-6 operative as well as a physician. Wynn was his boss, and he followed orders.

"Okay, Jason. We're going to close you up now." Vargas returned to the remote hand controls and sealed Wynn's chest. In the background, a surveillance camera recorded everything.

Clown sat in Wynn's chair with his feet up on the A-6 director's desk. He was watching the surgery on the wall-screen. He reached into a greasy bag, pulled out a large worm that wriggled in his hand. He dipped it in a jar of mayonnaise and plopped it into his mouth. He smacked his lips as he chewed loudly.

"Tic goes the heart . . . tock goes the world. Oh, this is sooo frigging sweet. Hm, needs more salt." He looked back at the screen again as he munched on the worm. "This procedure is really boring. No blood, no guts. Let's see what's on the Snuff Channel."

Clown tapped Wynn's touchpad and the surgery scene

was replaced by raving circus clowns who attacked a startled crowd in the bleachers with oversized baseball bats. Clown giggled and slapped his knee as one of the clowns pounded an old woman on the side of the head and another bit a man in the neck as frightened children screamed. In a matter of minutes, a full-scale panic erupted as several people were trampled to death in the rush to escape the mad killer clowns.

"Crazy stuff . . . crazy stuff," Clown chortled. "Hope it's all real."

The scene shifted to a video of mangled accident victims being pulled from wrecked cars, derailed trains, and crashed airplanes. That was followed by a show on videotaped suicides, including a man who was beheaded by a fast-moving train.

Clown waved a hand at the screen, dismissing it all. "Ah, I've seen worse. I've done worse."

He nudged the touchpad, turning off the system. "I'm still bored. Think I'll go see what Wanda and Terry are doing tonight before I check up on Spawn." He glanced at his oversized pocket watch. "The time is getting closer and closer." He placed a hand behind his ear. "I can almost hear the army galloping into town."

The evening was chilly and Spawn wrapped his greatcoat around his bulging shoulders. He pulled the hood low as he sat against the alley wall behind the Emergency Deliverance Church. The coat protected him from the stares and the fearful looks of the homeless as well as provided him a buffer from the cold. He'd come here because it was one alley that was safe. Even if the cops showed up and cleared everyone away, he would have enough warning to escape undetected.

There was another reason he came here, too. Camaraderie. He knew he could never return to Wanda. It had been a mistake to go see her speak at the school. Now his mind was filled with images of her at the podium. She seemed so fresh and alive. And what was he—dead? Dead, but alive. He'd been re-animated and blasted out of Hell and back into this world. Yet he had been human and he still remembered what that had been like. In spite of everything, he still longed for human companionship.

He looked up as a large-boned man walked past him, followed by Zack, the ten-year-old kid he'd met here. Neither of them noticed him as they headed across the alley to the Dumpster that was fed by a nearby restaurant. Spawn could see the resemblance between the two and guessed they were father and son. But the father's sunken eyes and hollow cheeks were more pronounced than the boy's, as if he'd given up hope.

The man reached into the Dumpster and pulled out a sandwich. He wiped it off and took a bite of it, then handed the rest to his son, who made a face. "It's kind of moldy, Dad."

"Just eat it."

Zack took a bite of the sandwich while his father fished around and found an open tuna container. He fingered out the contents and ate it with a scavenger's relish. Zack gagged and spat out the rest of the sandwich.

"Hey, what the hell're you doing? You puking up decent food, boy?"

"It's rotten," Zack protested. "The bacon was bad. Really bad."

"Tasted fine to me. You know how much they charge for a BLT in that restaurant over there? A lot. More than we got, that's for sure."

"It didn't taste good."

The man grabbed his arm. "You think we eat so good that you can just spit up whatever you like? Huh?"

"No!" Zack shouted defiantly.

"Don't you go talking back to me in that tone of voice." He angrily raised his hand and was about to swap

Zack when his arm was snatched in midair.

Spawn lifted him off his feet and pinned him to the nearby wall. His eyes burned deep green as he leaned close to the man, whose pale blue eyes now seemed to bulge from their deep sockets. His voice literally chilled the already cool air.

"The kid doesn't want eat it, pal."

"Who the hell are you?"

Spawn viciously hurled the man across the alley and into the far wall. He tumbled onto a heap of garbage, and his arms and legs flopped in the air as if he were swimming. Spawn loomed over him and fished him out of the slimy filth. He was getting ready to administer another dose of pain when Zack rushed up and tugged at Spawn's massive arm as he shouted for him to stop.

"Please, please. Leave him alone. . . . He didn't mean anything. He's my Dad!"

Spawn peered down and saw the naked fear in Zack's eyes. His father trembled and Spawn dropped him back into the trash and stepped away. Zack moved over to his father and helped him lean against the wall. The man looked diminished now, as lost and frail as a child himself as his son tried to comfort him.

Spawn sagged, knowing that he'd done more harm than good. Maybe that was all he was capable of doing. He wasn't sure of anything anymore. He walked away to look for a new place to rest, and Spaz trailed after him. He felt lost and useless. He just wanted to find Wynn, kill him, and return to the oblivion.

He picked up the dog and climbed a series of fire escapes until he reached the roof of the old Gothic church. He shed his overcoat and pulled back a couple of roof tiles to reveal his weapons cache. He began organizing the weapons and ammunition. He ripped open an ammo pack and loaded a grenade launcher. The weapons felt good in his hands. They gave him a purpose. Spaz pranced nimbly along the roof, getting used to his new surroundings.

"Kiss it good-bye, Jason." Raw vengeance rippled through his voice.

He heard footsteps and spun around, his weapon ready to fire. Zack was making his way across the roof. His eyes widened in fear. Spawn lowered his smart-gun as Zack approached and closely examined the state-of-the-art ordinance.

"Whoa, awesome hardware!" His jaw dropped. "What're you gonna do with it?"

"Throw someone a going away party."

A beat passed.

"Sorry about what happened down there," Zack began. "Things have been kinda rough lately. We didn't always live in the alley, you know. We had a house and a real life. Then my mother was killed, shot by a stranger for no reason. Dad just sort of lost it. He didn't care about anything anymore. The house, his job, the bills. Nothing. He barely heard me when I talked to him." He shrugged. "We ended up down here, eating out of garbage cans."

Spawn packed up the arsenal. He listened, but didn't comment on the kid's story.

"Need any help?" Zack asked.

Spawn looked up at him. "Look, kid. I'm not looking to make friends."

Zack looked down, his shoulders slumping, but he held his ground. Spawn appraised the kid for the first time and saw that he was aged beyond his years. He was tough and resilient.

"The first time we met you told me you're name was Zack."

The kid looked up. "Yeah, that's it."

"I'm Al. This is Spaz."

Zack dropped to one knee and petted the dog. "Hi-ya, Spaz."

The little dog wagged his tail. Spawn smiled for the second time. For the moment, he was at peace with himself. But he had the feeling his sense of tranquillity wasn't going to last.

Cyan kneeled next to her bed, her hands folded as she prayed. "God bless my Mommy and my Daddy, my teacher at school and all my friends, except Jennifer who wasn't very nice . . ."

"No exceptions, Cyan," Fitzgerald said as he stood at her bedside.

"Okay, God bless Jennifer, too. And God, will you please return my little dog, Spaz, to me? I love Spaz and miss him. Thank you."

"That's a good girl," Fitzgerald said as Cyan crawled into her bed. But he had a bad feeling about Spaz. He figured the dog must have gone with Simmons. Somehow he'd recognized him. If anything, it gave Fitzgerald more reason to believe that the beastly thing that he'd talked to at the embassy had actually been his old friend. Or, rather, his remnants.

"Daddy, can you tell me a story before I go to sleep? Please. But not a scary one."

Fitzgerald sat down at the chair next to Cyan's bed. As soon as she was asleep, he planned to take a closer look at the files he'd removed from the Wynn's office, which told true horror stories. "Of course, I will, and don't worry, I won't make it scary."

Cyan smiled and cuddled her favorite teddy bear as she waited for him to begin.

"Let's see, how about The Three Bears?

"I'm kind of tired of that one. I'll tell it to you, okay?"

"With your eyes closed."

"That's silly. I don't have to see the story to tell it to you. But okay, I'll keep them closed." She began the fairy tale that she'd been told over and over again since she was a toddler. As she retold it, Fitzgerald's mind started to drift to the recent jarring events when something Cyan said caught his attention.

"What was that about the Daddy Bear, sweetie? I didn't catch that."

"Oh, Daddy Bear was very, very big, and he had a black face that was all burned and scary looking. But he was really a nice Daddy, because Baby Bear loved him a whole lot."

Jesus, the Simmons thing was infecting his entire family. Wanda was disturbed by Cyan's mention of Mr. Spawn and was mystified and frightened by the idea that the derelict who knew her name had found Cyan again. He was waiting for Cyan to go to sleep before he would tell Wanda what he knew about Mr. Spawn.

"... and Baby Bear looked at her bowl of porridge and said, 'Somebody has been eating my ... somebody has been eating ...'"

Fitzgerald looked over and saw that Cyan was sound asleep. He gazed at her innocent face as she drifted off and for a moment wanted to wake her up and talk to her some more. But he kissed her on the forehead and slipped quietly out of the room.

The computer screen in Fitzgerald's den displayed a world map with multicolored dots scattered across the continents. There were particularly heavy concentrations of red dots in the Mideast, in parts of Africa and Asia. Mixed among them were green dots in Europe. A few blue dots were spread across the U.S. and Canada, from the Arctic Circle to North Dakota, Oklahoma, and Nevada.

"Do you mean this HEAT-16 is spread all over the world already?" Wanda, wearing round tortoiseshell reading glasses, leaned forward on the chair next to Fitzgerald and studied the screen.

"That's what I'm still trying to figure out," Fitzgerald answered. "I don't know what the different colored dots mean."

"How deadly are these weapons?"

"From the specs I read on another file, each weapon consists of a packet of six canisters, each one about the size of a large Thermos—all packed with a deadly virus soup. When detonated in a populated area, one of these HEAT-16 weapons could easily kill a million people within a week."

"I can't believe he's done this in secret. How could he get away with it?"

"He's a powerful man, Wanda. Some other people do know about it. They're in on it with him in one way or another. It's just old-fashioned greed combined with the old-fashioned Cold War idea that nobody will dare fire one if they know the enemy is also armed with the same weapon.

"What about these blue dots in North America? What do you think they mean?"

"My guess is that they're either storage dumps or new manufacturing facilities. Maybe both. I wouldn't doubt if weapons could be deployed from those points as well. Wynn wouldn't be so foolish as to only sell the weapons abroad. I'm sure he's made secret deals with the U.S. military, using black-bag budgets."

"Is any of this legal?"

Fitzgerald turned away from the computer. "Wanda, people like Wynn consider laws as petty annoyances. You work around them. Or just ignore them. It's a power game. The more power you obtain, the less you worry about technicalities. After all the death and destruction he's caused, you can be sure that he believes he's above the law. Way above it, because he gains power by his illegal activities."

"What about the president? Do you think he knows about HEAT-16?"

"Of course he does. But he's running scared. He knows he's just a pawn now. Same with Congress. They all know that something bigger and more powerful has moved into town and there's nothing they can do about it right now. They don't even try anymore."

Wanda shook her head. "And Wynn has sold the other weapons to the highest bidder."

"That's right."

Fitzgerald hit several keys and brought up another document. "Look at this. He's got a plan to announce the formation of the HEAT-16 Consortium of Nations as soon as he completes his final deals. Wynn is the facilitator of the consortium, essentially making him the most powerful person in the world."

Wanda shook her head. "I don't get it, Terry. Doesn't he realize that he's self-destructing the world? Once some hothead dictator uses one of these weapons, it'll start a chain reaction."

Fitzgerald mulled over her question. "That's exactly what I've been thinking about. Somehow it's all tied up with Al and his death five years ago."

"Why do you say that?"

"I know this sounds crazy, but I think Wynn has sold out to some powerful entity. He's not acting alone on this consortium plan. Maybe he's even been brainwashed. I don't know."

"Entity? I don't understand. Do you mean like a corporation or something?" Wanda took off her glasses and frowned at him.

Fitzgerald shook his head. "I'm not sure what it is, but it's bigger than the A-6, bigger than anything else we know of. This entity has brought Al Simmons back to life to do their work."

"Terry, you're scaring me now. You're talking crazy."

She rubbed her arms against a chill that had invaded the room. "How could Al really be alive? It doesn't make any sense?"

"I know it doesn't. But that thing that assaulted the embassy and that stole the weapons from the A-6 headquarters claims it was Al Simmons. He, it, whatever, knows us. He knew me. He knew your name, and he's taken an interest in Cyan."

"You mean that Mr. Spawn she keeps talking about? No, Terry. I can't . . . I don't want to believe it." She shook her head.

"I don't, either. But there's more to it. This entity, this evil thing that brought Al back to life, is double-crossing Wynn. Either that or Al isn't taking orders very well, because he was definitely out to get Wynn."

"I'm afraid, Terry. What if he comes into the house after us . . . or Cyan?"

"You know, for some reason, I'm not afraid of the Simmons creature. It's whatever's behind him that I'm really worried about. Whatever it is, it's coming closer. I can feel it."

"Oh, how perceptive, Terry," Clown said as he peered into Fitzgerald's den through a window.

He had watched and listened to all the conjectures. "Yup, ol' Fitzy is right on the money," he said to himself. "Now I know why he was an analyst."

He took another look at Wanda as she wrapped an arm over Fitzgerald's shoulder and kissed him, nearly knocking him off his chair. Clown smacked his lips. "Oh, she's a hot number. Yum, yum."

He pressed his mug against the window, leaving a clown-face imprint. "Too bad I can't stick around for the bedroom scene. A little eye-shot of hokey-pokey would be worth a few jollies for the ol' Clown. But I got that funny ha-ha feeling that I'll be back for some real fun later."

SEVENTEEN

COGLIOSTRO CROUCHED near the top of a low hill and gazed out across Connecticut Avenue and over the city. A chill wind blew and with it came a brooding smear of darkness across the face of the waning moon. He rose to his feet, braced himself against the wind, and watched a ghastly shadow bleed across the sky. It passed over the Washington Monument, cast a dark finger at the White House, then closed in on the barely visible spires of the old Gothic cathedral.

"It's time."

He steadied himself, mentally preparing for what was coming, and slowly, resolutely walked away.

Spawn pressed his back to the cathedral's steeple and snapped fully loaded clips into his two smart-guns. Spaz had settled on a narrow, flat shelf at the base of the steeple and rested his chin on his paws. Zack absently petted the dog and stared out toward the tangle of inner city underpasses.

"Sometimes I wake up at night, down in the alley with the smell of garbage around me, and wonder if this is Hell," Zack said. "It certainly seems that way. No one has any hope for the future. Not my father. Not any of them. They're all just waiting for the end.''

Spaz started to growl as a shadow fell across Spawn and Zack. The chill in the night air turned frigid and seemed to penetrate Spawn's armor. Clown's head appeared over the edge of the roof, his electric-blue grin a vision from a nightmare. With no effort whatsoever, he vaulted up onto the roof and climbed surefooted toward the steeple, his oversized shoes making plopping sounds with each step. He snapped his fingers and added a dance step or two, then shuffled closer with his chin tucked toward his chest and his gaze focused on Zack.

''No, kid, this ain't Hell, but if you look really hard, you can see it from here.'' He turned to Spawn. ''So, making new friends are we, Spawny? How cute. Did you tell 'em about your new job as underboss of the dark dominions and destroyer of humanity?''

He laughed and looked down at himself. ''It's almost time for the end of the world and I don't have a thing to wear.''

He took a step closer to Spawn, then jerked his thumb toward Zack and Spaz. ''Now, kill 'em and let's go. Your army's just a few short hours from being ready, and you don't have time to sit here with your thumb up your butt, big guy.''

Spawn motioned to Zack. ''Get outta here, kid. Take Spaz with you.''

Zack cringed as Clown leered at him. He stood up, scooping up Spaz, and quickly moved to the edge of the roof and to the nearest fire escape. He looked back once at Spawn, and that was when Spaz wriggled out of his arms and dashed back to his master. Zack started to go back for him, but Spawn motioned for him to leave.

Spawn climbed to his feet. He'd had enough of Clown and his antics. He locked his gaze on the fiendish dwarf, lifted his smart-gun, and leveled it at him.

"So Wynn killed me because you told him to do it. That's what I heard."

Clown shrugged, turned up his palms. "It was nothing personal, you know."

"Nothing personal here, either," Spawn said, tightening his finger over the trigger. "Before I blow your fat ass to that circus in the sky . . ."

"Hey, I'm a little bit sensitive about that circus thing."

". . . I wanna know why you picked me to lead your evil minions."

"Me? Oh, well. I'm just the boss's little demon, you know. As far as the evil goes, it's been part of you since you were soup in your mama's crotch. You had the raw talent, even as a kid, and we nursed it along. All those black-bag ops were just training for what's coming, and like I said, it's coming fast."

Maybe what Clown was saying about him was true. Maybe the seed of evil was planted in him even before his birth. He didn't want to believe it. Sure, he was good at killing, but he had never wanted to take lives just for the thrill of it. He had followed a moral code. He had believed in it. He was a patriot.

Clown chuckled as if reading his thoughts. "Of course you had to justify what you were doing, Spawny. We knew that. That was what made you so good, so vicious. You believed in what you did. Heart, mind, and soul. You convinced yourself that you were a killing machine and the killing you did was good. But now you're not alive anymore, so you don't have to believe in anything but death, death, and more death."

Clown paced back and forth in front of Spawn. "We can finally get down to business now that Wynn's hot-wired to the HEAT-16. We made it especially for you, so you could start things off with a big infectious bang." He looked out over the city. "They say the world is sick, but we're going to make it sicker."

He shrugged. "Personally, I would've preferred a megafusion bomb. Nothing like human confetti to kick off a party."

Spawn was stunned by what he'd just heard. He was starting to grasp the scope of the horror. They wanted him to kill Wynn, to exact revenge, and the death would set off the Apocalypse.

Clown seemed to enjoy Spawn's reaction. "And all we need is for you to lead us to the holy land . . . so we can burn it down."

The gruesome dwarf laughed nervously as Spawn retrained his smart-gun on him. Spawn's eyes narrowed with a new resolve. "You can take that army of yours and shove it," Spawn snarled.

Clown looked genuinely stunned. His blue grin turned down. "I'm sensing a little hostility. You've got that 'I want to beat the fat little man' look in your eyes. How about a group hug?"

Spawn cocked his gun. Spaz growled at Clown's feet and took a disrespectful pee on his ankle. Clown reached down and swiftly scooped up Spaz into his arms.

"I don't know why I put up with this kind of disrespectful crap."

"Put down my dog," Spawn ordered.

"Your dog? Do we have dogs following us around in Hell? I don't think so."

"You heard me!"

Clown clutched Spaz by the neck and held him up, but out of Spawn's reach. "You are not gonna screw things up for me, Mr. 'I'm-too-good-to-be-a-Hellspawn.' No, I don't think so."

Clown's fingers seemed to grow and then his hands suddenly transformed into lethal talons. The sound of their growth was like screeching nails on a chalkboard. Spawn watched, stunned, as the talons merged and formed a Venus's-flytraplike cage around Spaz. The dog whimpered as the cage completely encased Spaz's body in a shiny ball of flesh.

"I'll put down your dog, Spawn. No problem. Nice doggie. Heel, fetch. No, I got it . . . play dead!" Clown shouted.

The talons started to squeeze down on the dog. Spawn had never seen this side of Clown. He knew if he lunged for Spaz, the dog would be instantly crushed.

A rock thumped against the back of Clown's head. Clown turned in surprise just as Zack ducked back down below the roof.

Spawn recovered and fired a shot that hit Clown in the shoulder. The dwarf's hands returned to normal and he dropped Spaz. He stared at his wound with total surprise and indignation. He looked up at Spawn with burning, rage-filled eyes.

"So, you want to do it the hard way," Clown said in a raspy, anger-filled voice. "I warned you, Spawny, old pal. Now it's time to get nasty."

Spawn took a step back, sensing that something truly bizarre was about to happen. Clown's laughter grew into a roar, and then grew louder still until it sounded like an approaching storm. It ended with a screeching cry as horns burst out of the sides of his skull. His jaw and eyes transformed into a heinous vision of Hell. His outer flesh hideously melted away and shifted into greenish insectoid skin.

Clown's body shook as it grew. It pulsed into a new being, something with powerful elongated double-boned, tri-jointed limbs and razor-sharp steel talons: a massive, hulking beast with blood-red compound eyes and huge double-hinged, multifanged mandibles. He was now the ultimate necroplasmic killing machine, standing ten feet in height.

You can call me Violator.

The words echoed inside Spawn's head, although he

wasn't sure that Clown—or what had been Clown—had actually spoken. Violator cackled and stretched its extremities, testing its power.

Spawn snapped out of his shock. He swung around, aiming the gun. But Violator moved quickly, slapping it away. His head smashed through an archway rising from the cathedral roof as he grabbed Spawn with one talon and pinned him against one side of the arch. Spawn screamed in pain and in response, his armored mask moved into place.

Violator leaned close and licked Spawn's leathery chin, with characteristic Clown glee. Spaz growled and barked and snapped at Violator's feet. The insectoid beast kicked the little dog, sending him flying off the roof and down to the alley.

"Spaz!" Spawn yelled.

Violator squealed and screeched in anger and delight. Spawn struggled harder and managed to fire off a series of shots that missed the creature and merely blasted away part of the roof beneath its feet. They twisted and turned around and around in a strange lethal dance.

Finally, Violator lifted Spawn up overhead, but his weight and momentum sent him stumbling backward until they were both rolling toward the edge of the roof. Then abruptly they were falling through the air, spilling earthward along with part of Spawn's weapons cache.

Spawn crashed onto a village of cardboard condos, which instantly flattened. Their residents screamed in panic and crawled free, struggling to escape the pair of menacing, nightmarish creatures that had dropped in for a visit to the downside of human existence.

Spawn, stunned by the fall, heard a high-pitched screech and turned to see Violator impaled on an electrical hydrant, struggling like a pinned insect. The vile creature jerked the hydrant from its base, letting loose a stream of sparks and steam that ignited the remains of the cardboard village.

Spawn searched for his gun in the rubble and confusion of rags, garbage, and leftovers of humanity. He found one of the smart-guns a few feet away, next to the remains of a putrefied chicken carcass. He quickly seized the weapon and turned around to fire. But Violator was gone.

A shadow rose behind Spawn. Nearby, Zack stood up from his hiding place near a Dumpster and pointed at Violator. "Al, watch out!" His father grabbed the boy and pulled him down, sheltering him with his body.

Violator rose to his full height. The hydrant had left a gaping hole in his thorax, but the wound suddenly sealed over with a wet sucking sound. Violator lunged forward, his horns tearing utility wires to the building. He reached down and swept up Zack's father.

Spawn whirled around and fired as Violator hurled Glen at Spawn. The impact knocked him back to the wall near the Dumpster. Spawn gently rolled the battered man aside, then spun around, aiming his weapon one way, then the other. But Violator was again nowhere to be seen.

A screech shredded the night and Spawn rushed in the direction of the noise. He moved down a side alley leading to a subterranean labyrinth of passages that was part of the underbelly of the Metro. He passed beneath a shaft of light and fired as Violator darted above him along a catwalk. The blast struck a thick cable, severing it. The cable hissed and whipped back and forth like an injured giant anaconda.

Spawn ducked as the cable lashed down at him, then raced ahead, reacting to every sound. He reached a fork in the passageway and saw something moving toward him. He turned and was about to fire when he realized that it was two rag-tag men backing away, their arms held up, their hands shaking in fear. Then they turned and rushed away. One fell and yelled for help. The other one grabbed him and pulled him to his feet as he looked back at Spawn.

"Run!" one of them yelled as he dashed down the passageway. But at that moment, a wicked talon shot down and the straggler disappeared into the superstructure above the passageway. His screams echoed through the dark channels. Spawn raced in the direction of the sounds until they died away. He followed a trail of blood, then glimpsed blood dripping from above.

He moved forward and spotted Violator, but he held his fire when he saw that the body of the man was blocking his shot. A moment later, the headless body toppled down, barely missing Spawn. When he looked up again, Violator had darted away.

Spawn continued on, searching one passage after another. Just when he thought that Violator had disappeared, he heard a keening behind him. He spun around, squeezing the smart-gun in his hands. Violator stood in a shaft of light blocking the passage, daring Spawn to fire on him.

Spawn growled angrily and squeezed the trigger. Violator screeched and leaped upward in a flash as the shot struck a man who Violator had been hiding behind his broad back. Spawn ran forward and saw it was the other subterranean dweller who had escaped earlier. Spawn flew into a rage and fired his weapon repeatedly overhead, hoping one of the bullets would find the heinous creature and destroy it.

More screeches echoed through the passageway and Spawn moved toward them, but with a wariness now. He scanned left, then right, then above as he reached a point where another passage crossed. He twitched nervously, uncertain which passage to follow.

He heard a chattering sound behind him. He spun around and fired, decimating several scampering rats. He continued searching, but there was no sign of Violator. Finally, he abandoned the labyrinth and returned to the surface, where he made his way back to the alley.

Earlier there had been fifteen or twenty people back there, but now the alley looked as if a tornado had ripped through it. The residents had scattered in fear or in search of a quieter, safer hideout.

Something vaguely familiar glistened in a puddle under Spawn's feet. He bent down and picked up Spaz's rhinestone collar. He turned it over, rage simmering inside him again. He smashed his fist against the nearest wall and the bricks crumbled beneath his hand. He almost didn't hear the whimper of a dog coming from a nearby Dumpster.

He moved toward the sound and peered into the heaps of garbage. "Spaz? You in there, boy?"

He reached into the Dumpster, but suddenly a huge talon burst through the garbage and grabbed his arm, pulling him down into the Dumpster. Spawn fired helplessly and dropped his gun as Violator, then lifted him above his head and whimpered like a hurt dog.

The creature squeezed its talons with crushing pressure, compressing his armor. Spawn struggled and chest spikes burst out of his armor, puncturing Violator's hands. The insectoid beast screamed and hurled Spawn against the wall, impaling him on the spikes of a wrought-iron fence that blocked the entry to another side alley.

Violator leaped out of the Dumpster and taunted Spawn as he hung in agony on the prongs. He roared with hideous laughter, licked and drooled over the spikes protruding from Spawn's chest.

Then the beast twirled around and around. Its arms folded in a fetal insect pose as its flesh glistened and shrank. The green insectoid skin melted away from the spinning creature, and as it stopped, Spawn glimpsed the familiar rags, a blue tattooed grin and worn-out makeup. Clown stretched and wiped the filmy ooze from his cheeks and chin, the transformation from demon-beast to demon-dwarf complete.

"Yah, you've been violated," Clown said in an Arnold Schwartzenegger accent. "I have sooo much fun as Violator. You gotta admit he is a real fun bunny. Ha ha ha."

Clown laughed hysterically, then inspected Spawn's helpless situation. Reveling in his victory, he strutted back and forth in front of him in his version of a touchdown dance.

"Thought you were a tough guy, didn't you?" Clown asked, returning to his normal sneering, clownish tone. "Look at your sorry ass now. Twinkle, twinkle little Spawn, you look like crap, so fertilize my lawn. I coulda killed you like that."

He snapped his fingers, disgusted with the ease of it all. "And to think that Malebolgia thought some fancy-pants armor was better than good ol' necroflesh . . . *I don't think so.*"

Spawn grunted in agony and anger. Clown howled with abandon. "It's time to stop jerking around and get down to business. I'm going to give you another chance, and you'd better not blow this one or it's Hell's dog kennel for you, Bub."

He looked around mischievously. "I wonder where that little Spazy dog went, anyhow."

Spawn looked down and locked his burning eyes on Clown. He wanted nothing more than to be freed from his predicament so he could strangle Clown until his beady little eyes popped out of his head.

Clown leaned close to Spawn, exhaling his garbage breath. "Maybe you need a little more inspiration." He shifted his voice, mimicking Wanda as he held his hands up with his palms turned out and shook his head. "No, no! Help, please . . . somebody. Oh, God, no . . . Nooo!" Wanda's words trailed off in a hideous scream.

Clown straightened his back and crossed his arms. His

voice now sounded exactly like Wynn. "Wanda, forget Terry. It's my turn on the carousel of love. I'm ready and willing to hop aboard for a ride down the love tunnel."

"Stay away from her!" Spawn bellowed at Clown, at Wynn, at whatever nameless creature of Hell was causing Wanda any pain or anguish.

"Like I said, last chance, Spawny old boy. You better be ready to get in the saddle or else Wanda gets to entertain the troops."

Clown's insidious laughter echoed through the alley-way as he ambled away with a cocky little hitch to his walk. He stepped on the end of Spawn's rocket launcher, which had fallen from the roof, flipped it up, and caught it. He twirled it like a baton as he walked off, chortling with inner glee.

EIGHTEEN

WITH A look of disgust, Cogliostro watched his former partner pass by. Clown always reminded him of his days—or rather his centuries—of depravity, and the feeling sickened him. Clown was hopelessly vile, a demonic offspring of Malebolgia who had never experienced human existence, who believed love and compassion were simply human frailties, weaknesses that could be used to cajole, entrap and manipulate.

As soon as he was gone, Cogliostro stepped out from a darkened niche in the alley and walked over to where Spawn was hanging from the pipes. Without a moment's hesitation, he reached up and pulled him down. Spawn cried out in pain and crumpled to the ground. His armor was deeply gashed, and a dark substance leaked out of the ragged holes.

"It seems that the truth has exacted its toll on you," Cogliostro said to the prone figure.

Spawn raised his head. He was weak and only semi-conscious. "I'm gonna kill that asshole as soon as I get my hands on him."

Cogliostro shook his head. "You still haven't learned, Al."

He helped Spawn to his feet. "Remember what I told

you before. Closely consider all of your actions. Your anger and hate just works against you, unless you really want to lead Hell's Army.''

"Who are you, anyhow?" Spawn asked in a gravely voice.

"Ah, well. Now that's the question, isn't it? Call me Cogliostro. I've been many names, many people. But right now you need to heal and prepare yourself, not listen to my ramblings.''

Cogliostro walked away.

As Spawn huddled behind the Dumpster where Violator had caught him, he felt his armor slowly tending to his injuries. Bullet wounds healed quickly, but Violator's vicious assault had left him considerably weaker, and the wounds were going to take more time to heal. Next time he would be ready for Clown. He'd destroy him before he had a chance to transform himself into that malignant insectoid creature.

When he saw some of the alley people returning, Spawn wrapped his cape around himself, making himself seem like just another shadow on the wall. He spotted Zack, who started digging through the flattened cardboard houses. The kid seemed desperate as he pawed deeper and deeper.

"Dad? Where are you?"

Spawn was about to go help the boy, but several other alley people joined him in digging through the debris where Spawn and Violator had fought. The distant sound of an ambulance siren grew gradually louder and louder.

Zack kept digging and a head appeared. He pulled away the rubble, uncovering the rest of his father's body. "Don't worry, Dad. I'm here with you. Hang on. The ambulance is on its way."

Seconds later, police vehicles and an ambulance turned into the alley. Flashing red lights illuminated the faces of the alley people who were huddled over Zack's father. He was gasping for breath. Spawn knew that he was near death, and Zack knew it, too.

"Don't die, Dad," he cried out, wrapping his arms around him and holding him close. "Please don't ... you're all I've got."

The emergency medical technician moved in next to Zack and placed his hand on the man's neck, searching for a pulse in his carotid artery. A few seconds later, he removed his hand and shook his head.

"Sorry, kid. He's gone."

"No! No!" Zack screamed. Several of the alley dwellers tried to comfort him and moved him slowly away from the body.

Spawn felt heavy and lethargic, both from the wounds and what he'd just witnessed. He sunk deeper into his corner and closed his eyes.

The image was soft, dreamlike, and surreal. The figures moved slowly as if they were underwater. Wanda and Cyan were sitting in the grass, laughing and playing. Suddenly, Spawn appeared in front of them, and as Wanda looked up, her smile turned to a horror-stricken expression. He was dressed in clothes like Simmons used to wear, but he wasn't fooling her. He would never look like Al Simmons again.

Wanda started to scream, and that's when Spawn's features shifted and his body transformed so that he was now Terry. He smiled and held out his hands to them. Wanda and Cyan laughed, relieved that it was really Terry. They leaped up and into his open arms. Wanda was so happy, so in love.

In love with Terry.

Spawn moaned and rolled over on the dirty mat that was jammed behind the Dumpster. His eyes fluttered open as gray morning light washed over him. He closed his eyes again and tried to retreat to the dream. He wanted to hold Wanda again, to feel her in his arms. But his legs were cramped and sore. He stretched his stiff armored body and winced at the pain. His wounds were healing slowly into ragged, oozing puckers.

He focused his gaze and saw the bearded old man again crouched over him. He looked different. His eyes were glazed, and he was holding an ancient spearhead that literally glowed in his hand. Spawn realized that the old man was about to kill him. He tried to spring up and push him away, but he was immobilized like a fly in a web.

He knew he was about to die. Again. Like before, there was nothing he could do about it.

Cogliostro's dark eyes were furrowed in soul-felt conflict. Spawn was his best hope, the one who could lead the way to victory over Malebolgia. But from everything he'd seen so far, it looked like Spawn was going to follow the same path as the others he'd tried to turn. If he did, the results would be devastating, so devastating that he didn't want to think about the possibility.

He couldn't let him live. "I can't chance it," he muttered.

Spawn struggled to no avail against the powerful psychic web that held him in place. Cogliostro pressed the magical spearhead against Spawn's throat as he prepared to make a clean, swift decapitation. It was the only weapon that could kill Hellspawn.

In that instant, he relived his connection to the ancient spearhead. All the events flashed before him compressed in a mere moment of time. He saw himself breaking into a museum in Austria in 1918 to obtain the artifact. At the time, Cogliostro had been shadowing the man who Malebolgia thought would one day lead his army to victory.

Cogliostro followed the man as he preached on street corners and wrote political tracts.

With growing concern, he searched for a way of stopping the man. He confronted him, displayed his powers by transforming a piece of lead into gold. Once he had captured the man's attention, he attempted to persuade him to join his effort and overthrow Malebolgia. But Adolf Hitler, in his twisted mind, turned good into evil and evil into good. He was convinced that he was being haunted by a demon and ran in fear every time he saw Cogliostro.

Still, the old man continued tracking him as he grew more and more concerned that Hitler would indeed be the one who fulfilled Malebolgia's master plan. He sensed the enormous loss of lives, the massacres and gas chambers, the battles, and he saw Hitler moving across Europe winning, victory after victory.

He saw it all coming. But then he observed that Hitler had a peculiar obsession. Day after day in Vienna, the future German leader visited the Treasure House of the Hofburg, and spent hours staring, as if in a trance, at the Spear of Longinus. Hitler was mesmerized by the spear and convinced by the story that it was the same spear that had pierced the side of Christ.

Cogliostro knew he was right. He knew because he had been the Roman soldier who had wielded the spear two thousand years ago. His own human life, of course, had ended countless centuries earlier. To his surprise, the blood of Christ had altered the spear and had planted the seed within him that would one day transform him from demon to archangel. But the spear had been taken from him by his legion leader as a trophy and that was the beginning of its journey through the hands of many legendary figures.

The spearhead became renowned for its powers and it changed hands generation after generation, passing from one chieftain to another. Theodosius I tamed the Visigoths with it in A.D. 385. Alaric the Bold, the savage convert to Christianity, claimed the spear after he sacked Rome in A.D. 410. Aëtius and the mighty Visigoth Theodoric rallied Gaul with the spear to vanquish the barbaric hordes at Troyes and turn back the ferocious Attila the Hun in A.D 452.

Charlemagne, who became the first Holy Roman Emperor in A.D. 800, lived and slept within reach of the spear. But after returning from victory in his forty-seventh campaign, he accidentally dropped the spear and died a short time later. Altogether, forty-five emperors possessed the spear from the time of Charlemagne to the fall of the old German Empire, exactly a thousand years later.

Cogliostro had watched how the Spear of Destiny had shifted hands from century to century and was attached to so many historic events that altered the world. But he had avoided taking control of it himself until he found out that Hitler yearned to possess the spear, and would do anything to obtain it. While Charlemagne associated the spear with the Blood of Christ, Hitler was linked with the Anti-Spirit. With the Spear of Longinus in his control, Hitler undoubtedly would conquer the world.

Cogliostro realized there was only one thing he could do. With the help of a blacksmith, he fashioned a duplicate of the magical spear. Then he broke into the museum and swapped weapons. Since that day, he had kept the Spear of Destiny with him day and night. With it in his possession, Malebolgia or his agents could never harm him.

He gazed down at Spawn, still debating what he should do. Killing him would stop Malebolgia once again. But if he spared Spawn, there was the chance that he would shift his allegiance from the Dark Lord to the Light Master and his illuminated agents.

Slowly, he withdrew the spear from Spawn's throat and

stood up, slipping the magical spearhead back into his sleeve and out of sight.

Painfully, Spawn climbed to his feet and angrily staggered out into the alley, away from Cogliostro. He surveyed the wreckage of smashed boxes and scattered belongings, vestiges of lost lives, leftovers of the mayhem he'd ignited. *Not my fault,* he thought, but blame didn't mean anything to Zack's father, who had been killed in the melee.

"Your vengeance . . . their pain." He turned to see the old man standing beside him. "Wynn, Wanda, none of this is worth the cost."

Spawn grabbed the old man as if he were the physical manifestation of the guilt he felt. "Don't you understand? That's all that matters to me now—helping Wanda and killing Wynn."

"Al Simmons is dead—let go of him," Cogliostro said in an admonishing tone. "There are other things you should be doing now."

Spawn was stung by the rebuke. He let go of the old man, took a step back, and glared darkly at the hooded figure who seemed lost in his oversized coat. "Maybe you don't know it, but I *am* Simmons!"

"You're Spawn now." He scratched the name with his heel in the muddy alley. "But that doesn't mean you have to be what *they* want."

Spawn pushed the old man aside and stumbled down the alley. He stopped after a few steps when he saw Zack with his back to the wall, softly crying and holding a battered boot that his father had worn. He wanted to comfort the kid, but knew he couldn't do anything for him.

Spawn turned away, only to find the old man staring at him like a judge about to pass sentence. With the heel of his boot, he brushed the *S* away from the name he'd scrawled in the mud. "That's what you are—their *pawn.*

Don't let them fool you into believing you're anything else."

Spawn eyed him coldly. "I'm not working for anyone. Wynn is the one who's working for them, and I'm going to stop him."

Cogliostro stepped closer and met Spawn's gaze. "Don't fool yourself. It's not that simple. Your anger is your weakness. They know it and they'll use it to rob you of any humanity you have left."

"What do you think I should do, let Wynn have his way? What good is that?"

"Simmons knew that violence only leads to more pain and suffering, no matter which side gives the orders." Cogliostro spoke firmly and with an earnest resolve. If Spawn had thought he was a weak, babbling fool, he was changing his mind now. He didn't agree with him, but he grudgingly admitted that he respected the old man.

"He tried to quit killing and give himself a second chance," Cogliostro added.

Respect shifted to suspicion. Spawn grabbed Cogliostro by his coat and lifted him off the ground. "How do you know so much about me? Who are you, anyhow?"

He smiled darkly. "I'm a killer like you, only I killed for a kingdom that has been buried for millennia. No trace of it remains. I killed without remorse. I went out of my way to cause pain . . . and then like you I died and came back, and I kept killing and killing. But then I stopped hating. I turned against the dark force that drove me and still drives you."

Spawn was stunned by the old man's speech. He couldn't believe what he was hearing. Slowly, his anger began to rumble deep inside him, like a smoking volcano ready to explode. "Are there any normal people left on Earth?" he shouted. "Or is everyone just back from Hell? Someone please tell me."

Cogliostro remained calm in spite of Spawn's uproar.

"Your old life is gone . . . accept it. You won't be going back to live with Wanda again."

"But I still love her."

"Put her in the past. It's the only way to free yourself."

But Spawn was adamant. "You don't understand. She's the reason I'm here."

Cogliostro shook his head sadly. "All you can do is haunt her like the ghost you are."

"I'm not a ghost. I have a body. I feel pain." All of Spawn's wounds seemed to shriek in agreement. He still felt weak from his combat with Violator. "I sleep, I dream, I wake up."

"You're a ghost in a physical form. I'm sure you've noticed that you have no appetite. Your energy comes from elsewhere."

Spawn turned and walked painfully away from Cogliostro. He didn't care to hear any more from him. But the old man was right at his side, shadowing him, and he wasn't finished talking, either.

"The war between Heaven and Hell can turn on the choices we make, and those choices require sacrifices," Cogliostro said.

Spawn considered what he'd just heard, then turned as he heard someone approaching. Zack, still teary-eyed, walked down the alley, seemingly unaware of Spawn or Cogliostro. Then he looked up and stopped. For a moment, Spawn thought Zack was going to scream at him.

"That thing killed my Dad," he said in a quiet voice. "I don't know what I'm going to do."

"I didn't want this to happen," Spawn said, crouching down to the boy's level.

"I know."

"I'm going to nail that scumbag," he said, standing up again and peering toward the end of the alley. "I'll finish him off once for all."

* * *

Fitzgerald couldn't sleep. He turned from side to side, stared at the wall, the ceiling, the darkness that surrounded him. How had he let this happen to himself? He was the spokesman for the man who might turn out to be the greatest criminal and mass murderer of all time, who would make Hitler look like a street punk.

What kind of world was being created with the proliferation of these biological weapons? Not one he cared to live in, and not one that would be a place worth living. Would Cyan even have a chance to live a happy life? Not if these weapons were in the hands of terrorist nations and power-hungry leaders.

The weapons were being shipped all over the world and there was no doubt in Fitzgerald's mind that some of them would find their way into the hands of international terrorists. No country would be safe. Wynn was out of his mind. Something evil had taken possession of him. That was the only way he could look at it.

He got out of bed, moving as silently as possible so as not to awaken Wanda. He walked back to his den, turned on the computer, and began going through the files again one by one, looking for some way to stop Wynn.

"What are you doing up, Terry?"

Fitzgerald started at the sound of Wanda's voice. He'd been so focused on his work that he hadn't heard her come into the den. She stood to one side of him wearing the knee-length T-shirt she slept in.

"I've found something important." He turned back to the computer and switched files.

"What is it?"

"The dots. I found out what the colors mean. The green are the weapons that have already been sent. The red ones are ones that are about to be shipped. The blues are just what I'd guessed—the manufacturing plants and storage depots."

"There were a lot of red dots on the map, I remember," Wanda said.

"That's right. So far only our allies have received the weapon. The next one is a major shipment, and it's going out to a lot of unstable countries in the Mideast, Africa and Asia. Look at this."

He pointed to the screen. "It's a shipping order, supposedly for a large shipping container of cleaning solution. It's going out of the Port of Norfolk on a Liberian freighter.

"You think that's it?"

Fitzgerald smiled wryly. "I'd say so. They call the cleaning solution HEAT-16."

"When does it leave?"

"It's scheduled for a midnight departure."

"What are we going to do?" Wanda asked.

He stood up from his desk, saw that it was dawn. "I don't know. But we've got to stop that shipment one way or another."

NINETEEN

SPAWN FRANTICALLY checked what remained of the arsenal he'd hidden on the rooftop of the old cathedral. He snapped on his ammo belt and the remaining smart-gun. He was ready to lead a one-man army to track down and eliminate the enemy—Clown and Jason Wynn. He knew he had to hurry before either of them one, or both, got to Wanda.

Cogliostro had followed him up the fire escape to the rooftop. He shook his head in disappointment. "This is just what the denizens of Hell want, you know. Wake up, Spawn. You're playing their game."

Spawn loaded the ammo into the smart-gun, then looked around for any other weapons that hadn't toppled into the alley. "Then, I'll play dirty."

"Guns are useless."

Spawn looked up at him with disdain. "You got any better ideas, smart guy?"

With an amazing display of grace and dexterity, Cogliostro circled Spawn and let loose a series of rapid feints, barely touching Spawn's armor on the front, sides, and rear. Annoyed, Spawn spun around and reached out for the old man, but his armor seemed to turn against him. Chains shot out, twisted around him, and sent him sprawling to the rooftop.

Spawn looked up to see Zack standing at the edge of the roof, watching, surprised that the old man had so easily bested the powerful armored being.

"I might," Cogliostro said.

Cogliostro finally seemed to have captured Spawn's attention, and he wasn't going to let the opportunity pass by. It might be his last chance.

"Your armor has trillions of neural connections. It is a living extension of your own instincts, instantly translating your thoughts into physical reality, but only as long as you stay clear and focused. Once you lose your focus and allow yourself to become confused, you tumble into chaos, as I just showed you."

Spawn nodded thoughtfully and ran his fingers over his wounds, which were no longer ragged eruptions, but smooth, tender mounds that were gradually sinking into place as the armor repaired itself. He stopped when his fingers touched the locket with the picture of him and Wanda together that was imbedded in his chest plates. Slowly, he dropped his hand away.

"So that's how it works."

"So far you've just used your armor in its automatic mode, but you can also direct it by your own volition," Cogliostro explained.

"How?" Spawn listened closely now to everything the old man said.

"Focus your attention and try to release the spikes from your hands."

Spawn stared at his hands in concentration. At first, nothing seemed to happen. Spawn felt awkward and uncomfortable. Then the spikes began to emerge, slowly rising from the back of his hands. He smiled and they started to retract.

"More!" Cogliostro said. "Focus."

The spikes forced their way out and gleamed in the

early morning light. Spawn held up his fists in triumph. "I understand now. It's all in the attitude. I can control the armor."

"Now try your chains."

Spawn looked at the spots on his chest where the chains emerged and scowled as he focused his full attention on the task. Nothing happened. Then he tried again. When he didn't get any results, his concentration started to wander. That's when a coil of chain burst out from his lower back. It was too fast for him to control, and it quickly tangled on itself.

Cogliostro and Zack tried hard not to laugh. Spawn grimaced as he unwound the chain from his legs. It instantly retracted on its own. But when he tried to send it out again, nothing happened.

"You must visualize your objective," Cogliostro said. "If you want the chains to come out, give them a target. Your armor will take it from there."

"All right, Yoda, just give me a second. I'm starting to get the hang of it."

"Good. Let's see your aim." Cogliostro hurled a bottle into the air, out over the edge of the roof toward the building on the other side of the alley.

Spawn concentrated, his eyes glowing intently. Two lengths of hooked chain unfurled from his chest. It flew out into space, veered around the cross, and smashed the bottle into shards of glass just before it struck the far wall across the alley.

Spawn grinned, enjoying his moment of success as the chain quickly retracted. "Not bad."

"Don't get cocky," Cogliostro said as Spawn started to walk off. "You've got a lot more to learn. Your cape has its own powers."

Spawn shrugged. "I guess I'll have to learn the rest on the job."

*   *   *

The key fit snugly into lock, just as Wynn remembered from what was quickly becoming the good old days—the times he and Chapel got together at her compact Georgetown apartment. He didn't feel a bit awkward about entering the apartment. After all, he was the one who had obtained it for her.

Housing in Georgetown was expensive and difficult to come by. But when Wynn found out that Chapel wanted a place near Wisconsin Avenue, he'd arranged it. He'd told her to call the manager of a six-story luxury apartment building that had been constructed a few years earlier on a former parking lot.

There just happened to be an opening in the apartment building because one of its residents, a Japanese diplomat, had been arrested for his role in an industrial spying scheme. Wynn had followed the man's spying career, waiting for the best time to expose him. That moment came after he found out that the manager of the building was playing a minor role in the scheme as the diplomat's well-paid messenger. Wynn allowed the manager to escape prosecution in exchange for providing an apartment at a very reasonable rate.

He stepped into the stark, hi-tech apartment and paused by the door as he flipped on a light switch. Even though it was midmorning not a hint of sunlight entered the apartment. He smelled a faint scent of her perfume, and it was almost as if he expected her to step out from the bedroom and greet him in one of his favorite selections of sexy negligee.

He pushed away the thought. She was dead and her body by now was on its way to some small town outside Detroit, where she'd grown up, where her parents still lived. They would be told that she had died in an accident in the capital, but he doubted that they would ever find out the details.

He moved into the living room and adjusted his cast. His arm was starting to itch. The apartment was furnished in black leather and shiny metal-frame furniture. The carpeting was black with white highlights, like a sprinkling of snow on blacktop. It was definitely a masculine decor, but it worked well for Chapel. The sharp-edged design contrasted the soft curves of her body. The same could be said for the finely honed steel blade on her sleek, black-handled knife. Her targets only saw the curves, never the blade— until it was too late.

Wynn avoided the bedroom. Too many memories there. He went right to her office. Chapel worked at home and in the field, only visiting her Spartan cubicle at headquarters on days when she was required to attend a meeting. She'd called the office her cave, but when Wynn stepped through the doorway he felt as if he were entering a planetarium. The walls and ceiling were painted black and a dramatic display of the Milky Way spilled across three walls and the ceiling. Black Berber carpeting covered the floor.

He sat down at her metallic desk and turned on her computer. She was supposed to destroy all classified files as soon as she received her assignment and memorize the related data. While Chapel was effective, she was independent and he knew she bent the rules for her benefit from time to time. He needed to check the computer and delete everything associated with the A-6 and especially anything related to HEAT-16.

He was relieved to see that she had apparently been following orders. There were a few letters to her parents and old friends. He read them over and found them to be inconsequential. They even made him laugh because they revealed a humorous side to her personality that he'd never known about.

She played the role of a slightly dipsy executive secretary to an undersecretary of state and even made up stories of how she had bungled important messages being sent overseas so that the meanings were slightly twisted and suggested that the undersecretary didn't really know what was going on. Of course it was exactly what Chapel had thought of men and women in those positions, and this was the only bit of truth in the stories.

He rummaged through the desk drawers and found a case of disks. Most of them turned out to be programs that she'd installed on the computer. He flipped quickly through them and was about to move on when he found a disk labeled J.WYNN.

He held it in his hand a moment, wondering if it was going to be a diary of private thoughts about their relationship. If that was the case, he was glad he'd taken the time to come here. He didn't want any record of their relationship to remain, and of course he was curious about what she'd written about him.

He slipped the disk into the slot in the computer and loaded the directory. The files were innocuously named Doc.1, Doc.2, Doc.3, and so on. He opened Doc.1 and as he read its contents and the contents of the other files, his concept of Chapel as loyal agent and lover was shattered. All the leaked documents were here, along with a record of her e-mail correspondence with the *Washington Herald* reporter who had published the secret documents and caused him to go through months of hell.

When he opened Doc.13, a graphic image appeared— a grinning blue-mouthed clown. "What the hell," he muttered and scrolled further down to a letter.

Hiya Chapel,

Lovely, lovely work. You are sooo deadly efficient, you almost scare me. Ha-ha-ha. Keep it up. In no time Jason will be out of the way, and you'll be moving into that fancy big office and all the goodies that come with it. Yum.

Kisses & Laughs,
Clown

P.S. Don't worry about the weasel, Fitzgerald. We'll get him soon enuf. Har-har!

"I don't believe it," Wynn said to himself. "Chapel and Clown." He knew all along it wasn't Fitzgerald. He was too smart to try something like that. And he wasn't sneaky enough. It wasn't his style.

He sat back in the chair, suddenly feeling exhausted and literally deflated. There was nothing he could do about Chapel now, but Clown was another matter. "That sleazy little dwarf is dead meat." He shouted the words at the computer.

His thoughts about Chapel were more complex. He felt betrayed in a far different sense. He'd trusted her and confided in her. He'd told her things he would never reveal to his wife. They were good together, but she'd turned on him. She wanted more. She actually wanted his job. He should've known.

He tried to push aside his anguished thoughts as he continued reading the e-mail exchange with Clown. But he couldn't help wondering now if she had ever loved him. Maybe in the beginning, he decided. No, she'd never loved him. But so what? She was worm food now. Just what that double-crossing killer-wench deserved.

He forgot all about his feelings about Chapel as he stared at the last e-mail message from Clown, written the same day Chapel died.

Guess what? It's hide-'n'-seek time! Ha-ha. I moved the HEAT-16. Sorry about that.

I put it in a real funny place, too. Wynn will be so surprised.

As always,
Your silly Clown

P.S. Hey, don't try to be more sneaky than me. It just ain't possible. This silly Clown has fangs.

```
                              """" """"
                               0   0
                                 o
                                V V
```

"What?" Wynn shouted, bolting upright out of the chair. "No!"

The shipment was scheduled to be shipped tomorrow at midnight. How could that little creep destroy his plans? "That sonuvabitch! I'll kill him twice."

"Hey, Wynn. You should give me a medal!"

He spun around and saw Clown grinning behind him. His hands, covered by dirty white gloves, rested on his ample hips.

"You! What have you done?" Wynn started forward, literally ready to strangle the depraved dwarf. "Who's side are you on?"

"Now, just wait, Mr. Bigshot. Before you start getting violent with me, let me tell you the whole story. You see, your honey of an agent, Ms. Chapel, was doing a little in-and-out on the side with a certain terrorist. You know the guy, what's his name?" He pounded the side of his head with his open palm as if realigning his memory. "Oh yeah, now I remember, the Hyena. Him, do you think he laughed when did it with her?"

"What?"

Wynn didn't want to believe it, but slowly he was coming to realize that he didn't know Chapel at all.

"You know, the Hyena, the guy who was not supposed to get HEAT-16. Wrong. Chapel set it all up on her own. Sort of balancing the powers, you could say, and making a quick buck on the side, too."

That explained why the Hyena had been so quiet. He'd made no attempt to persuade Wynn to sell him the supervirus.

Clown flashed a blue smile. "That's our Chapel. Always on her toes, even when she was on her back. Although from those photos, it looked like she was the cowboy and you were the horse."

"Stop it! Cut the crap! Get to the point. Where is the HEAT-16?"

"I moved the entire shipment before Chapel could get her hands on any of it. I didn't want you delaying our plans. We've got to get moving."

"Damn it, Clown. Where is it?"

"In a nice quiet country spot." Clown leaned closer to him and whispered. "The basement of your little country home. Only half an hour from the port. You've got plenty of time to get it to the ship."

"What? You didn't! You did! You idiot! My wife and daughters are there right now!" The entire shipment was labeled as soap. Muriel or one of the girls might wonder what all the soap was doing in the basement and open up a canister.

"Oops! Guess the wife wanted a breather from hubby after seeing those photos. Hee-hee. Sorry, I just couldn't help it." Wynn's whole body was trembling with anger. Clown took a step back from him and looked at him out of the corner of his eye. "There were some nice shots, though, don't you think?"

Wynn lunged for him, but Clown sidestepped him, grabbed the back of Wynn's shirt, and sent him flying forward onto his elbows and shins.

"Ouch. I bet that hurt. No time to wrestle a dwarf,

Jason. You've got to get the shipment to the docks. Now, get up and get going. Put your useless bodyguard to work. I'd help you, but I don't want to interfere with your family life, you know.'' He shrugged. ''But that's just me.''

Clown darted out the door before Wynn could tackle him. Wynn wasn't finished with that disgusting creature. Not yet. But Clown was right about one thing. There was no time to waste.

''Oh, one other thing,'' Clown said, sticking his head back into the door. ''You better take along those fancy white suits you used in North Korea. You know, just in case.''

It was late afternoon when they turned onto the dirt road five miles from the house outside of Norfolk. Wynn signaled Marcus to pull over. He got out and stopped the armored truck, the decontamination vehicle, and the two A-6 Suburbans that had followed them. Everyone immediately put on their biohazard suits.

''Isn't this sort of overdoing it?'' the burly bodyguard asked. ''I mean, I just saw someone out in her yard gardening a mile or so back, and we passed some kids playing right around there, too.''

Wynn did feel odd about approaching his own house in the suits, as if he were part of an invading army of spacemen. It certainly wasn't going to help his tenuous relationship with Muriel, but then again he had gone to Lichon and seen the victims of the predecessor to HEAT-16. He wasn't about to take any chances. There was nothing in the world quite as insidious and deadly as HEAT-16, especially since it was much easier to use than a thermonuclear weapon. That was precisely why he was wearing the suit.

''As soon as we see someone alive at the house, we'll take off the masks,'' he answered. ''At least until we begin moving the canisters. Then we cover up again. But first we get Muriel and the girls out of there.''

Marcus shrugged and climbed back into the vehicle. Wynn sealed his face mask and turned on the internal air tank, which would give him at least forty-five minutes worth of oxygen with a five-minute reserve. He checked the radio to make sure it was working.

"Okay, attention. Everyone get ready to go in with your suits fully on and the oxygen engaged. Over.''

A couple of beats passed. "Jason, what if your wife has a weapon? Over?'' An agent in one of the Suburbans asked.

"Don't worry,'' Wynn responded. "She won't be armed.''

"She hates guns,'' Marcus cut in.

Wynn slowed as he approached the house a few minutes later. He saw Muriel's minivan parked in the drive. He was hoping he could reconcile with her, but this obviously was not the time for it. He would tell her that they were here to remove some toxic waste that was being temporary stored in the basement.

He figured that when Muriel saw the biohazard suits, she would think about the safety of the girls and do whatever he said. The incident would give him a good reason to call her later and apologize for the inconvenience, and that was when he would attempt a reconciliation.

He stepped out and headed toward the front door. He watched the front door, waiting to see the girls. What if they panicked and screamed? He recalled that he did once show Muriel where he kept a semiautomatic. What if Muriel came out firing? No, she would recognize the Lexus. She hated the color, which she called tarnished gold.

He stopped and looked down at a dead robin. *Birds die,* he told himself. One just happened to die here. He moved on, suddenly hoping to see the door to burst open, to glimpse someone looking out the window, to hear voices, even a scream. Some sign of life.

All was quiet, still.

Next to the door was a black cat. It lay curled up as if asleep. He touched it with his foot. It didn't wake up. It was stiff.

"What's going on, Mr. Wynn? Over." Marcus's voice was tight.

He looked at the cat again and felt as if the wind had been knocked out of him. He didn't want to believe it. It couldn't be. "Oh, shit. Oh, shit. No, please. It just can't be."

He rushed up to the house. The door was unlocked. He pushed inside. The living room was empty. Same with the dining room and the first-floor bedroom. His heart pounded and his stomach was knotted in anxiety as he moved to the kitchen. And there they were.

Two chairs had toppled over. The basement door was open, and three bodies lay on the ceramic floor.

"Nooo! Oh God! Oh God! No! No! No!"

He crumpled to the floor, touching Muriel, then the girls, with his gloved hand. They were not only dead, but he could never touch any of them again. Their bodies were contaminated, too dangerous to even bury.

His personal life was destroyed. Why should he even bother to go on? Why not take off the mask and go with them? Take half of North America with him.

But then he mentally stepped back and tried to take control of his wildly rapid breathing. He raised his head up. *Stay calm. Relax, Jason. You've been through rough times before. You're a survivor.*

He could deal with it, he told himself. He could still enjoy life. This part of it was over. That was all. He still had his work. That was what was important. He would be all right.

They had come prepared for the worst with special

body bags that would seal in the contamination just as their suits sealed it out. "Get three body bags up here right fast. Over."

It felt good to give orders, to take control. He would be okay, he told himself again.

He looked around and saw a canister lying near his youngest daughter. One of them found the crates, opened one, and took out a canister. She'd brought it upstairs and unsealed it. He picked it up, examined the broken seal. He tested the top. It had been tightened again, resealed, but too late.

He announced his discovery and passed the canister back to one of the men, who carefully placed it into a protective container that would eliminate the possibility of any further leaks.

Wynn stepped out of the room as two men with body bags moved into the kitchen. *Life would go on,* he told himself. Sure it was a cliché, but it was one that meant something to him right now.

He flicked on the radio. "Okay. I want the rest of us to head downstairs to ground zero and begin uploading the cargo."

He glanced at his watch. "Fifteen minutes and we're out of here. Let's go to work."

He moved past the bodies, but this time didn't look. The past was dead.

TWENTY

SPAWN LUMBERED down the alley toward the street. Clown's remarks about Wanda were still on his mind, eating away at him like a cancer. Maybe Clown was just trying to make him mad, but he couldn't relax until he knew that Wanda was okay. He'd started the day intent on decimating Wynn and Clown and making sure that Wanda was all right. But now he saw it was late afternoon and realized Cogliostro had occupied most of his day.

As he crossed the street, Cogliostro moved to his side. "It's better to defend and protect than to assault," the old man said.

"That's exactly what I have in mind." Spawn pulled the hood of his greatcoat over his head as he saw people on the sidewalk outside of a biker bar.

"Then use your powers wisely," Cogliostro said, keeping pace with him. Remember that when you've drained them, you die."

"I'll keep that in mind," Spawn said, then with a snicker, added: "It wouldn't be the first time."

They crossed the street to a biker bar and Zack ran after him. Spawn surveyed the neat row of gleaming motorcycles parked out on the street. "It must be happy hour."

He was tired of walking everywhere and was still frustrated by his lack of control over his cape. No matter how hard he tried to fly, the cape wouldn't form wings. He needed some wheels, he decided. Two would be fine. He picked out a high-performance bike as if he were at a sales lot. He grabbed the helmet from the seat and tossed it aside. "Don't think I'll need this."

He climbed onto the bike with his bulky weapon in hand. He looked at the smart-gun, then at Cogliostro. He tossed the weapon to the old man.

"No guts, no glory."

"Now you're catching on."

The bike roared to life as Spawn settled onto the seat and throttled the engine.

Zack ran up to Spawn, waving his hands. "Let me go with you," he shouted over the sound of the engine.

Spawn shook his head. "You don't want to go where I'm going." He reached into his coat and handed Zack the sequined collar he'd found in the alley. "I want you to find Spaz and bring him back to me. No matter how you find him."

Zack nodded with a serious expression on his young face as Spawn accelerated away on a black carpet of burning rubber.

Cogliostro watched Spawn speed off with profound concern. "It could still go either way with him."

A bald-headed, bearded biker in leather chaps and jacket with a skull and crossbone insignia ran from the bar out into the street, shaking his fists. "Hey, come back here with my bike, you sonuvabitch!"

He turned Cogliostro, grabbed him by his coat, and lifted him off the ground. "Was that guy a friend of yours, old man?"

"A passing acquaintance."

He put Cogliostro down. "I'm going to kick his ass when I catch him."

Cogliostro watched the burly biker retreat to the bar. "I hope his insurance is paid up."

The cool night breeze whipped against his armor as Spawn raced down a straight stretch of road on his borrowed bike. It almost made him feel alive— really alive— again. He imagined that the bike, like the armor and his cape, was an extension of his body. But the euphoric sensation was short-lived.

Suddenly, a garbage truck appeared out of nowhere and cut in front of him. Screeching and careening, it nearly ran him off the road. Garbage spewed out of the open back-end, striking him and the bike; for a moment he nearly lost control.

"What the hell!"

Gritting his teeth, Spawn tried to overtake the truck on the left. But as they approached an underpass, the truck swerved hard to the left, throwing Spawn against the underpass divider. He struggled to control the bike and keep from being crushed. Sparks flew from the bike's frame as metal struck metal and a metallic screech ripped up his spine, through his head, and down his arms.

Finally, Spawn managed to pull out to the right and the truck drifted away, rumbling alongside him. He looked over at the driver. Clown smiled and waved from the cab. Spawn responded by picking up speed and passing him. But the garbage truck accelerated and nudged the bike's back wheel. Spawn spun out into the opposite lane and barely avoided hitting an oncoming car.

Spawn recovered in time to stay on the road, but now a pickup truck was coming right at him. He swerved over to the right and off the road, darting between a fence and a wall. He sped past the garbage truck on his left, but suddenly the truck pulled into the fence and began ripping it down as Clown picked up speed in his wild chase.

Spawn accelerated, trying to stay ahead of the truck.

Then the gap between the fence and the wall began to narrow, until the fence rubbed his elbow. It looked as if he were about to get squeezed between the fence and wall when suddenly a ramp appeared. He drove up it and found himself on an elevated platform running parallel to the road. Below him, the truck turned to the left, pulling back into the road. It smashed into a slow-moving car, spinning it around and around, as Clown continued on.

Clown leaned out the window of the truck with a grenade launcher that he'd taken from the alley. He aimed and fired. Spawn squeezed the brakes and swerved, and ducked low; the grenade exploded several yards behind him.

A wall suddenly appeared directly in his path, forcing him to drive off the platform. He flew over the road, over the truck, and landed in the left lane. Clown stayed ahead of the motorcycle and pulled in front of Spawn. He fired another round that blasted a crater in the asphalt to the left of Spawn. Flames and black smoke rose up around him.

"I just love the smell of burning asphalt," Clown yelled. "Reminds me of home."

Spawn was ready to jerk Clown out of the garbage truck and drag him down the road. His green eyes burned brightly as he concentrated on the thought, testing Cogliostro's training on the use of his armor. He tried to send out his chains to snag Clown, but suddenly he had to swerve around something lying in the road. His anger and his shifting focus caused the message to be misdirected.

Instead of chains, his cape emerged and wrapped around him. For a moment he thought that he was going to crash, but then he realized the cape encased the motorcycle in an impervious projectile. Only his enormous, green glowing eyes appeared through the cape's protective veil.

Clown leaned out the window of the truck and fired

another salvo over his shoulder. This time he scored a direct hit. Spawn's new form shed the blast debris as if it were merely a hailstorm.

"Hey, that's no fair!" Clown yelled as Spawn emerged unscathed from the explosion. Like a whining kid upset that his toy doesn't work, he tossed the grenade launcher out the window.

Spawn saw his chance to get away from the demonic clown and accelerated into the passing lane as the truck headed under an overpass. But Clown swung the wheel to the left, blocking his path. Then he pulled down on a chain and released a tank of toxic waste onto the road.

Spawn's bike-projectile hit the slick, gooey substance and went into a skid. He went down, tumbling head over heel across the road. His armor maintained its shape, and he rolled to a stop uninjured. He got up and was starting to lift the bike upright when he heard tires squealing.

He looked up and saw the truck spin around one hundred and eighty degrees. It's engine roared, and then the truck charged toward Spawn, spewing a cloud of smoking rubber and liquid toxins.

He saw Clown's wide, neon-blue grin through the windshield as the truck rapidly approached. He could hear the dwarf's hoots and hollers as the front grill of the truck rushed toward Spawn's face. He turned, but there was no time for him to dive clear.

He concentrated, directing his mind into a single-pointed focus, ordering his armor to protect him. He had no time to think about how it would happen, but suddenly his armor molded over into a thick black wedge with a sharp leading edge that anchored itself deep within the bed of asphalt.

The truck hit Spawn at seventy miles an hour and stopped dead as it struck the blunt side of the wedge. Clown had no time to consider what had happened. The massive truck exploded on impact, catapulting him through the windshield. He sailed into a nearby intersection, where he crashed headlong through the ragtop of a Volkswagen Beetle. He hung head-down through the roof and face-to-face with a stunned forty-something woman, who screamed when she saw the grinning clown face.

"Let that be a lesson to you, lady. Always wear a seat belt. Or you could end up like me."

He somersaulted into the passenger seat. "Ah, that's better. Except I'm in the wrong seat. Lady, time to take a hike. I need some new wheels and, you know, I need my space."

Her mouth moved, but she didn't say anything. He grabbed her by the shoulder and leg, and tossed her out of the vehicle through the gaping hole in the roof.

"Good-bye."

He slipped behind the wheel and drove away. He glanced at the flaming wreckage of the truck through his rearview mirror and laughed. "Good job, Spawn. Bet that hurt, though. Just bet it did."

Then he saw Spawn step out of the flaming wreckage. "I knew he'd be okay. What's a little fire to a guy like him who's seen it all. But I bet he's mad and ready to kill. That's what important."

Fitzgerald slipped the disk he'd taken from Wynn's office and brought up list of files on unauthorized field-op reports, surveillance video, intelsat recon, mug shots, of Wynn's international contacts.

"What have you got, Terry?"

Fitzgerald clicked an icon in the corner of his monitor to reveal an image of Natalie Ford, the high-profile investigative reporter who had interviewed him several times during her ongoing investigation of A-6.

"Okay, I've got black-bag ops, assassination lists, just about everything you've ever asked about," Fitzgerald said as he talked to Ford via a televideo hookup. "Wynn's been using the A-6 to form some kind of criminal consortium," he began and told her what he'd found out.

"Jesus!" Ford interrupted more than once. "The rumors are really true."

"I'm e-mailing a copy of the disk to you. Should be enough there to bury Wynn. But the important thing is stopping the shipment tonight."

"What about the port officials at Norfolk, the inspectors?" Ford asked.

"Wynn has probably paid off everyone who has the power to interfere with his plans. None of the authorities or security people can be trusted."

"Well, I can make it hot for him. I'll see what I can do, Terry. But we don't have much time."

"Good. See you later."

Fitzgerald began e-mailing the files to Natalie Ford, hoping that she would be able to do some good. But he wasn't stopping there. He knew it was dangerous, but he'd go to the port himself and do whatever he could to stop Wynn from shipping his deadly cargo.

Tranquil, soothing jazz washed over Wynn as he drove the Lexus down the highway heading back to the capital from Norfolk. He was pleased that the recovery operation had gone smoothly. He kept telling himself that the transfer had gone flawlessly. But a part of him knew that he was in denial, that there had been a serious glitch—the death of his family.

He was doing everything in his capacity to push away any thoughts of Muriel and the girls. He had cherished that part of his life that was separate from the political-power wars and the intrigue. But now he was no longer a father or a husband. He had to focus on what he was and that was pretty damn impressive. He was a power broker, a world leader who could never be toppled by an election, whose very heartbeat controlled the destiny of the entire world.

He couldn't let the loss of his family destroy everything. He had to remain strong. He had already figured out a plan to explain their disappearance. There would be a fiery accident tonight. Marcus was taking care of it for him. The Cherokee, with Muriel and the girls in it, would run off the road a few miles from the country house. It would plunge over a cliff and explode. Clean and simple.

The HEAT-16, meanwhile, was back at the port and the A-6 team was staying with it until it was time to load the freighter. He didn't expect any more problems now. He'd taken care of everyone who was a potential problem: the union people, the night dockmaster, the inspector, even the security people who patrolled the docks. Everyone was primed and happy, ready to do their parts.

He wanted to be home tonight when he received the unhappy news about the accident, and he'd be there in just half an hour. He would drive back to Norfolk immediately to meet with authorities and answer any questions, and make sure they didn't carry their investigation too far. Fortunately, the house was relatively isolated, so that no one would've noticed the strange convoy of vehicles arriving at the house, or the men in bio suits cleaning up the surrounding area. Besides, they were in and out of the place in a mere twenty-three minutes.

His car phone rang and he answered on the second ring. "This is Carrie at CNN."

For a moment, Wynn was confused. He was about to ask how she got his number, when it clicked. Carrie was a low-level A-6 mole that he'd planted in a secretarial position at the network to watch Natalie Ford. He'd almost forgotten about her.

"What is it?"

"Ford has just received some A-6 documents, classified

stuff, by e-mail. They were sent to her from Terry Fitzgerald.''

"What else?"

"That's all I know right now."

"Okay, keep an eye on her. Let me know if she's going anywhere."

"Oh, one other thing. I heard her say something about getting a chopper to go to somewhere tonight. Norfolk, I think.''

"Shit." He hung up.

"That sonuvabitch," he screamed. Fitzgerald was going to pay. "Oh, was he ever going to pay."

He thought a moment. Ford could cause a stink at the port, but she couldn't stop the shipment. Not now. Everything was wired. No one would tell her anything.

He popped out the jazz CD and reached way into the back of his built-in storage case and found what he was looking for. He slipped the Black Sabbath CD into the player and turned up the volume. He didn't listen to raucous rock 'n' roll much any more, but now was the time. The only reason he had the CD was that it had been sent to him a week ago. It had arrived unexpected with no accompanying note, except for a grinning clown in the return-address space.

Wynn bobbed his head to the pounding beat as he gripped the steering wheel. Traffic slowed and he passed a burning garbage truck that somehow seemed to fit right in with the music. His thoughts drifted to Wanda and he smiled. He wouldn't be home when the authorities called, but so what. He couldn't wait to get to Fitzgerald's place. As soon as he took care of Fitzgerald, it was Wanda's turn. She would be his prize.

Wanda rested in Cyan's bed next to her daughter, who had just fallen asleep. She was starting to drift off herself when a shadow fell across her face and she blinked her eyes open. A burn-scarred face stared down at her, inches from her face. She screamed a silent scream. Her body was frozen in terror. She wanted to run, to escape, but no matter what she did, she couldn't move.

"Mommy, wake up!"

Her body jerked and she woke up. Cyan was standing next to the bed, exactly where Spawn had been standing. "Sweetie, what are you doing awake?"

"I'm thirst. I want a drink of water."

"Okay," Wanda said, relieved that the image had been a dream. But she couldn't shake off the feeling of being watched.

Fitzgerald didn't care any more about taking precautions. He dialed the number to connect his modem with the A-6 modem and worked his way into Wynn's files. He was looking for something new—anything that could give him a way to stop the shipment from leaving the port.

He looked over the long list of files, checking the dates of each one. He stopped when he found one that had been opened just yesterday. It was a file labeled, Monitor-Implant, that had been sent to Wynn from the A-6 medical/laboratory section. He had no idea what the name referred to, but he was going to find out.

He tapped into the file and saw a three-dimensional graphics of the HEAT-16 molecular structure. He watched it slowly revolving for a few seconds, then scrolled down. The files contained a design plan for a pacemaker that linked to the HEAT-16 virus. The plan indicated that the pacemaker had been installed in Wynn's chest the day before and was operational.

"Oh, Christ."

Fitzgerald whispered the words as he realized the full implications of the operation. Wynn was a time bomb.

His death would result in the automatic detonation of the weapons.

"He is out of his mind."

He scrolled back to the top of the file and stared at the HEAT-16 graphics again.

"What did you say, hon?"

He turned to see Wanda with Cyan who was drinking a glass of water at the doorway. "I'll tell you later." Frowning at Cyan and playacting the stern father role, he said: "It's past your bedtime, young lady." He tapped his watch. "Off to bed with you or the big, bad wolf is going to get you and eat you up."

He raised his hands into claws and Cyan screamed and laughed as she ran off to her bedroom.

"Terry, you're going to give her nightmares," Wanda admonished.

"Well, Wynn is giving them to me, and unfortunately I'm awake. Take a look here."

"Let me tuck her back into bed first." Wanda turned and nearly ran into Cyan.

"Mommy, mommy. There's a man with a big gun in my bedroom."

"What?" Wanda shouted.

Fitzgerald leaped to his feet and hurried across the den.

"She's right, Wanda," a voice said from the darkened hall.

Wynn moved down the hall toward her, the barrel of a smart-gun leading the way. She cried out as Wynn motioned her back into the den.

"Good evening. Nice to see you both. Surprise. Surprise."

Fitzgerald positioned himself in the doorway. His hands curled into tight fists.

"Just take it easy, Terry. Step back. Do what I say, if you want your family to stay healthy. I'm sure by now you've figured out that I'm capable of terminating their existence and yours.''

"What are you doing here?'' Fitzgerald asked. He moved back and stood between Wynn and the computer, hoping the screen saver would quickly engage.

"We've got some unfinished business to take care of, Terry.'' He motioned with the gun. ''Move aside.'' Fitzgerald hesitated, then stepped away from the computer.

Wynn moved forward, staring at the screen. "So, I see you've been working at home. What have we here, some classified materials?''

The HEAT-16 graphics were still on the screen. He raised his smart-gun and blasted the monitor and CPU, destroying the files.

"You disappoint me, Terry.'' He viciously backhanded his cast across Fitzgerald's jaw, sending him down to the carpet.

Fitzgerald slowly rose to his feet as Cyan whimpered in Wanda's arms. "You can't release the virus, Jason. Millions of people are sure to die.''

"Only in the countries that refuse to join me. The rest will be protected by the ability to retaliate. It's simply survival of the strongest and smartest. Nothing new there, Fitz.''

Wynn turned to Wanda and smiled as he softly brushed the backs of his fingers along her supple cheek and long neck. "You're a lucky man, Terry.''

Cyan cringed against Wanda's leg. "That man hit my daddy.''

Wanda stiffened, but she refused to allow Wynn to intimidate him. "Whatever it is you want . . . just take it and go.''

"I intend to,'' Wynn said.

A pounding erupted at the other end of the house.

"What was that? Who's out there?'' Wynn demanded, moving to the hall as he pulled Wanda and Cyan with him.

"It sounded like the front door," Fitzgerald answered from the den.

"Move!" Wynn ordered the three of them down the hall ahead of him.

The pounding started up again as they reached the living room. Wynn forced Fitzgerald to his knees and grabbed Cyan as he motioned Wanda with his smart-gun to answer the door.

"Get rid of whoever it is."

Wanda moved over to the door and slowly pulled it open. Suddenly, the door was kicked out of Wanda's hand and slammed against the wall. Clown poked his grinning head around the door jamb.

"Peek-a-boo!"

A Volkswagen Beetle was parked on the lawn behind him. He stepped inside and slammed the door. He took a big sniff of Wanda and licked his lips with a tongue that nearly reached his ears.

"You smell *terrific.*"

Wanda cringed.

Clown pursed his lips, then turned and noticed Wynn holding Cyan. "What's a matter, scared this little girl's gonna shoot off your pee-pee?"

Wynn loosened his grip and Cyan rushed to her mother's side. She looked warily up at Clown. "You were at my birthday party."

Clown twisted his face into a crazed look, with his tongue lolling to one side, and curtsied. "Ah, the memories of childhood."

"What are you doing here?" Wanda asked in a tensed voice.

"Oh, sorry, did you want me to leave you alone with this maniac with the fancy gun? Okay, no problem. You guys have fun. I know when I'm not wanted." A beat passed. "Naw, just kidding."

He folded his arms over his heart. "I'd never leave you

in a time of need. Actually, this is my encore performance. So sit back and enjoy the show folks!''

Fitzgerald kept a close eye on Wynn. He was looking for an opportunity to take away his weapon. But Wynn must have sensed Fitzgerald's interest in him, because he suddenly tightened his grip on the smart-gun and swung it toward Fitzgerald.

''Hey, pay attention, guys!'' Clown yelled as he gyrated in a belly dance. Then he pulled out a balloon and inflated it in his hands while his head simultaneously deflated. The balloon started laughing and the laughter turned psychotic and menacing. Suddenly, the balloon exploded and Clown's head was its normal size again.

''For a minute there I was wondering if my hat size was going to be a fraction.'' Clown felt his head. ''Does wonders for my asthma.''

''Where's Spawn?'' Wynn asked. ''Did you take care of him?''

''Actually, he's taking care of himself these days. He's a big boy now, you know.''

''Answer my question,'' Wynn demanded, sounding annoyed. ''Where is he?''

''Spawn, Spawn, is that all you ever think about? What about Clown?''

He grinned and wiggled his eyebrows. ''He's on his way. The real question is . . . are you ready, Jason? He hasn't made his undying commitment to Hell's Army yet, and that's very troubling.''

Wynn glanced at Wanda. ''I'm ready for him. I can deal with him.''

Clown gave Wynn a patronizing smirk. ''We'll see soon enough.''

TWENTY-ONE

SPAWN KNEW something was wrong from the moment he reached Wanda and Fitzgerald's house. A Volkswagen had smashed through the iron fence and had stopped in the front yard a few yards from the sidewalk. The front door creaked open as he gave a slight push against it. He stepped warily inside.

The house was quiet, nothing was disturbed or out of place. A warm inviting glow danced along the wall across the living room as he eased into the house. But then he saw it was all wrong.

Odd blue and crimson flames blazed in a misshapen opening in the wall where the fireplace had been. It was as if a flicker of Hell had poured into the room, transforming it into a bizarre cavelike domain that blended into the rest of the house. The floor was gooey; strange growths hung from the ceiling.

Spawn moved into the room and suddenly crimson flames roared into the center of the room, licking at his legs and feet. Then they retreated back into the portal, leaving the room in a flickering shadow. On the far side of the portal was a figure, bound to a rack made from braided barbed wire, decorated with black horns, spikes, and images of twisted faces caught in the grip of extreme anguish.

"Wanda!"

The horrific sight startled Spawn. Her eyes were red with tears and she looked terrified. She was trying to say something to him. Her mouth moved, but no words came out.

Another figure moved through the gloom, and before Spawn had the chance to react, the man had darted behind Wanda. He held a long serrated blade to her tear-stained face and grinned at Spawn. It was Wynn and he looked totally mad.

"Please . . ." Wanda gasped.

Her head hung to the side, as if she could no longer hold it up. The torturous rack pressed into her skin, and welts had risen on her arms and legs from the heat of the flames.

"Get away from her!" Spawn bellowed, edging closer to Wanda.

The shifting glow of the fireplace turned Wynn's features jagged and loathsome. His mask of coolness had given way to something raw and wholly evil. Every evil act Wynn had ever committed was reflected in his hideous features.

"I can't do that, Simmons. Can't you see? She wants me." He leered at Spawn and brought the blade to Wanda's throat.

"Touch her and you're dead! Spawn vowed.

"No, you're dead," Wynn snapped. "You've been dead five years and counting."

Spawn took a step closer. He wanted to lunge for Wynn, to snap his neck like a toothpick, but he knew it would be too late for Wanda. "I swear, I'll kill you."

Wynn twirled the knife and gazed fiendishly at Wanda's neck. "Careful, don't make me nervous. I might nick something vital." Wynn leaned closer and took a seductive whiff of her neck. "You wouldn't want me to do that, would you?"

"You're out of your mind, Wynn. What's happened to you since I've been gone."

Wynn laughed. "And what's happened to you? What the hell are you, anyhow, Simmons? Or should I say, Spawn? Dead and buried and back from Hell with the burns to show for it."

"You know where those burns came from, Wynn. And now you want to cause more pain and death, just so you can play your little power games. I've had enough of it."

"There's a bigger picture that you're ignoring, Spawn," Wynn said in a cool, sly voice. "You're well aware of your role in it. Why else would you be back?"

A beat passed as Spawn remained silent. What Wynn said was true, but he was confused by his own desires to exact revenge and Cogliostro's warnings that he was playing into Clown's game by following those craving for payback. He was being pulled in two directions, and the revenge factor was winning.

"You're not the only one who has suffered. My wife, Muriel, and the girls are dead now." Wynn seemed to wilt and Spawn was about to pounce when Wynn abruptly jerked upright and turned to Spawn with a cruel grimace.

"The fun and games are over, Spawn. Either you finish the deal with Clown or she dies." He grinned like the maniac that he was. "After I'm through with her, she'll be ready to die."

He pressed the side of the blade to Wanda's neck. "So what's it going to be?"

Spawn didn't say anything. Finishing the deal with Clown meant killing Wynn, and he would be glad to do that. But he wasn't going to commit himself to Clown, either. He couldn't say yes, but he didn't want to say no.

Wynn smiled and shook his head. "Time's up, Spawn. No answer is the same as a no answer. Say good-bye to your Wanda."

He tightened his grip on her. She screamed as he

plunged the serrated blade into her chest and blood pumped out, turning her white T-shirt a deep red.

"Noooo!"

Spawn exploded forward. He rammed Wynn aside, knocking him into the wall, and then tried frantically to stop the bleeding. But it was already too late. He screamed in disbelief as shock waves of pain slammed against him.

He hugged her limp body that still hung on the garish rack. "Wanda. Wanda."

He didn't want to believe what he knew was true. "Nooooooo!!"

His anguished bellow seemed to shake the foundation of the house, setting off tremors that raced out in every direction from his tormented body.

Wynn, cradling his damaged cast, watched with smug satisfaction. "It's all your fault, Spawn. You know it, too. Wanda was doing just fine until you showed up and destroyed her life."

His words flayed Spawn, ripping him apart from inside out. His sanity was quickly fading. His eyes grew dim as he crumpled to the floor. Maybe he'd never left Hell. Maybe this was it, just another version of torture. What could be more painful than to see his Wanda reject him, then witness her death?

"Now you've got nothing left to lose, you soulless corpse . . . *nothing.*

Spawn slowly pulled himself together. He looked up with burning demonic eyes, glowing dark green with hints of red. He surrendered himself to the pain, madness, and rage. "I've still got you!"

"Where's Mommy, Daddy? What did that man do to my Mommy?"

He tried to quiet Cyan, but the gag in his mouth prevented any sounds from coming forth. He and Cyan were tied together in the den, and Wanda was gone—vanished as if she'd never been in the room with them.

Fitzgerald struggled with the bindings on his wrists. He knew something strange and horrible was going on in the living room, but he had no idea what it was, except that it must have something to do with Wanda.

He was still confused by what had happened. One moment, Wanda was bound and gagged next to him, then the clown had waved his hands and they were both gone. It was like another one of his magic tricks, but now Fitzgerald was well aware that he was no ordinary clown, that he had some extraordinary powers.

Maybe he wasn't a clown at all, but rather some otherworldly creature masquerading as one. Somehow Wynn had started dealing with the fiendish gnome, and Fitzgerald suspected the relationship had something to do with Wynn's rapid rise in power as well as the demonic twist that his espionage work had taken.

He heard voices in the living room. One was Wynn, and after a moment he recognized the other deep voice. Simmons raged in his living room.

He craned his neck as he heard screams and shouts. Something had happened. Wanda. She was dead, he thought. *No, she couldn't be dead. Not Wanda.* Something else had happened. He had to hold that thought, no matter what.

"What happened, Daddy?"

He tried to calm her with his gaze, but he didn't think it was working. She saw his own concern in his features. Ironically, he was not only worried about Wanda, but also about Wynn. He had to try to keep Spawn from killing him.

Spawn's frame shuddered as he raised himself up from Wanda's body. He was ready to pounce, to tear the limbs from his former boss as if he were shredding newspaper. Nothing would get in his way now.

Wynn's sneering cynicism vanished as he realized that

he was the target of Spawn's fury. "I guess I've over-estimated you, Spawn. You can lead Hell's Army to a great victory, but instead you choose to spend your energy attacking me."

Spawn smashed Wynn in the face and sent him flying across the room and down the hall. He stalked after him, picked him up, and slammed him into the door of the study. The hinges broke and Wynn fell into the room and started crawling away.

Spawn trailed his prey into the room. But two steps in he was distracted by the sight of Fitzgerald and Cyan bound and gagged in one of the corners. Fitzgerald was trying to say something, but it just sounded like murmurs. Spawn met Cyan's inquisitive gaze for a long moment, then moved after Wynn again.

He grabbed Wynn's ankle and dragged him out of the closet where he was trying to hide. Wynn shook and kicked his leg, trying to free himself. But Spawn booted him in the gut. Wynn tumbled across the room and crashed into a wall.

Spawn was enjoying every moment of the beating. He didn't care if it continued for hours. As long as Wynn was still alive, he would beat him and take great pleasure in doing it. Then he noticed Cyan cringing in fear and terror at his brutality. Fitzgerald was shaking his head about something, trying to get his attention. He paused in his pursuit and again recalled Cogliostro's words of warning.

Wynn crawled out into the living room as Spawn untied Cyan's and Fitzgerald's hands. "Are you going to hurt us?" Cyan asked.

"I'm not here to hurt you."

"D-Don't kill Wynn," Fitzgerald stammered as he pulled off the gag. "He's connected to the virus."

"Good reason to kill him."

"You don't understand . . ."

But Spawn had already stalked off after him. He knew

he couldn't turn his back on Wynn for long. He found him in the living room, crawling toward his smart-gun.

"Not smart!" He grabbed Wynn by the back of the neck and lifted him off the ground just as he was about to reach the weapon.

"You can't kill me," Wynn snarled. "You'll kill everyone on the East Coast."

"I think you'll be enough for me."

Spawn squeezed his neck, compressing his spine. All he had to do was twist hard one way or the other with his huge armored hand and Wynn's neck would snap.

"If I die, the virus is released." Wynn spoke in a wheezing, choking voice. He knew that Spawn was about to make good his vow. "It'll kill millions right in this country because a shipment is still here."

Spawn didn't believe him. It was just a ruse. Why would killing him release the virus? "Like you said, I've got nothing to lose."

"Al, it's me, Terry. Please, listen to me. He's telling you the truth." Fitzgerald stood at the end of the hallway, holding onto Cyan. His right cheek was swollen and purple and his eye was barely open. "He's connected to a pacemaker that's linked to viral weapons. If he dies, the weapons go off."

"Why should I believe you? You've protected Wynn for years."

He squeezed tighter, digging his fingers into Wynn's throat. Wynn waved his hands in a frenzied panic and uttered a choking gasp. "Clown . . . he's killing me! Do something! Hurry!"

Spawn hurled Wynn into the flaming portal. Wynn screamed and rolled out of the flames. His arms and legs moved wildly as he frantically extinguished the flames on his clothing. He rolled to a stop and clasped a hand over his pounding heart.

Spawn moved forward toward Wynn again. He heard

Cyan crying and glanced momentarily in her direction. "Get her out of here, Fitzgerald. She doesn't need to see what I'm going to do next."

"I want you to stop, Al," Fitzgerald pleaded. "You don't understand what you're doing."

"Al's dead."

He knelt down next to Wynn and lifted his head by the hair. "Feel the burn?" he whispered hoarsely. "Get used to it, because you're going to be feeling a lot more of it where you're headed."

Clown watched from one of his most inventive hiding places. He had a wonderful surprise for Spawn. He couldn't wait to show him. But first Wynn had to die.

It didn't matter to him that the weapons hadn't been spread to all the countries that had ordered them yet. Once the good ol' U.S.A. and a few other countries that had the weapon were taken out of the picture, there would be worldwide confusion. A massive struggle to be the next Big Guy. No one would win. No one except Hell's Army, and the army would be on the march by the time the virus was being inhaled by its first victims.

"Enough of this slow, gruesome death stuff," he said to himself. "Just get it over with Spawny. Kill da bum." He was getting bored being so still and quiet. He wanted to see the future set in motion. Now. "I'm waaaaiting."

The flames in the portal began to grow and move, making squealing noises, becoming more and more violent as Spawn's revenge approached. He grabbed Wynn by the arm, jerked him up, and held him at arm's length. Wynn gasped for breath as Spawn raised a spiked hand.

He was shaking with rage and his boiling anger caused more blades to emerge from all sides, turning his fists into a fearsome oversized mace. He reared back his arm and ooked over at the pitiful, pleading Wynn. "See you in Hell, Jason."

Wynn shook his head and gulped for air. "You'll . . . you'll kill everyone. Think about it . . . please. Not for me, but for your daughter."

Spawn hesitated just a beat. *His daughter.* That was what he'd said. Everything slowed down as that thought touched him.

He turned to the portal and saw the roiling, screaming flames. He closed his eyes, but the flames of Hell burning brightly right through his eyelids and seemed to sizzle his eyeballs. The roaring wails of Hell's hordes pounded in his head. Spawn's entire being had reached the crossroads. His existence and the world's would be defined by his next move.

He knew he could easily satisfy his vengeance and feed his limitless rage, but in doing so he would also cast aside his morality and forever surrender his soul. As he hesitated, his brutal, spiked hand began to transform back to its normal armored appearance.

He heard Cyan's terrified whimpers. He turned and saw her staring right into his eyes, crying, terrified. They were fused together at that moment at some deep, unspoken level.

Spawn noticed for the first time that his hand was normal again. It surprised him, but then he realized that his armor was doing exactly what he was telling it to do. Just like Cogliostro had told him it would.

He turned back to Wynn and his feeling of disgust nearly overwhelmed him again. He hesitated, but then tossed him back to the floor with both hand.

"I'm through doing Hell's dirty work," Spawn proclaimed.

"Yes!" Fitzgerald said with a loud sigh of relief. "You don't need to kill him."

Wynn rolled over onto his back, wheezing on the floor,

barely conscious. The flames in the portal died to a faint flicker and the wailing became a distant echo. Spawn looked back at Cyan, who had stopped crying and was staring with wide-eyed wonder at him from behind Fitzgerald's leg.

Then her gaze shifted to the rack near the portal. "Mommy . . . is that my Mommy?"

Spawn moved between Cyan and Wanda and motioned Fitzgerald to take her out of the room. He scooped her up, glanced toward the rack, his brow deeply furrowed, then moved back toward the hall.

Spawn turned to Wanda, his face filled with grief. He moved over to her lifeless body, intent on removing her from the rack. He hugged her, venting his pain through his quiet sobs.

Then, to his utter surprise, he felt her move beneath him. "Wanda?"

He raised his head in hope and anticipation. She abruptly pulled up her legs and kicked him off her with astonishing strength. Spawn sprawled to the floor and looked up in shock. Wanda climbed off the rack, the knife still buried in her chest.

"You worthless bag-a-crap!" she shouted at him. "That puke just murdered me! The single most important human being in your entire freaking universe! And you are just gonna let him get away with it?"

"Wanda?"

Spawn stared in disbelief, his armor paralyzed by his confusion as Wanda whirled and struck him in the face with an adept and powerful karate kick. Spawn staggered back and crashed to the floor. He was amazed and baffled by her strength, and uncertain whether she was alive or dead. Or what she was.

He started to get up, but she pushed him down again as if he were the size and strength of a child. She snapped up Wynn's smart-gun and walked toward Spawn, firing off a vicious salvo. Caught off-guard, Spawn screamed as each shot blew him backward until he fell against a wall and slumped to the floor badly wounded.

Fitzgerald looked over his shoulder as he reached the hall, and he nearly dropped Cyan when he saw the knife sticking out of Wanda's reanimated body. He couldn't believe what he was seeing. She tossed Spawn around as if he were throwing a rag doll. First, Al Simmons returned from the dead . . . now Wanda? He'd hardly registered her death in his mind, but she must be dead.

He hurried back to the den with Cyan before she saw her mother, who Fitzgerald was sure was not Wanda at all. She wasn't acting anything like Wanda. She didn't sound like her, and her strength was overwhelming. It was as if a demon had taken control of her body.

To his surprise, Cyan had seen her, too. "Don't worry, Daddy. That's not Mommy." She shook her head as he set her down. "I know Mommy and that's not her."

"You're right, Cyan. You're absolutely right. It's not her."

"Come on, be a man!" Wanda yelled, urging Spawn to get up. "Pop that little puke's head like a zit! Do it now before I blast you back to Hell for eternity plus a hundred thousand years."

Spawn looked up to see Wanda's entire body growing fuzzy as a dark energy swirled around and around her, whirling faster and faster. When the whirlwind died away, Wanda was gone, and Clown stood in her place. The knife fell to the floor. Of course. It was Clown the entire time. He'd shape-shifted to look like Wanda.

But then, where was Wanda?

"Good trick, huh?" Clown grinned, then turned dead serious.

"Come on, Spawnie. What's the big holdup? Finish the deal and kill the man who took everything from you, your life, Wanda, your future. Kill Jason Wynn! Do it now, the army is waiting to cross over. You must be deaf if you can't hear them.''

''What army?''

''What army, he asks,'' Clown muttered, then pointed toward the flames in the portal. ''You want to inspect the troops? Okay!''

Spawn's vision suddenly expanded as a part of himself was zipped through the fiery portal and down into Hell's inner gullet. He saw flames and a burnt, wasted landscape that resembled a dead planet lacking water and life. Planet Hell hovered close to a sizzling death star that scorched its rugged surface and fried its ghastly condemned inhabitants.

Then his vision shifted and he realized he was staring at a writhing, slathering army of Hellspawn—a horde of fiends with bloodlust in their eyes. They were a blur of savage, wanton killers just waiting for more. Then his vision focused and he glimpsed Chapel moving forward, smoldering and seething, her hate-filled eyes sensing his presence, seeking him out. She was wearing one of her skin-tight op outfits, except that bursts of flames shot out from under her arms and between her legs, as if a part of Hell's internal combustion engine had been embedded inside of her, fueling her hate and anger.

''Give the order!'' she shouted. ''Give the order and we'll cross over.''

Spawn blinked and was back in the living room, staring into Clown's dark, beady eyes. But he still felt the presence of Chapel and the army ready to charge forward. They were urging him on, ready to plunge into the physical world and slaughter all in their wake.

''Do it! Kill Wynn now,'' Clown shouted.

''Never!''

TWENTY-TWO

"**WHAT DO** you mean 'never'? Didn't your mother teach you to never to say never? Do you know how long I've been working on this thing, preparing for this moment, you pansy-assed bacon crisp?''

Clown placed a hand behind his back and a glistening blade flew out of the portal and into his grasp. He started slinking toward Spawn, circling one way, then the other. He held the knife in one hand, the smart-gun in the other. ''You can recover from the stab of an ordinary knife, but this one is different. Very different.''

Clown grinned, showing his bloody fangs. ''It's a dark-magic special. That's a trade brand from down below, by the way.''

Spawn eyed the knife warily. His armor was beginning to heal the wounds, and the bullets were being pushed out one after another. Clown heard them as they plunked to the ceramic tile floor. He knew Spawn wasn't ready yet to fend off another attack. He had him now right where he wanted him. Spawn would pay the price for defying him. Then he'd do what he was told.

''You were wrong about me, Clown. I'm not the heartless killer you thought I was, and I'm not taking orders from you.''

Clown threw down the gun and screamed in outrage. He couldn't believe it. He didn't care anymore what he did to Spawn. He charged him with the dark-magic blade raised above his head. It glinted in the red light from the portal flames, then sparkled with luminous green energy as he plunged it toward his target, aiming for his neck, where his armor was weakest.

Spawn's chains responded instinctively, snapping out in defense. But Clown deftly avoided them by ducking low. Then he rose up and stabbed the injured Spawn through the neck. He plunged hard and deep. He turned and twisted the blade until it came out the back of Spawn's neck and penetrated the wall.

Spawn cried out in pain as the dark green energy spread out from the wound. His armor turned a dull dead-gray and his legs and arms wriggled helplessly. Clown knew Spawn was in pain, serious pain. Just what the disgusting excuse for a leader deserved.

"This isn't funny, Palsy!" Clown shouted near his ear to make sure that Spawn heard him. "Malebolgia is gonna fry my fat ass unless you complete the deed." The dwarf shook his rear end from side to side. "You're gonna do it, even if I have to hold your hand."

Wynn stumbled over to Clown. He looked angry and confused. "Why are you trying to get him to kill me? Are you out of your mind?"

Clown scooped up the smart-gun and pumped a couple of rounds in Wynn's direction. Wynn leaped back and crashed into a bookcase. "The only reason you got that bioweapon pacemaker was so that when Spawn *did* kill you, we got two birds with one stone."

Wynn cringed in a corner as Clown moved toward him, waving the gun. He stopped in front of him. "You still don't get it, do you?"

Clown shook his head as if he were looking at the most pathetic excuse for a human that he could imagine. "It's this way. Hell's Army gets its leader when he kills you, and Armageddon gets cranking with HEAT-16! Now do you get it, you spunk-sucking-dipstick?''

Clown turned back to Spawn, whose breathing came in painful gasps. His armor wasn't pushing the blade out of his neck and Clown knew that every time Spawn tried to move, he felt another burst of sharp pain. The knife from Hell had overpowered the armor's healing properties.

Spawn grasped the knife with both hands and tried to pull it out, but he sank back down, nearly losing consciousness as the green energy seared through his neck and spread across his body.

''I told Malebolgia to choose me to lead his army, but would he listen? Nooo.'' Clown kicked Spawn in spite and shook his head like a drill sergeant who was fed up with his wimpy recruits.

''I shoulda killed you in the alley, but I was such a bleeding heart I gave you another chance.'' He crossed his hands over his chest and cocked his head to the side. Then, dropping his hands to his hips, he shouted: ''Well, now I'm taking over and Malebolgia will thank the little fat dwarf when it's all over.''

He looked at Spawn with a vicious smile. ''But first, I'm gonna have me a little *crème de Wanda*.''

Clown laughed and turned to the hellish portal. Long fingers of fire reached all the way out of the portal to where Clown was standing across the room. When he snapped his fingers, the flames retreated and there was Wanda, tied and gagged to a black wrought-iron chair. Shiny pitchforks pointed up from the corners and the center of the chair's vertical back.

''Another little Clown trick. The real Wanda returns, although she was never really gone.'' He looked around at his audience. Spawn stared in startled amazement. Wynn was preoccupied with his own thoughts and barely noticed her. Fitzgerald looked ready to leap out and save

Wanda, but Cyan was holding his leg, pulling him back.

"How come no one's clapping? I thought it was a good trick."

Clown leaned over the quaking Wanda and licked her cheek with his impossibly long black tongue. He smacked his lips and savored her smell as if he were about to eat a meal.

Fitzgerald stepped forward and saw Wanda bound and gagged. If Spawn couldn't help her, he would do it himself. This time he knew it was her. He turned to his daughter and crouched down. "Cyan, you stay back. I'm going to help your mother."

"That's her," she said, nodding. Then she frowned. "That's a bad clown. I don't like him."

"I don't, either."

Fitzgerald crept forward. The air grew warmer with each step, and he felt a sense of foreboding coming from what had been his fireplace. It was just a trick, he told himself. Another trick by the vicious clown. But Wanda's predicament was no ruse. She was tied to the chair and in pain. He met Wanda's gaze and tried to reassure her that he was here to help.

Suddenly, the clown spun around dragging his gaze away from Wanda. A gleeful grin was plastered on his face as his beady eyes focused on Fitzgerald.

"Terry. Oh, Terry. Coming for a look? I thought husbands were supposed to watch from the closet. I guess you wanted a closeup shot." Clown's voice turned dark. "I don't think so." He raised a hand and pointed a finger at Fitzgerald.

For a moment, he couldn't move another inch forward. Then it was as if he were standing on a fast-moving ramp that was pulling him away, back to the hallway. He tried to walk, but couldn't move his legs. He kept going backward, faster and faster until he slammed into the wall and slid to the floor. He tried to get up, but he felt as if a magnet were holding him down.

"Daddy, are you okay?"

Cyan crawled over to him and hugged him. "I'm fine," he said, stroking her hair. You stay right here with me, and don't look at Mommy. The clown is acting bad again."

She frowned at him. "But Daddy, can't you go get her away from the mean clown?"

He wished he could tell her that he was going to do it, but he knew he wasn't going anywhere.

"Ahh, dinner is served," Clown said, turning back to Wanda. "Did you know that one serving of Wanda's brain has the nutritional value of all four major food groups? Well, it's the truth."

He pulled a gruesome curved knife blade and a fork from behind the chair and raised them over Wanda, who was squirming and shaking her head from side to side as she screamed into the gag.

"Oh, let's not get all hysterical, lady. For jolly jumping beans, it's just a meal." Clown cackled and rubbed his fork and knife together as a frisson rippled through him.

Spawn began to pant and tried with all his might to pull himself free from the wall where the malignant blade was holding him. But it was useless. He was pinned like an insect, as good as dead.

A sharp metallic rasp rang out, filling the room with sound. Clown spun about, his eyes widened, and he stutter-stepped to avoid a glistening blade that swept in an arc toward his head. He caught his breath and quickly retaliated with the fork, but the tall dark figure spun and sliced his left arm, cutting deeply to the bone. Clown howled out in genuine pain, dropped the fork, and stumbled backward cursing and leering at the all too familiar face of his assailant.

"Mind if I cut in?"

"Cogliostro, I thought you were dead," Clown croaked as he huddled against the wall.

"Not quite."

The old man loomed in front of Clown. His spearhead extended from his right hand. Clown's beady eyes looked up at the renowned weapon and then at Cogliostro.

"You wouldn't hurt a helpless little clown, would ya, mister?"

Cogliostro had learned long ago not to listen to anything Clown said. The demon-dwarf used words like he did magic, to baffle and confound. He responded by leaping forward with surprising speed and swung for the dwarf's head. Clown shrieked and twisted aside narrowly avoiding decapitation.

He turned to Cogliostro with red eyes. "You and that old spearhead," Clown sneered. "It ain't gonna do you no good this time."

"We'll see about that." His voice was confident and assured, as was his manner.

"I was sure you were dead."

"That's what I wanted you to think," Cogliostro responded.

Clown growled, looked around the room, then twisted his good arm back and hurled another wicked-looking knife. Not at Cogliostro but at Wynn. The blade sailed through the air, turning over and over as it zipped toward the wounded A-6 director. The blade struck something just an inch from Wynn's face.

It was Spawn's cape. The blade pierced the cape, but stopped short of Wynn. Spawn, still pinned to the wall, collapsed and the cape dropped to the floor with the blade still embedded in it.

Clown cursed and ran toward the back hall. He kicked Fitzgerald as he passed him and stuck his tongue out at Cyan. Then he disappeared into the rear of the house. "Cogsy, come get me!"

Cogliostro started to charge after Clown, but thought better of it. He quickly moved over to Spawn and adeptly removed the dark-magic blade from his neck, freeing him from the wall. Spawn groaned and slumped to the floor. His breath came in hard short rasps.

Cogliostro hurled the blade into the flaming portal, then turned his attention back to Spawn. "Concentrate on healing. I can't hold him off alone. You must recover while there's still time."

"I'll do it," he said in a raspy voice. "I can already feel the armor healing." He closed his eyes, concentrating, but blinked them open again at the sound of Clown screaming and laughing simultaneously.

Cogliostro raised the spearhead as he searched for Clown. The scream was followed by a gruesome sound of bones cracking and shifting, but Cogliostro still couldn't detect where the sound was coming from. Then, suddenly, the floor boards splintered and ruptured and Violator burst through the gaping hole and into the living room. His red compound eyes flashed with hell-fueled rage and he let loose a loud, unearthly screech that momentarily paralyzed Cogliostro with dread.

Cogliostro pushed aside his fears and slashed the spearhead at Violator. The insectoid creature avoided the attack and swiped at his opponent. Cogliostro dodged away, then leaped toward Violator, aiming the point of his weapon at him. The spear was about to plunge into the miscreant's thorax when Cogliostro plunged through the hole that Violator had blasted through the floor. The spear missed its target as he fell into darkness.

Cogliostro found himself in Hell's basement. Below the living room fireplace, the gullet of Hell passed through the basement. Hellish goo was pouring out of the gullet and seeping across the basement floor, infecting everything it touched.

He looked up through the hole just as Violator stretched

a barbed leg toward him. Cogliostro responded by slashing off the creature's leg with the razor-sharp edge of the famed spear. Violator screamed and leaped into the hole, darting one way, then the other in search of his enemy.

Cogliostro dived under the staircase as Violator rushed past him. As the creature spun around and peered through the darkness searching for his prey, Cogliostro saw that the severed leg was already growing back. He wasn't surprised. He had seen Violator in action many other times. In the distant past, they were even allies.

Violator served as Clown's alter ego: a demon-dwarf who transformed into a giant menace. Clown was cruel, cynical, and devious, a sadistic trickster at heart, while Violator was a killing machine who emerged when Clown's dirty tricks ran out.

He had heard once that Violator was born from the Great Work of Dr. John Dee, a sixteenth century alchemist. Dee may have encountered Violator in his nightmares, but his legacy dated much farther back into time. Cogliostro vividly recalled Violator striking terror in the world in the ninth century, during the final meltdown of the Roman and Greek cultures, the heart of the Dark Ages.

It was a time relished by Clown/Violator and his kind, when centers of learning disappeared and the tribal sense of community nearly vanished. Malebolgia was accorded great power in that time, and most believed that he held rightful dominion over mankind. Malebolgia assumed his barbarity would rule forever. But to his surprise mankind began to awaken and denied the Beast his supremacy.

During that era, Cogliostro and Clown and a host of Hellspawn had roamed the countryside spreading terror and making sure everyone knew the devil ruled. But when the Renaissance emerged, Cogliostro realized that mankind's spirit was stronger and more resilient than he'd imagined. Humanity had survived the dark path and he too began to slip from the deadly grip of Malebolgia.

Cogliostro adjusted his position as the vile goo crept toward him. As soon as he moved, Violator spotted him. Now he was cornered under the stairs.

But Violator was wary of the power of the spear. He circled around the old man, moving right, then left, then right again, taunting him with vicious swipes of his legs. Cogliostro jabbed the spear at Violator's eye, then moved agilely away from the staircase.

The creature screeched and stalked its prey. Cogliostro crouched in a dark corner, invoking a shield of invisibility. He watched as Violator edged behind a column of hellish goo, then Cogliostro moved warily out into the basement. He appeared now as nothing more than a shadow among shadows. But the malignant creature's compound eyes detected his movements.

Cogliostro heard a noise above him. He looked up to the ceiling, which glowed red as if the fires from the gullet of Hell were heating it up. He didn't see anything else at first. Then he spotted the creature, who was color camouflaged, matching the reddish tint. Violator cackled, then screeched as he dropped down on top of the old man, crushing down on him with his massive frame.

Cogliostro swung the spearhead at the attacker and cut deeply into Violator's mandibular horns. Violator screamed in pain and jerked his head upward. The spear slipped from the old man's grasp as the beast swung his head from side to side. The heinous creature yanked out the spearhead and threw it across the basement, where it stuck in the floor. Cogliostro was stunned, his power gone.

Violator grabbed Cogliostro with his huge talons and rammed him into the wall, pinning him there. Cogliostro girded his strength and remaining powers, but he was helpless against the enormous creature and its overwhelming might. There was nothing he could do but wait to see how Violator was going to kill him.

The brute moved his head close to Cogliostro's as his articulated horn moved in for the coup de grâce. He growled as the tip of his horn shot out toward Cogliostro's forehead. The old man jerked his head to the side and the projectile grazed his cheek, then slammed into the wall.

Violator emitted a screeching laughter and pinned Cogliostro's head with his talons. He pulled back his head, aimed his horn again for the old man's forehead. He was about to ram it through Cogliostro's skull and brain, when chains suddenly wrapped around the horn, holding it back.

Violator grunted and whirled about in confusion. Cogliostro followed the chain up through the hole in the floor just as another chain rippled down and snagged Violator by its throat. The pair of chains tightened and Violator's talons ripped away from Cogliostro and the creature struggled like a harpooned whale.

Instead of being reeled up and out of Hell's basement, Violator pulled down hard on the whaler. Floorboards popped and suddenly Spawn burst through the ceiling, crashing down onto Violator's back.

The creature screamed, hurled Cogliostro aside, and tried to untangle itself from the chains and buck Spawn off his back at the same time. Spawn, his face armor engaged, rode the hulking demon, hanging on to its articulated horn and pounding its leathery neck with his spiked fist.

Violator spun about and smashed Spawn into the wall. He grabbed his leg, ripped him off his back, and hurled him across the basement into the far wall. Spawn slid through the goo, then bounced off the wall. Just as he started to get up, Violator grabbed him with his huge talons and smashed him again and again into the buckling ceiling.

Cogliostro crawled through the hellish goo, which burned his hands and legs and made him feel heavier and heavier as if he were made of stone. In spite of the pain, he struggled ahead even closer to the Spear of Destiny. Finally, he reached out, but his hand fell short.

The entire basement shuddered again as Spawn was thrust against the ceiling. Cogliostro tried again to reach the magical spearhead and this time his fist curled over it. He wrenched the point out of the floor. Instantly, the painful, burning sensations eased and his body felt lighter and more powerful than ever.

Violator held Spawn high over his head, screamed, then pulled him down toward its jaws. He was about to chomp on Spawn's neck when Cogliostro shouted and hurled the spearhead. The creature turned just in time to see the sparkling projectile hurtling toward its head.

Violator jerked away and the spearhead sailed past him. But it was stopped in midflight, snagged by one of Spawn's chains. The chain retracted, whipped about, and plunged the spearhead deep into Violator's neck. Instantly, a dark green energy burst from its throat like a sun.

The creature roared and twisted in pain. It dropped Spawn and staggered across the room, weaving from side to side. Then with a final scream it crashed through the gullet and disappeared amid the flames.

The portal's hellfire roared and blazed. The entire basement lit up in tones of deep green and dark red. The gullet swelled and seemed on the brink of swallowing the entire basement when the flames transformed into the horrendous continence of Malebolgia, a seething, malevolent face that swelled with the knowledge of every evil deed ever committed, and craved more.

It was Cogliostro's master coming to take him back, Cogliostro thought. After all these centuries of ignoring his existence, as if he never was, Malebolgia was about swallow Cogliostro's soul and crush his being into nothingness and return him to the hell's fires. It was what he'd always feared would happen.

The entire house shook as the green goo was sucked back into the gullet. Cogliostro felt as if he were on a rug being dragged forward by invisible hands. Next to him, Spawn was being pulled toward the portal in similar fashion.

Cogliostro grabbed Spawn's chain and found the Spear of Destiny. He gripped it with both hands and lifted it boldly above his head. The spear glowed; the room turned so bright he had to close his eyes.

When he opened them again, the slimy goo had vanished beneath them. The portal and gullet shrunk smaller and smaller and disappeared. The house—except for the extensive damage—had returned to normal.

Cogliostro looked up at Spawn, who gave him a respectful nod.

TWENTY-THREE

SPAWN PULLED Cogliostro out of the hole, then walked over to Wanda, who was huddled in a corner of the living room. He bent down to her as his face mask retracted. She shrank back against the wall in fear as she saw his burnt face. But when she saw he wasn't going to hurt her, she seemed to relax and looked curiously at him.

"Do I know you?"

"You used to."

Spawn picked Wanda up and carried her down the hall and into the study. Even though the pounding and shaking and screaming had stopped for several minutes, Fitzgerald was still hiding under his desk, cradling and rocking Cyan in his arms. He looked as if he were shell-shocked from everything that had happened. He seemed only vaguely aware that someone had entered the room.

"It's okay. It's over," Spawn said in a soft voice. "You can come out now."

He set Wanda down on the floor as Fitzgerald slowly crawled out. He looked around warily as if expecting Clown or Violator to charge out and assault them at any moment. Wanda collapsed into Fitzgerald's arms and pulled Cyan close to her. They held each other tightly, tears welling in their eyes. They were incredibly relieved and overjoyed to be together again.

"Oh God, Terry. I don't know what happened. It was so horrible. I don't even want to think about it."

"Neither do I," Fitzgerald said, stroking her dark hair. "It's over, baby."

A sense of profound sadness swept over Spawn. He forced himself to look away. But Cyan reached out and grabbed his hand. Her innocent smile filled him with a momentary sense of belonging.

"I knew you'd save us," she said.

Spawn smiled sadly. Wanda pulled Cyan back to her and Fitzgerald. She kissed her daughter on the cheeks and forehead. Their embrace bound them together and helped them expel all that was horrendous and frightening and beyond their comprehension. Their nightmare had come to an end, or so it seemed.

Spawn walked away from them and with each step his melancholy deepened as he moved further and further out of their world. His love for Wanda was still strong, but he knew that he could never return to the past.

He entered into the battered living room again and walked past Wynn, who was slouched against a wall. Spawn stopped and glowered down at the man who'd killed Al Simmons. A fit of rage raced through him and spikes emerged from his hands and feet again. He raised his spiked foot over Wynn's head and slammed it down, striking within an inch of his face. Wynn raised his arms, cringed, and then tried to crawl away.

"Stay away from me," Wynn gasped in a hoarse voice. "Just stay away."

Spawn grunted in disdain and walked over to where Cogliostro was slumped against another wall. He collapsed next to him. He could see into the den, where Wanda, Fitzgerald, and Cyan were still huddled together.

"They belong together," Spawn said. "There's no place for me here."

*　　*　　*

Cogliostro relaxed and slumped further toward the door. He was old and tired and ready to give it up, and now he saw that his judgment had been correct. His last hope had survived and not given in to Malebolgia. He nodded slowly. "Maybe you are the one after all."

"The one? What are you talking about?" Spawn gave him a wary look. Cogliostro knew that Spawn didn't want to escape one trap and fall into another one. But he blundered on, anyhow. There was nothing else he could do.

"I'm all worn out . . . I've been fighting this war far too long. It's time for someone to take my place. To lead my army."

He smiled as Spawn gave him a wary look. "The army of one. It's a lonely battle being Hell's traitor, but you weren't swallowed whole, like so many others. You have the chance to pick up where I left off and find other Hellspawn to join you."

Cogliostro gave Spawn a questioning look. "What do you think?"

Spawn considered what he'd just heard. "I remember when Al Simmons saw you way back in Hong Kong, and I think he might have seen you before that, too. So I guess you've been checking me out for a long time."

The old man smiled and chuckled softly. "Considerably longer than you realize."

"Are you saying you knew what was going to happen to me in North Korea?"

Cogliostro chose his words carefully. "What I knew was that forces much more powerful than you were conspiring to end your career with the A-6."

"If you knew what was going on, why didn't you warn me? Why didn't you stop them?" Spawn's anger flared. "How are you any different from them?"

"Al Simmons wouldn't have listened to me. You know that. I could have stopped Clown once or twice, but he would've eventually gotten you, anyhow. It was one of those things that was destined to happen once you made certain decisions in your life. Believe me, if I could have prevented you from falling into his hands, I would've done it.''

''And what if I would've sided with Clown from the start and did whatever he wanted?''

Cogliostro's response was blunt and offered without the least bit of hesitation. ''I would've killed you.''

Spawn shook his head and laughed. Cogliostro joined him, enjoying the moment.

The telephone rang.

Fitzgerald looked up at the sound and finally released his embrace of Wanda and Cyan. It seemed odd to hear something so commonplace as the phone after all the extraordinary and horrific events that had happened in the house. He was amazed that the phone worked at all. He picked it up, but couldn't bring himself to say anything.

''Terry, are you there? This is Natalie Ford.''

He hoped she didn't ask what was going on, because he didn't know, and what he did know, he couldn't explain. At least, not in any way that would make him sound credible or sane.

''I was able to verify some of what you told me. There is a Liberian freighter leaving the port of Norfolk at midnight, and there's a shipping container of a cleaning solution called HEAT-16 listed on the manifest.''

It took a moment for Fitzgerald to gather his wits. He'd nearly forgotten about the shipment. Maybe Clown was gone, but Wynn was still around. The scenario really hadn't changed much. Wynn was putting deadly weapons in the hands of the worst leaders in the world. He was doing it in some perverted scheme to gain more power for himself in the world scene.

He looked at his watch and with a sinking feeling saw

that it was 11:15. He knew there wasn't much hope now. But there must have been some reason that Ford had called. "Have you found anyone with the guts to try to stop the shipment yet?"

Ford paused. "Yeah, me. I believe you, Terry. It took me some doing, but I've got a chopper. We're on the ground now about half an hour from the port. I'm going to drop on that freighter with camera and lights before it leaves the dock. Maybe I can stop it."

"I don't know, Natalie. It's going to be dangerous," he responded. "Extremely dangerous."

"Don't worry about me. I won't be the only one there. I've alerted the local media, telling everyone that Wynn is shipping illegal weapons to our enemies from the port tonight. I'll lose my exclusive, but I might save my life with other reporters around."

"Natalie, that place is going to be full of A-6 agents. They're following orders and they're dangerous. They could feasibly eliminate all of you and by morning have created some watertight cover story about an accident. Believe me, you're dealing with topnotch experts in cover-ups. They're the best."

Fitzgerald could hear her taking in a deep breath. "Okay. I understand. I'll see if I can get some firepower on our side. I'll take a chance that the local cops aren't involved."

He knew there was a chance she was just alerting Wynn's team that she was arriving. He was about to say so when she interrupted him. "Don't try to talk me out of it, Terry. You know I've been after this story. I'm committed to it. I'm going in."

"Then you better go. Good luck."

Spaz limped into the house through the open front door. The little dog looked as battered and bedraggled as his master. Zack followed the pooch into the room and looked at the hole in the floor.

"Spaz!" Spawn shouted, feeling lighter at the sight of the dog.

He wagged his tail, limped over to Spawn, and climbed into his lap. He pet the injured dog gently as Spaz licked Spawn's chin affectionately. Somehow the little dog had survived and his survival gave Spawn hope. He might be adrift, but Spaz would follow him down whatever road or alley he took.

"I tried to get him to a vet, but he wouldn't stay put," Zack explained as he sat down wearily next to Spawn. "He wanted to find you more than anything. In fact, he led the way."

"Thanks, kid."

Cyan walked toward Spawn, her eyes locked on him with preternatural fascination. He returned the gaze, staring deeply into the little girl. Spaz growled, sensing that something was about to happen. Cyan's mouth moved forming a word, but at first no sound came out. Then in a whisper, she gasped: "Daddy!"

Spawn knew it was true. Al Simmons, not Fitzgerald, was Cyan's father. She was his girl, always would be.

Fitzgerald suddenly loomed behind her. The fright and confusion, even the relief he'd experienced, was gone, replaced with a new sense of anxiety that literally rippled through him. "The HEAT-16 shipment is going out tonight. We've got to stop it. It's our only hope. Otherwise . . ." His voice trailed off.

Spawn let out an audible groan. The night wasn't over yet. In his concern to stop Clown, he had forgotten about the viral weapon. He definitely was earning his wings, or whatever it was that turncoat Hellspawn gained for their efforts.

Spawn took another look at Cyan, then climbed to his

feet and turned to Fitzgerald. "Anyway that you can get the shipment postponed?"

"No, but he can do it!" Fitzgerald pointed to Wynn who was trying to crawl out the front door.

"I thought the battle was won a little too easily," Cogliostro said, standing up. He patted Spawn on the shoulder. "Your first challenge. At least the first since the last one."

Spawn took two enormous steps, grabbed Wynn by the back of his collar, and pulled him to his feet. "How about it, Jason? Are you going to cooperate or are you going to make me angry again?"

Wynn laughed. "Do you think I would do anything to slow down that shipment? I've made the deals and I'm going through with them. You can beat me up some more, but it ain't going to do you any good. And if you go too far, you know the results."

Spawn lifted him over his head. "Are we going to start this again?"

Cogliostro walked up to Spawn. "He's right, you know. He's not going to talk, no matter what you do, and if you kill him, Clown and company get their wish after all. It's quite a fix."

Spawn lowered the battered A-6 chief, but didn't let go of him. He looked over at Cogliostro. "You got any suggestions?"

"You know, there were certain advantages to the old days," the old man said, reminiscing. "In all the centuries that I've lived as Hellspawn and betrayer of Hellspawn, this is the only one where one person could destroy the entire world."

"So what are we going to do about it?" Spawn asked, impatiently.

"Let me think about this. Ah, yes, maybe . . ." he muttered. "But it would be so much easier if he just cooperated.'' Cogliostro turned to Wynn again. ''No, no chance of that.''

''What is it?'' Fitzgerald asked. ''We don't have much time. The freighter leaves at midnight.''

Cogliostro nodded, then turned to Wynn. ''Okay, I see your point, Mr. Wynn. You don't want to give up a good thing. Now I'll show you my point.''

He reached into his greatcoat and pulled out the Spear of Destiny. ''This remarkable spearhead has some unusual properties,'' he began. ''One of them is the capacity to get people to cooperate. I don't use it often for this purpose. It's not a very wise way to get things done, but this is clearly an emergency.''

He stepped back and held the spearhead with both hands, pointing it at Wynn. He glanced at Fitzgerald and Spawn. ''I just hope that it hasn't lost some of its powers with the abuse it's taken tonight.''

He closed his eyes and recited an ancient invocation in Gaelic. The spearhead bobbed up and down as he spoke. When he completed the invocation, he opened his eyes and looked at Wynn, who was staring back at him.

''Hm, sorry. Nothing. I haven't used that one for a long time.'' He looked at Wanda, who had walked into the room and smiled. ''That's it.''

''What?'' Spawn asked.

''Hold him still. Everyone think about Wynn and his awful weapon. Focus. Concentrate. I need a group effort on this one.''

Wynn struggled as Spawn squeezed his shoulders, trying to hold him in place. Cogliostro pointed the spearhead at Wynn's forehead. He could literally feel the energy being focused on Wynn. He seemed on the verge of cooperating. Then Wynn broke the spell.

''Get that thing away from me. I'm not going to . . .'' Wynn suddenly looked confused. His eyes glazed over and his shoulders slumped. He stared straight ahead, slackjawed, waiting for his orders.

"Ah, the power of the group," Cogliostro said softly. "Very interesting. I'll have to remember that." He turned to Wynn. "Go down the hall into the den and call the pier. Tell whoever you know there to hold up the ship and get the HEAT-16 off immediately."

Wynn stood up and seemed to float as he moved to the den. He dialed a number and asked for the portmaster. He identified himself and said that there was a change in plans and explained what he wanted done.

Spawn watched in fascination. But hypnotized or not, he still didn't trust Wynn. He grabbed the phone from him and listened.

"What? You want us to remove your shipment now and return it to storage? Are you sure, Mr. Wynn?"

Spawn clapped his hand over the mouthpiece and leaned closer to Wynn. "Tell him you are sure. Very sure." He handed the phone back to him.

Wynn did as he was told.

"Wonderful. I guess that's that," Cogliostro said, slipping the spearhead back into his sleeve.

"Not quite," Spawn said. "We can't stop now. We've got to go take control of the shipment before it goes out on some other ship. There's no time to waste."

"I've got one of the A-6 Suburbans in the back," Fitzgerald said. "We can all fit in."

"Wynn's going, too," Spawn said. "I want to keep my eye on him." Cogliostro sighed. "I guess I'll postpone my retirement."

"We're going, too," Wanda said, holding Cyan. "I'm not going to be left here alone."

"It might be dangerous, Wanda," Fitzgerald said.

"Hey, it was dangerous here, too," she responded. "I don't want to stay here alone."

"Okay, let's pack everyone in and get rolling," Fitzgerald said.

"Spaz can sit on my lap," Zack said.

Wynn sat in the front passenger seat next to Fitzgerald. Spawn was right behind him with Cogliostro. Wanda and Cyan, along with the kid and the dog, were in the rear. He adjusted his position in the seat. His body ached. He had several broken ribs, possibly a shattered cheekbone, and his broken arm felt as if it had been fractured again when Spawn shattered the cast.

In spite of the injuries and the pain, he was feeling surprisingly pleased with himself. Everything was working out in his favor. As Fitzgerald swung into the street from the driveway, he laughed, a cruel, devious chuckle. He couldn't contain himself any longer.

"You fools, that old spear didn't make me do anything I didn't want to do." He laughed again. "I got news for you. That wasn't the portmaster. That was one of my men, my bodyguard. As soon as he heard me call him portmaster, he played right along."

"What exactly does that mean?" Fitzgerald asked, his shoulders tensing.

Wynn glanced over his shoulder at Spawn. "What it means is that the shipment will be long gone before we get even close to the port. In fact, it's leaving in half an hour, right on schedule."

"Don't believe him," Fitzgerald said. "He's trying to distract us."

"Believe what you want."

Wynn smiled smugly, even though it hurt his cheekbone. He turned in his seat and looked over at his astonished audience. "You guys were kind enough to get Clown and that other thing off my back, so now I can carry on with my business without their interference. Clown was an annoyance, a necessary one for a while.

But now I don't need him, and everything is working out quite well."

The vehicle filled with silence as it cruised aimlessly down the street. "Clever guy," Cogliostro said after a few seconds. "But I've been around longer than you. It's not going to take four hours to get to Norfolk."

"What do you mean by that?" Wynn asked, suddenly feeling uneasy.

Cogliostro clapped his hands once and a green fog filled the car. Wynn felt light-headed for a moment, then he brushed away the haze, and peered out the window. He couldn't see much through the darkness, but he sensed something was different. The road wasn't the same one. The surroundings were different. They were no longer driving along a tree-line boulevard, but along a road in an open area with a high fence on one side.

"Ah, here we are, the docks at Norfolk," Cogliostro said as the fog cleared. "That wasn't bad. About four seconds, instead of four hours."

A guardhouse appeared and armed guards stepped out, blocking their way. "Now what?" Fitzgerald asked as he slowed to a stop.

"Oh dear," Cogliostro said. "I guess I should have put us on the other side of the entrance. Just tell them who you are and what you're doing. That should work. I'll keep everyone out of sight back here."

Fitzgerald rolled down the window. He reached into his pocket, took out his A-6 ID, and flashed it at the guard. "I'm here with Director Wynn to check on our shipment at Pier 22."

The helmeted guard, who carried a rifle and sidearm, peered into the back of the vehicle. Wynn looked back and to his surprise didn't see anyone at first. Then he saw them, but didn't see them clearly. It was the oddest thing. If he hadn't known they were there, he was sure he wouldn't have seen anything.

The guard returned to his booth and came back with a clipboard. He flipped through several pictures and looked at Wynn. Then he nodded, and saluted. "I'll call and tell them you're on your way."

"Wait a minute!" Wynn said, gesturing for the guard to come around to the other side of the Suburban. But even as he spoke, he felt Spawn's chain slide over his arm, around his throat, and squeeze.

"Yes, sir?" the guard inquired.

Wynn shook his head. "Nothing. It's okay."

The guard nodded, opened the gate, and Fitzgerald drove through. It didn't matter, Wynn told himself. When they got to the pier, his men would stop the vehicle and they wouldn't be so easily fooled. They would recognize right away that something was wrong.

The vehicle moved slowly ahead. Fitzgerald stopped at a quiet pier where no activity was taking place. "Wanda, take the kids and dog and wait here for us. I'll be back for you as soon as I can."

"Read that as never," Wynn said as Wanda got out with Cyan, Zack, and Spaz.

She ignored Wynn. "Be careful, Terry." The Suburban continued on, passing pier after pier.

As they approached Pier 22, Wynn saw a refrigerated cargo box being lifted by a crane from the deck of the ship. The A-6 truck that had delivered the cargo was backed up to the pier. He cursed under his breath. He couldn't believe it. The HEAT-16 was being downloaded.

Two vehicles rolled in front of them and Wynn recognized several A-6 operatives as they rushed forward. He smiled as Marcus approached and prepared to leap out of the vehicle. "What the hell's going on, Marcus? Why is the cargo coming off the ship?"

"I stopped it, sir. Like you said."

"What?"

Marcus was trained to detect when someone was being coerced. He should've realized Wynn was speaking under duress, especially when he called Marcus the portmaster.

Wynn felt something piercing the back of his neck. He knew it was the spearhead. "You underestimated the power of the Spear of Destiny, Mr. Wynn," Cogliostro rasped in his ear. "He heard differently."

He knew that the old man was somehow connected with Clown and his out-of-this-world scenario, but until a moment ago, he'd figured old Cogs didn't have an iota of Clown's powers.

"Now tell him he did the right thing," the old man continued. "They can't load it on this ship. They've got to put the box back on the truck."

Wynn glanced back, but to his surprise didn't see either the old man or Spawn. He opened the door and stepped out of the vehicle. "What happened to you, sir?" Marcus asked when he saw Wynn's torn and bloodied clothing. "Do you need help? Are you all right?"

He wanted to tell his bodyguard to take Spawn, the old man, and Fitzgerald into custody, that they'd beaten and kidnapped him. But that's not what came out of his mouth. In spite of his thoughts, he said: "Don't worry about me. Just get the cargo down off that crane and into the truck. We've run into a problem."

"Yes, sir."

Wynn couldn't believe what he'd just said. He'd spoken against his will, saying exactly the opposite of what he'd intended to say. It was as if he were hypnotized and fully awake and aware at the same time.

"So let's do it!" he added.

"Right away, sir." Marcus hurried away. Less than a minute passed when a burly man in a navy blue shirt and pants climbed down the steps from the upper level of the pier and hurried over to Wynn.

"What's going on here?"

"You tell me," Wynn answered and identified himself. "Who are you?"

"I'm the dock foreman," the man said. "This shipment is already registered, Mr. Wynn. You can't take it back now. Too late."

Wynn just stared at the man. Inwardly, he was cheering his intervention. But outwardly, it was impossible to agree with him or to say anything, for that matter.

The foreman moved closer, his dark eyes scrutinizing Wynn from head to foot. There was something familiar about those eyes. "Look at you. It must have been quite a brawl, and from the looks of it, I'd say you were on the losing end."

Cogliostro appeared by Wynn's side. "Mr. Wynn is the boss. He says put that crate back so you do what he says." He was tapping the spearhead against his palm as he talked, and the foreman's glistening dark eyes watched it.

"Let me see that thing," the foreman said, holding out his hand.

"I'll do better than that." Cogliostro suddenly jabbed it toward the forman's gut.

The man stepped back, but too late before the spear touched his belly. He looked down at himself and his whole body seemed to shudder.

"That was a mistake," the foreman said in a threatening tone. "Big mistake."

TWENTY-FOUR

THE DOCK foreman suddenly started to shrink in height and at the same time expand in girth. He ripped off his shirt and pants, revealing Clown's attire. He savagely pulled off his face as if it were a rubber mask, revealing the neon-blue tattooed grin.

His arm shot out impossibly far, as if his shoulder was equipped with an extension, and his hand snatched the spear from the startled Cogliostro. Then he spun in a circle, his features blurring. A leg flew out and the heel of his foot caught Cogliostro under his jaw, sending him tumbling onto his back.

Clown put one hand on his hip and twirled the spearhead in his other hand like a baton. He took several marching steps, raising his knees high, kicking out his feet. His grin stretched to his ears. "Damn, I should've rented a marching band."

Then he turned serious, and stared down at Cogliostro, who was still stunned by the blow. "Well, well, Cogs, aren't you ever going to give up? Determined old fart, aren't you. But you're really just a misguided fool. No one is going to stop the shipment from leaving port tonight. Ain't gonna happen."

He frowned, looked off to the side, and under his

breath, added: "No wonder he's so attracted to my devious deviant defect, otherwise known as Spawn. But two
fools are no better than one. They don't even make good
company on boring days."

He turned to Wynn, who remained speechless. He made
a circle with the spear in front of the A-6 director's face.
"Snap out of it, Wynn, ol' buddy. I'd hate to see you die
while you were still in a trance."

He grabbed Wynn by the throat and raised the spear.
"Consider it an honor to die by this weapon." He laughed
and leaned close to Wynn's face. "You'll go first class
to Hell. Here, catch."

Just as his arm started to plunge the spear down toward
Wynn's heart, a thunderous body blow struck Clown. He
flew back and the spearhead flipped end over end. Cogliostro reached out and pulled it in, clutching it to his
chest.

Clown lay on his back, kicking his legs and pounding
the air with his fist, like a kid in a tantrum, as he cursed
angrily. Then he vaulted onto his feet. Still groggy from
the blunt attack, he looked around warily. As his vision
cleared, he saw Spawn stalking him.

"I guess you're asking for more trouble, Spawn. Well,
you've got it."

He snapped his fingers, spun around and around, faster
than his earlier spinning. His body twirled into a shapeless
blur of color. Then as it slowed down, it twisted at odd
angles, bones crackled and lengthened. His head grew
enormous mandibles and a pair of horns. The jaw lengthened to reveal two jagged rows of saliva-covered teeth.
The legs and arms grew longer and the hands and feet
turned into deadly talons.

Violator was back again.

Spawn charged the green-skinned beast, but Violator
leaped high in the air and landed on top of his enemy.
His mandibles reached down and seized Spawn's head.

Violator lifted Spawn ten feet in the air and was about to slam him into the road when Cogliostro darted forward and stabbed him with the spear.

Violator screamed and fell sideways, the spearhead sticking into his back. Green liquid leaked from the wound. But he quickly rose up and pulled the weapon out and waved it in front of him. Enraged, he targeted Spawn and aimed the weapon at his heart.

Wynn backed away, recovering his senses. He took in everything around him and signaled a couple of his startled men. "Give me that gun," he said to Marcus, taking a smart-gun from him.

Marcus quickly pulled out a semiautomatic pistol. "What is it, sir? What are those things? Should we shoot them?"

"No, let them kill each other. But don't let anyone get away."

Wynn smiled in spite of the pain in his arm, sides, cheek back and leg. He was hurt, but he would recover, and he was ready to take charge again.

Violator hurled the spearhead at Spawn, who ducked under it, but the insectoid creature charged and grabbed him around the chest with his talons, lifting him up and squeezing hard.

Spawn thrashed and screamed in agony as the talons crushed him. He was trapped and Violator seemed stronger than ever. It was as if the spear wound had simply released a reserve supply of energy.

"Use your armor!" Cogliostro shouted, sliding away from the action.

Violator's massive lower jaw dropped with a bone-cracking shudder. He pulled Spawn's head into its maw and prepared to deliver the decapitating bite. Spawn struggled, but realized it was no use.

He relaxed, concentrated, and visualized his armor coming to his aid. He had no idea if it would work, but he forced himself to let go of his doubts and give in completely in his armor. Time seemed to expand, split seconds changed to minutes, and all motion lagged, as if life itself were stuck inside a clogged catsup bottle. He felt the armor reinforcing itself to stop Violator's powerful jaw from chomping down on his throat and head. He didn't know how he would escape, but he was confident that the armor would find a way.

Instantly, yet still inside the expanded time frame, the armor unleashed a vicious barrage of lances from his skull. Violator screamed and whipped about in pain and Spawn was catapulted back into real time. The lances pierced the insectoid creature's upper and lower jaws and locked Violator's jaw open. But the lances also kept Spawn trapped between the creature's filthy jaws.

Suddenly, Violator unleashed noxious, overpowering fumes from its gullet and Spawn gagged. But he refused to pull out the lances. Instead, his chest chains lashed out and encircled tightly around the beast's neck. Razor-sharp barbed hooks burst out of every link of the chain. The chains tightened even more, digging the hooks deep into Violator's scaly green skin.

Violator whipped his head from side to side to no avail. Its shrill screams blasted Spawn's ears. The motion cleared the fumes, though, and Spawn took in a deep breath of air. Violator's red eyes bulged as he seemed to sense what was coming. His armored captive had turned on him, and the results would be crushing and final.

"Give my regards to your boss. Tell him . . . he's next," Spawn shouted.

He pulled back the lances from his armored head and the creature's jaws closed down over him. But Spawn didn't panic. Instead, he focused and visualized. Time expanded, then collapsed as the chain hooks revved into a chain saw and ripped through Violator's thick neck as if it were a dead tree stump.

Violator's jaw shuddered, then relaxed its grip on Spawn as the vile creature's head was sliced from its torso. The skull hit the ground with a thud. It gasped like a fat green fish flopping on land, then it transformed back into Clown's head.

The creature's body jerked about violently for several seconds, then it slowly came to rest. Within seconds, it began to lose its shape and melt into a heaping pile of black goo. The disintegrating body released a noxious odor that forced Spawn to turn away.

But Clown head wasn't finished. It tried to turn itself upright using its long, black tongue. "Christ, what a mess. I told Malebolgia you couldn't handle it. I dunno. My family's gonna disown me. Look at me, will ya. I was short before, but now I'm . . ."

Cogliostro stepped forward and slammed the Spear of Destiny through Clown's mouth, finally quieting the fiendish demon. He withdrew the spear and the black goo rolled over the head and absorbed it. Within seconds, the head bubbled away and disappeared.

Spawn's face armor retracted and he turned to Cogliostro. "Not bad for a dead man."

"Beginner's luck," Cogliostro answered and shrugged. Then he smiled and they both laughed.

"Yeah, I agree. Good job, Spawn," Wynn said. "Good job." He held a smart-gun and several armed guards flanked him, aiming their weapons at Spawn and Cogliostro. "Now that you've really got him out of the way, I can move ahead with my business."

Three more operatives pushed Fitzgerald, Wanda, and the two kids toward the others. Wanda gripped Fitzgerald's arm and Cyan clung to her mother's leg. Zack looked around as if he were searching for Spaz.

Wynn moved forward, jerked Wanda away from Fitzgerald and Cyan, and aimed his weapon at her head.

He looked over at Spawn. "Do I hear any objections to my sending this shipment on its way?"

Spawn was silent, trying desperately to control his anger. He'd no sooner conquered Clown and Violator when Wynn was back on his feet and running the show. He wanted to hurdle himself into that despicable excuse for a human being, but he knew that Wynn would kill Wanda before he could reach him.

Wynn turned to Cogliostro. "As for you, if I see that spear again, I'll blast it into a thousand bits along with your arm. Then I'll take care of the rest of you, and send you back where . . ."

The roar of a helicopter engine silenced the A-6 director as he looked up and shielded his eyes against the blinding light of its spotlight. He crouched down amid a rush of air and swirling dust that stung his face. Slowly, the chopper landed.

Spawn covered his face and stepped back so that the chopper landed between him and Wynn and the A-6 agents. He took advantage of the chaos by slinking off into the darkness.

"What the hell?"

Wynn glimpsed the CNN logo on the side of the chopper as it landed. Then, before he could react, a news crew leaped out of the chopper. A television camera was pointed at him and more lights shone in his face. Then a familiar face stepped forward with a microphone in her hand.

"Hello, Mr. Wynn. Natalie Ford of CNN News here." She yelled above the sound of the chopper, which finally cut its engine. "Glad to see you here. You're just the person I want to talk to."

"For chrissake," Wynn muttered to himself. He should've had this woman put away months ago. If he could get away with it, he'd do it right now.

"I can't talk now," Wynn said as he ran a hand through his mussed hair.

Ford ignored his comment. "Could you just tell us what's going on here tonight? Why are you here at the Port of Norfolk with all these armed men?"

"No comment. This is not a public matter." Wynn started to turn away from the camera, but Ford pursued him, shouting questions.

"What happened to your face, Mr. Wynn, and why are you walking like you are injured? Were you fighting with someone?"

Wynn hit upon an idea to distract Ford and turn her attention away from him. "Yeah, I was. Where is he? Wait until you see the beast."

He shouted at his men to find Spawn.

Spawn crept silently through the shadows, moving from the road to an elevated walkway. He crouched down and watched the news crew following Wynn. Nothing seemed to stop him. He just turned setbacks to his advantage, and so far he was still getting his way. Spawn knew he had to do something about it.

He heard a yelp and glanced back. Spaz was wagging his tail, looking up at him. He petted the little dog, who licked his hand. "What are you doing here?"

Spaz yelped again.

"Shh!"

"What was that?" a voice said.

Spawn glimpsed the silhouettes of two A-6 operatives moving in his direction. He looked around for a hiding place, but it was too late.

"Over there. There he is."

He scooped up Spaz, raced down the walkway and turned up the step, leading to another level of the pier. He was right below the huge shipping crate containing the

HEAT-16, and the crate was moving, heading back to the deck of the freighter.

He had an idea.

Ford finally backed away and Wynn moved out of the glaring light. What was taking his men so long to find Spawn? He couldn't have gone far. Then he saw Fitzgerald talking to Ford and started toward them.

Ford spun around with her microphone in hand. "Mr. Wynn, your own information director says that the container hanging up there from that crane is filled with a deadly virus that you're selling to nations that call this country their enemy. Is that true?"

"That's nonsense. That's just a container of cleaning solution." The crane was swinging out toward the freighter's deck. Once it was down, the freighter would leave and Ford's story would be mere hearsay.

But Ford wasn't about to give up. "Mr. Wynn, we have a report from a former associate of the notorious terrorist known as the Hyena that one of your agents, namely Jessica Chapel, was offering a supervirus called HEAT-16 to the Hyena."

Wynn refused to be intimidated by Ford. He knew her evidence was all hearsay. "I don't know what you're talking about. Chapel died in the Swiss embassy attack that was instigated by the Hyena, according to your own network's reports."

Two shots rang out from the pier, one after the other.

"Up there! Look!" one of the guards shouted, pointing toward the crane. "There he is! On the cab!"

"Watch where you're firing!" Wynn shouted. "Whatever you do, don't hit the container."

Ford moved to his side. "Why is that, Mr. Wynn? What exactly is HEAT-16?"

*   *   *

One bullet struck Spawn in the shoulder, the other whizzed past his head. He dropped to his belly and looked over the front of the cab and into the crane driver's startled face.

"What the hell!" the crane driver shouted as he saw Spawn's inverted head hanging over the side of the compartment.

"Get lost."

The driver didn't argue. He pushed open the door of the compartment and raced down the stairs, yelling and waving his hands, and pointing at the cab.

Spawn swung down into the compartment and put Spaz on the floor as he looked over the gears. The crate was about to drop its load on the freighter's deck, but now it was drifting out of place. One end of it was about to hit the corner of another shipping container. Spawn knew that could spell big trouble.

He grabbed a lever and pulled back. The crane shuddered and squealed. The container stopped its descent, but now it was swinging wildly and barely missed yet another shipping container. He pulled the next lever back and the container slowly began to rise from the deck. He turned the wheel and the container started moving away from the freighter toward the pier.

Several more shots pinged off the cab; A-6 agents rushed up the steps. The one in front stumbled on a step and the two men behind him tripped over the fallen man. But seconds later, they were all on their feet rushing toward the cab again.

Spawn stopped the container when it was fifty feet in the air above the pier. He climbed out through the window and mounted the roof of the cab. He looked back at Spaz. "You stay there. And stay down."

Bullets struck him in the leg and back. None of the bullets seemed to penetrate very deeply into the armor, but they still hurt. He ignored the pain as best he could and mounted the arm of the crane. He climbed higher and higher above the pier.

More bullets zipped past his head and he kept climbing out on the crane. Finally, he reached the end of the arm and slid down the thick greasy cable to the top of the container, which swayed gently from side to side.

"Don't shoot!" someone yelled.

He climbed down the side to the latched door and smashed his fist down on the lock, breaking it open. He looked down for a moment and saw a dozen armed men on the pier with their weapons trained on him. Wynn stood nearby watching him. A few feet away, at the top of the steps to the pier, a television camera crew recorded the action. Spawn waved and slipped inside the container.

"What the hell is he doing up there?" Wynn shook his head, puzzled and annoyed by Spawn's behavior. Whatever it was, he didn't like it.

Ford moved past him, this time without a word. Her eyes were focused on the container. Her crew followed closely behind.

Suddenly, the shipping container started to move down toward the pier. Wynn clicked on his miniature two-way wrist radio. "Hey, who the hell's doing that? What's going on up there?"

"Doing what, sir?" He recognized Marcus's voice and saw him standing near the cab.

Whatever happened to his competent operatives, the deadly precise killing machines? Were they all dead? These guys were a comedy act, not field operatives. "Who's driving the crane, goddamn it?" he barked.

Marcus moved cautiously up to the cab, his weapon ready. Wynn waited for his response.

Wynn heard static, then a response. "It's a little dog, sir. He's sitting on the lever."

"Well get him off it! Stop that container. Now!" Wynn shouted into the mike.

"The dog's barking and snapping at me. I can't get near it."

"Shoot it!"

A few seconds passed. "I can't do it, sir. I won't kill that little dog. I'm sorry."

"You're fired!"

As soon as the container settled to the pier, Wynn took charge. "No one opens it."

"But the man you're after is inside," Ford said. "Besides, I want to see the cleaning solution, and I want to know what the A-6 is doing exporting soap."

Sirens blared and a string of police cars and news vehicles arrived at the pier. A deep horn sounded and the freighter started to pull away from the pier.

"Wait a minute. Someone stop the ship," Wynn screamed. "It can't leave without the container!"

Spawn pushed out the top hatch on the container and crawled onto the roof. The entire pier was overrun by a confusion of police, A-6 agents, reporters, and television crews. He slipped down the back side of the container and dashed along the pier, away and into the night.

TWENTY-FIVE

SPAWN AND Wanda stood on a ramp a short distance from all the TV cameras and police activity. Nearby, Cyan and Zack were playing with Spaz, the little hero who had brought down the shipping container and inadvertently felled Jason Wynn.

It was ironic, Spawn thought, no matter what he did to overcome Wynn, his old boss just bounced back. But Spaz felled Wynn by simply climbing onto a lever. No doubt he was trying to get out of the cab, and then was frightened when the lever moved the crane and the guard rushed him.

Cogliostro was seated above on the ramp, watching the activities below. They could see what was going on, but couldn't be seen. Everyone was busy trying to find out what had happened. There were no bodies, only a dark oily spot on the road that had once been Clown and Violator. But Spawn knew that the contents of the shipping container, which was just being opened, would keep them busy.

"I hope they listen to Terry," Wanda said. Fitzgerald was standing in front of the container talking with the police.

"I think they'll take his word that they're dealing with

an extremely dangerous weapon. I don't know what they'll do about Wynn, though.''

Wanda impulsively reached out and touched his burnt face. She seemed confused about him and he could understand why.

"What I've been feeling." She paused, considering next words. "It's all true, isn't it? Somehow . . . you're Al. That's what I think."

Wanda cautiously stepped closer to him and Spawn met her intent gaze. Their eyes filled with tears, their visions blurred.

"Wanda . . ."

He reached out and touched her lip in a familiar gesture, the way he'd done it so long ago. His emotions were stripped raw, and it took every ounce of his strength to turn away.

"I never stopped loving you," Wanda said.

Spawn stopped. A beat passed as he looked back. "Al Simmons is gone . . . whoever . . . whatever I am now, belongs somewhere else. Not in your life."

Tears streamed down Wanda's cheeks. She nodded, knowing he was right. But the old pains of loss still came flooding back.

Spawn looked over at Cyan, who was hugging her mother and watching him. "But I won't be far away, either."

Cyan beamed. "You better not be."

Wanda looked wistfully after him. "I always knew I'd have to give you up."

They moved toward each other again and Wanda folded into his arms. They held each other for a long, heartfelt moment.

"I used to worry about your soul, Al. I'm glad I was wrong."

They finally drew apart and Spawn bent down to Cyan's level. His armor released the heart-shaped locket

with the picture of Al and Wanda. He smiled and handed
the locket to her.

"What is this?"

"The last piece of who I was . . . keep it safe. It's yours
now."

Cyan threw her arms around Spawn and hugged him
tightly. "I promise."

Spawn let go of Cyan, stood up, and took another look
at his family. Slowly, painfully, he turned and walked up
the ramp toward Cogliostro, who was now standing up as
if waiting for Spawn. Spaz followed behind him as Wanda
and Cyan made their way down the ramp toward Fitzgerald and all the activity.

Zack looked on expectantly, then turned and kicked the
dirt, feeling deserted.

"Hey, kid," Spawn called.

Zack looked up. "Yeah?"

"You've got some explaining to do."

"I do?" Zack asked. "What do you mean?"

"Like how did you teach ol' Spazy how to operate a
crane?"

"Oh, I didn't teach him that. He learned that on his
own, maybe from watching you."

Spawn turned away, then looked back. "Well, are you
coming or you just going stay there?"

Zack ran over to Spawn with a big grin on his face.
They joined Cogliostro and walked away; Spaz trotted
behind them.

Spawn looked over at Cogliostro, who looked tired and
worn out. "Let me get one thing straight. Just how long
have you known me?"

Cogliostro glanced over his shoulder toward Cyan.
"You and that little girl have something in common."

"I know. I'm her father. What's that have to do with
my question?"

"That's not all you have in common."

Spawn shrugged. "What else?"

"You both found your fathers today."

Spawn stopped and turned to Cogliostro. "Who? You . . . you're my father?"

Cogliostro smiled. "Well, in a manner of speaking. The man your mother had planned to marry walked away when he found out she was pregnant. I took his place and spent three years with the two of you. I couldn't stay any longer."

"Why not?"

"Because I was worried for your safety. I knew that Clown would kill you, if he found me."

Spawn nodded. "My mother never told me that she married an old man."

Cogliostro laughed. "I didn't look old while I was with your mother. I appeared to her and you as a man of about thirty."

Spawn stopped and watched as Wanda and Cyan headed toward the police lines and Fitzgerald. "Did you know I would follow in your footsteps?"

The old man was quiet a moment. "Yes and no. I knew it was no coincidence that I married your mother. I sensed who you might become, but I always hoped you wouldn't follow that path."

Spawn didn't know what to say. He didn't know whether to be upset with Cogliostro or happy to have found his father and solved the mystery of his disappearance. Finally, he put an arm over Cogliostro's shoulder. They turned from the pier and walked away.

Finally, the police handcuffed Wynn and led him away. The shipping container was sealed and under guard and the entire pier was cordoned off. But Fitzgerald couldn't relax, not yet. He needed to find Wanda and Cyan. When the police arrived, he'd told them that it was best to stay out of the way, but he hadn't seen where they went. He just hoped that some new tragedy hadn't befallen his family. He didn't think he could take any more. Not tonight. Not ever, if he had his way.

It had taken him nearly an hour of explanations, repeating his story over and over again, each time to a higher ranking officer until he finally spoke with the Norfolk chief of police and the mayor, who arrived at the scene together. The two officials also talked to Wynn, who was trying to cover his tracks as best he could. But finally, when Natalie Ford confirmed Fitzgerald's story, the mayor told the chief of police to take Wynn downtown for further questioning.

Fitzgerald was relieved that Wynn hadn't gone as high as the chief of police or the mayor. Apparently his power or sphere of influence was limited. Or so it seemed at the moment. He didn't have any illusions that Wynn would stay locked up, though. Maybe after Fitzgerald talked to a congressional subcommittee and presented them with evidence of his former bosses' activities, Wynn would be indicted. That was a big maybe. He wasn't sure whether or not anyone would be willing to take the lead in stopping Wynn.

He saw Wanda and Cyan and hurried over to them. He scooped up Cyan and embraced them both. "It's over," he said.

"Can we go home, Daddy? I'm really tired," Cyan said, yawning.

"I bet you are." He kissed her on the cheek. "Don't worry. We're going home, sweetie."

Two black Suburbans cruised into the pier area and stopped outside the police line. A group of gray-suited men and women stepped from the vehicles and hurried over to Wynn as he was being taken to a police vehicle. Fitzgerald recognized the new arrivals as A-6 internal security agents and moved closer. He immediately guessed what they were up to.

One of the agents presented a document to the lead officer. "This is a federal warrant for Mr. Wynn's arrest. We're taking charge of him."

The officer studied the document, nodded, then removed the handcuffs from Wynn's wrist and turned him over to the agents.

Fitzgerald tensed. They weren't taking him into custody. He started over to the group to confront the agents, but Wanda reached for his arm. "Terry, no, don't. Let it go."

He nodded and stepped back. "You're right, Wanda. It wouldn't do any good. They're duping the local cops, but he's going to get out, anyhow. They wouldn't have held him for long."

"You'll get him, one way or another," Wanda said in a comforting voice, putting an arm over his shoulder. "He won't get away."

They watched Wynn and the others slip into the two Suburbans and drive away. Natalie Ford and her camera crew recorded the transfer of custody from police to federal officials. After the cars disappeared into the night, she walked over to Fitzgerald.

"Terry, can we do that interview now?"

"Sure, why not? I'm ready to go on the record with everything."

The camera's light came on and Ford stood next to him with a microphone in hand. But before she asked a question, she was interrupted by a shout.

"Fitzgerald!"

He turned and recognized Marcus Garity, Wynn's bodyguard.

"Do you know what you're doing?" he called out.

"Yeah . . . something I should've done a long time ago," he called back.

EPILOGUE

FROM HIGH above, Spawn could see the alley behind the old church where the cardboard-box village had reassembled. He dove lower, sweeping above the rooftops and saw Zack leaning against a wall with Spaz resting in his lap. Next to him, Cogliostro held his spearhead in his hand, and Spawn knew he was telling him its history.

Spawn circled the church, gliding closer and closer on his long elegant wings. He landed on the cross at the top of the steeple and balanced on the precarious perch with the help of the wings, which twisted in the breeze.

A full moon hung over the city as Spawn looked out and contemplated his strange fate—an outcast from Hell, neither of this world nor that one. Neither demon nor human. A crusader for good, but spawned from evil. A lost soul who had found his own way on a lonely path.

The sound of a crash echoed from the chaos of the city. It caught Spawn's attention. He sensed that someone was in need of his help. His armor folded down over his face and his eyes glowed green in the darkness. He spread his wings and soared off his perch in the direction of the sound.